W9-CNC-518

Mary's Prayer

Mary's Prayer

Martyn Waites

PIATKUS

First published in Great Britain in 1997 by
Judy Piatkus (Publishers) Ltd of
5 Windmill Street, London W1

First paperback edition 1997

*A catalogue record for this book is available
from the British Library*

ISBN 0 7499 0398 8 (Hbk)
ISBN 0 7499 3028 4 (Pbk)

Set in Times by Intype London Ltd

Printed in Great Britain by
Mackays of Chatham Plc, Ltd

Thank you to Fabiola Hickson,
Kate Callaghan, Elenore Lawson, Hazel Waites,
and especially Caroline Montgomery.
Without you, etc. . .

Above all, this book is for Linda.

1: The End

I'm writing this just after you've gone. I didn't mean for this to be addressed to you; it didn't start out that way, but that's how it ended up. You know what I think of you – I mean, what I thought of you.

I'm playing your favourite song. Our song. At least, you once said it was your favourite, but since you lied about everything else why should you tell the truth about that?

You've made me hate you. Is that what you wanted? Well, if it was, you've succeeded, and what's more you've made me hate myself.

So I hope you're satisfied. I've nothing left. You've given me only one option. And this time I'm going to do it. I've pulled the arm out of the record player so the song will keep playing – my record player, the one you thought was so quaint – and that's how they'll find me. They'll hear the song and they'll say that's just how I was: a candle in the wind, never knowing who to cling to. I hope you'll be sorry. But I doubt it.

They'll find this, of course. And when they do, they'll know the truth.

They'll know that you killed me.

2: Killing Time

The clawhammer drove the spike in cleanly, expertly. Larkin screamed, jaggering his vocal chords.

'Shh,' the man said. 'You'll wake the neighbours. People have to get up for work in the morning.'

Larkin's screaming subsided into wracking sobs. He moved his head slowly to the right to see the damage. Slowly, because he didn't want to look, didn't want to see the body next to him on the mattress. He observed that his right hand was now nailed to the floor, palm upwards. He tried to keep a clear head, stay conscious despite the pain. The man looked at him lying there and smiled, light glinting off the tiny silver razors hanging from his nipples.

'Now try writing with that,' he said, and laughed; his two stooges did the same. Then he stopped abruptly; his face became set and mean. The stooges took their cue and immediately fell silent, expectant. The man straddled Larkin's immobile body. 'You're a naughty boy,' his impeccable public school accent continued, 'and we're the house prefects. We've come to teach you a lesson.' He grabbed Larkin's hair, pulling him off the floor slightly. Larkin whimpered as his hand strained against the nail.

'If you live – and to be honest, it's looking doubtful – you can take this as a warning. Stay away from me. Carry your scars as a reminder.' He stood up. 'I don't think I need add to that, do I?'

Larkin didn't reply.

'Then it's over to you, boys.' And with that he stood aside and the silent stooges stepped forward, staring down at Larkin, marking their targets, as their boss stroked his erection through his leather trousers.

The first kick gave him double vision. The next kick dislocated his jaw.

He felt as if he'd stuck his head in a bonfire. Instinctively he raised his hands to his face, but only the left one – the one that had been protecting his balls – came up. Pain rippled up his arm as his right hand wrenched against the nail. He tried to click his jaw back into place, rolling simultaneously to dodge a blow that would have put him on dialysis for life; the tear in his right hand grew bigger.

The boots recommenced their attack, stamping and grinding until he thought he would faint. Then the onslaught stopped and he heard the boots walking away. It must be over. For the time being.

He lay there for a long time – minutes or hours, he couldn't tell which – making up his mind to live rather than die. Then he turned his head to the left, and saw the clawhammer well within reach. Quickly, desperately, he stretched for it, his fingers scrabbling, not knowing where the boots had gone or when they would be back. And then he had it, and frantically he inserted the claw under the head of the nail in his right hand, knowing he had to endure the agony of release if he was to stand a chance. There was a sudden noise behind him; the boots were back. Larkin hadn't been quick enough. His feeble struggles continued until they snatched the hammer from his weak grasp and threw it into the corner of the room.

'Naughty, naughty.' He felt a whoosh of air next to his face as a heavy, solid object – a baseball bat? – came crashing down. Somehow he found the strength to twist his head, roll his body to dodge the blow. But he was defeated. They were playing with him. If Larkin had opened his eyes he would have seen them smiling.

Larkin had given up any thought of fighting back. In

4

fact, he was fast giving up any thought of living. As the uninhabited towerblock of his body began, floor by floor, to plunge into darkness, a peculiar thought struck him. It wasn't the whole of his life that was flashing before his eyes – it was just the last few bastard days . . .

Thursday had started off as usual. Days on which he couldn't be bothered to write – and they were on the increase – tended to follow the same well-worn pattern:

He'd got up, studiously ignoring the word processor on the table beside his bed, and got dressed. His clothes rarely varied in style: faded Levis, boots, plaid shirt and leather jacket. His armour for facing the world.

Next he'd collected the *Guardian* from his doormat. It offered the standard 1990s news diet: a man in North London tied to his bed, tortured and left to die while two boys went on a spending spree with his credit cards; talk of a peace deal in Northern Ireland; a crisis in an unpronounceable country he had never heard of; and a diatribe, from the Canute faction of the government, stating that Britain was an island and would never be part of Europe. Nothing special.

He took a final look round, as if to memorise the last place he'd been, and prepared to face the world.

He peered cautiously round the front door. It was vital to do this; too many times he'd stepped out and found an episode of *The Bill* taking place on his doorstep. Urban terrorism would be central to the plot, or, if the actor was black, drug-dealing. Larkin wasn't keen to incur the wrath of some hysterical luvvy director screaming that his shot was ruined. And he was a bit pissed off that the media viewed his home territory as a war zone. If it were true it might have been cause for congratulation; but Borough, South London, was not where the action was. And no TV producer was going to tell him otherwise. Just because it looked like Beirut with tube trains didn't make it hell on earth; more like an unimaginative Catholic's vision of purgatory, perhaps.

He walked down Great Dover Street to the tube. A

few abrupt halts in dark tunnels later, he was in the West End. Thankfully, with the onset of autumn, the tourist season was coming to a close so the city's supply of fat Americans, backpacking colonials and recession-proof Japanese had dwindled. Was he being mean-spirited or, worse, racist to think such things? He decided he was, but he wasn't in a mood to care.

He trawled aimlessly through the second-hand book-shops in Charing Cross Road. Larkin looked for everything and anything and was known to all the dealers. They had nothing to offer him today, though, apart from a slim, grey paperback on werewolves – a limited print run from a small press.

The author believed in his subject and that was good enough for Larkin. He'd read them all: from how the spatial geometry in certain East End churches could attract demons, to every conspiracy theory going on JFK and Jack the Ripper. For a man like Larkin, who had long since lost his faith in the truth, it was a glimpse into another world.

His routine took him on to a cappuccino in Old Compton Street and a look at the book he had pur-chased. If it was interesting, this would turn into two cappuccinos; maybe three.

Then came the walking, the observing. Soho was good for that. He was content now not to participate, to watch life from the sidelines. There was the furtive sex show crowd – single businessmen, usually; the prostitutes, posing as passers-by, walking round the same block every fifteen minutes and fooling no one; the sad couples with dead love lives hoping for an expensive cheap thrill. Then there were the newer arrivals: the anodyne ad-men, the media whores, the pickpockets. People trying to hustle, people trying to score, people confused by their own desires. Larkin thought if you stood still in Soho for long enough you'd see it all.

He felt hungry so he went to the cheapest Chinese restaurant he could find: one with a huge plate-glass window, enabling him to continue watching. Over the road, amongst the rubbish from Berwick Street market, an old, bald Greek, his coat tied around his waist, foraged through discarded boxes of soft and rotten fruit. He looked up, saw Larkin watching him; he stopped momentarily, gave Larkin a look that asked him to pity what he was reduced to. The look also said that if Larkin moved in on his pitch he'd slice his eyes.

Larkin finished his plate of sweet and sour carcinogens and moved off to the pub. He always frequented the same one: The Duke of Clarence, just off Brewer Street. It didn't look much from the outside so it didn't attract the tourists; and it wasn't much inside either so the Soho luvvies steered clear. It was a good place to drink.

Larkin drank to give himself strength and occasional inspiration. Plus he enjoyed it. And after swearing off drugs, it was the only vice he allowed himself.

Harold was behind the counter: never Harry, always Harold. Harold was the man who understood, everyone's best friend. A small man with an immaculately pressed white shirt, cufflinks, starched collar and bow tie. You could tell the days of the week by Harold's bow tie. Today it was yellow with small black diamonds – so it must be Thursday.

'Afternoon, Larkin. Usual, is it?'

Larkin nodded and Harold headed toward the Kronenbourg pump. Larkin felt no particular brand loyalty; all that mattered was that his lager should be draught, and as strong as possible.

Harold came back with the beer. 'How's tricks, Mr Larkin?'

'Mustn't grumble, Harold. Well I do, but nobody listens.' Harold laughed politely. 'The rent gets paid and I can still afford a pint, so I've not got too many complaints.'

'Glad to hear it, Mr Larkin.'

'How are you, anyway? How's Maeve?'

A shadow flitted quickly across Harold's bland face and was gone. 'She's doing as well as can be expected.'

Maeve, Harold's wife, had gone to the doctor

7

complaining of a stomach upset. He had told her to eat more roughage; she had done so, and the pain got worse. She returned to the doctor who, reluctantly, referred her to a specialist – who slit her open and found inoperable cancer of the colon, now spread to virtually every major organ and a few minor ones. All the hospital could do was to send her home 'to die with dignity'. She was now virtually comatose – which meant that Harold, in addition to running the pub, had to feed her, change her clothes and clean up when she soiled the bedclothes. That was the modern NHS's idea of dying with dignity.

Harold was bearing up well, but Larkin did notice his whisky glass was twice as full as usual. Still, he kept smiling – probably because he wouldn't know what to do if he stopped.

Larkin thanked him for the beer, sent his best wishes to Maeve and went to sit with his drink in a corner. As he was about to get settled, his pager sounded; the rest of the pub looked daggers at him, incredulous that a yuppie had invaded their sanctuary. He shrugged apologetically and trudged off to the pay phone.

He knew who it was. He dialled the only person who ever paged him: his editor.

'Is Lindsay there? It's Larkin. I've just been paged.'

The secretary put him through.

'Larkin. You want to see me?'

'Why else would I buzz you? It's the only way to get hold of you. That's why I bought you that pager, darling.'

'What d'you want?'

'So abrupt! Is that any way to talk to your lover?'

'I'm not your lover. I'm just someone you fuck when the mood takes you.'

'And what a good fuck you are. For a journalist.'

'Lindsay—'

'Sorry, darling – don't have time to get personal. This is more important. This is work.'

'If it's about the article, you can have it when I—'

'Oh, screw the article, darling. The world is hardly on

8

tenterhooks to hear that Elvis is alive and well and living in Beckton.'

'What d'you mean?'

'What d'you think I mean? You're going to be a proper reporter again. "Scoop" Larkin.' She started to laugh at her own joke, her merriment rapidly descending into a hacking cough; Larkin could hear her dragging on a Silk Cut to restore her equanimity.

'OK, Lindsay, what's the catch?'

'*Catch*? Lover, you disappoint me. There's no catch. It's a *story*. Remember what that is? You write it, the photographer gets some snaps, we print it. Now go and get your bag packed. You're off to Newcastle.'

'Newcastle?'

'That's right, loverboy. You're going home.'

3: The Rover's Return

'So there was Robbie, right? And there was this great big fuck-off Jamaican, big black bloke, right? Bending over him, and then suddenly the door burst open, right? And you know what? Whole fucking room went dead quiet – but Robbie, he never batted an eyelid. Never fuckin' flinched. Mind you, when he found out it was his boyfriend—'

'D'you want anything from the buffet car?'

'What?' said Andy, plainly irritated that his star-studded anecdote had been interrupted.

'I *said*, d'you want anything from the buffet car?'

'Closed, innit? Closed at Sheffield.'

'Oh.' Larkin paused. 'Well, I'm just going to stretch my legs.' He stood up and made for the aisle.

'Don't you want to hear the end of the story?'

'Save it for later,' Larkin said, and began to walk away.

He glanced over his shoulder and saw Andy gaze pensively out of the window for a couple of seconds before bringing his pony-tailed head round to bear on two pretty young girls who had joined the train at Doncaster. Although they had been pretending not to listen to him, the pitch and level at which Andy had been animating his stories would have caught the ear of Helen Keller.

'Hey ladies,' he charmed, 'you fans of Kevin Costner?'

They both giggled.

'Well, you won't be after you hear this . . .'

And off Andy went.

Larkin, meanwhile, stood in the corridor, staring blankly out of the window, watching the scenery rush past. Replaying his phone conversation with Lindsay.

'Why Newcastle?'

'Because that's where the story is.'

'Why me?'

'Because you're perfect, darling. You were brought up there.'

'What if I don't want to go back?'

'You do.'

'What if I don't?'

'You do.' Ice and steel had entered her voice; he knew it was futile to argue.

'What d'you want me to do?' he sighed in resignation.

'Believe it or not, there's been a gangland murder up there.'

'Gangland? You mean, drugs?'

'Yes. Very nasty. Some local dealer got knifed. Not all that exceptional in itself, but he was working for some very big hitters from a London firm. They've vowed revenge on the locals, and the stage is apparently all set for a potentially massive gang war.'

'And you want me on the front line.'

'Exactly.'

'So what's my angle?'

'The funeral.'

'The *funeral*? That's all?'

'For now. Wayne Edgell will get quite a send-off; I want you there to see it.'

Larkin thought for a moment. 'Wayne Edgell? That sounds familiar.' A mental lightbulb clicked on. 'I went to school with someone called Wayne Edgell—'

'I thought you might have.'

'But I went to school in Grimley. That's a small town, 'bout five miles outside Newcastle.'

'I know. That's where the funeral is. That's where he was murdered.'

12

'*Grimley*? Where I grew up?'

'Exactly, loverboy. See how this job's tailor-made for you?'

He was stunned. 'When's the funeral?'

'Monday. But I want you there before then to nose around – get some background. The locals should talk to you, since you speak the lingo.'

'I doubt that. North Easterners have very fixed ideas about founding sons who move away. Especially down south.'

'Well, see what you can do.'

'Will I have a photographer with me on this?'

'Of course. You don't know your arse from your Pentax! I know you like to work alone, but this time you've got a pal to keep you company.'

'Who?'

'Andy Brennan.'

'Andy Brennan? That little South London gobshite? He's a walking case for compulsory sterilisation.'

'Maybe so – but if there's a pic he's not allowed to get, he'll get it.'

'OK. Do I leave straight away?

'Tomorrow.'

'Why not today?'

'Because, darling, I have had the most godawful trying day, and what I really need is a good mind-cleansing fuck. My place. Eight o'clock sharp.'

And she rang off, leaving him to reflect on the inspired working relationship he enjoyed with his editor. Professional to the end.

Larkin had once vowed, in a dramatic, Scarlett O'Hara fashion, never to return to the North East. But as he stared through the window, reacquainting himself with half-forgotten landmarks, he found he was besieged by conflicting emotions. The places that had once marked the boundary of his whole world now felt strange, distant. It was like sleeping with a lover after a few

13

years' gap – the contours were familiar, but the quality of intimacy had changed.

The train passed Grimley. It had the same old greyhound track and chemical factory; the same church, shops, school and houses. Apart from being the unlikely focal point of a rather nasty little gangland war, it still struck Larkin as nothing more than a town for leaving.

The train sped on through Gateshead: a wasteland of industrial estates and row after row of dingy terraced houses interspersed with patches of bulldozed earth and rust-coloured tower blocks for a bit of variety.

Then the bridge. Despite himself, Larkin got quite a thrill seeing it again. The sharp drop to the Tyne on the north side, the steep sweep up from the Tyne on the south side – like passing over a moat into some giant medieval fortress. On the Tyne itself sat the floating nightclub he remembered from his adolescence. The lights were on all along the quay, casting the city in an unreal, romantic glow. Perhaps it was only because the lights gave it a rosy hue – but to Larkin, it looked like a place that could almost have possibilities.

He shook his head and walked back to his seat where Andy was cheekily inviting the two giggly girls to take a look at his equipment. He completely ignored Larkin, so Larkin collected his bags and prepared to leave the train. And as he stepped onto the platform he made a token effort to convince himself that he wasn't just a little bit excited to be back.

Larkin was lost. The city had changed and the hotel wasn't where he'd thought it would be; after plenty of asking around, he was eventually directed to the quayside.

Larkin had last caught a glimpse of Andy and his two new friends as they disappeared into The Forth on Pink Lane. Now alone, he walked through the darkening streets down to the Bigg Market, where he was greeted by a burgeoning mass of lads sporting shirtsleeves, pegged baggies and loafers, with styled, cropped hair,

Boss aftershave and chemically inflated grins. Herding from bar to bar, they were gearing themselves up for Friday night's fuck, fight or bag of chips, their broken noses and swollen stomachs testifying that two out of three wasn't bad for starters. The women were all perms and fake tans on microskirted gooseflesh, going through the rituals, playing the game. Everyone looked immaculately turned out, Larkin noticed; they'd clearly spent their wages if they had a job, or their dole money if they didn't, on trying to look and feel special. Either way the major growth industry seemed to be in Italian designerwear; and, of course, the black and white stripes of the born-again football fans.

He left them to it in the primal disco thud of the Bigg Market – more like a cattle market, he thought grimly – and went down the cobbled streets of the Side, past Scott's the Barbers, past the Keep and down to the quayside. He was surprised to find it gentrified; surprised and disappointed. Buildings once full of genuine character and individuality had been expensively refurbished and themed by big brewery chains. They bore names like, O'Hanrahan's, Flynn's: a phenomenon referred to by an Irish colleague of Larkin's as Plastic Paddy pubs. They had traded in their often unsavoury pasts for a cheap, pseudo-antiquity. Larkin didn't think it was a change for the better.

He walked along past The Red House and The Cooperage to find his hotel – another new building designed to look like an old one. Unfortunately it had failed to achieve the flat-roofed, red-brick warehouse style it strived for; it contained all the charm of a multi-storey car park.

He entered the reception, an area suffused with a beige opulence that even extended to the lightbulbs, checked in, and went up to his room. It was clean and impersonal, just like any hotel room. Just like his flat. The most pleasant thing about it was the view of the bridges.

He dumped his stuff, sat on the bed and flicked the

15

remote through the TV channels. There was nothing to stimulate him, so he switched it off. He took out a book, flopped on the bed and started to read. Soon he realised he wasn't taking in a word; he sighed, and put it down. It wasn't working. He knew what he needed. Picking up his jacket, he headed out.

The hotel bar was as welcoming and atmospheric as an airport departure lounge, so he struck out for the quayside where a suburban-smooth wine bar crowd flowed alongside him, their bankrupt smiles defying the recession even if it killed them. Larkin resisted the urge to push the smug bastards into the Tyne.

He eventually managed to get served in the Baltic Tavern; thank God somewhere still had an atmosphere of sorts. Plushly seated, with brick walls, it was noisier than he remembered, but it remained a place where a comfortable drink could be had.

Larkin took his beer and went to sit by the window. The last time he'd been in here, a row of old warehouses had faced the pub from the opposite side of the river; this had been razed and replaced by a steel, glass, concrete and brick monstrosity, seemingly designed by the creator of the Daleks. He looked closer: the new courthouse. He started to drink.

Half past eleven. The pubs were shut and Larkin was drunk. He had started the night trying to remember all he could about Wayne Edgell, which wasn't much; eventually he'd given up and let the alcohol take over. And it had done so with alacrity.

Now he was slumped over the rail at the river's edge, composing nasty little epithets for his Edgell piece about Newcastle's decline, singing snatches of old Elvis Costello songs. He swivelled his head to look along the quay to a spot where he had once taken photos of an old girlfriend. His first love: a law student, nineteen, blonde and gorgeous. It had been a tempestuous affair; they'd begun it ready to die for each other, and ended it ready to kill each other. The relationship had come to

16

its bitter conclusion shortly after they had traded punches on the Swing Bridge, when one of them had tried to throw the other off; he hadn't seen her since. She was just one of the ghosts he carried around with him.

He started to walk, after a fashion, stumbling up the road, telling himself, as all drunks do, that he was perfectly sober. As he went past the courthouse steps, a couple emerged through the main doors. They were well dressed, well heeled, and well pissed-off.

'I wish you weren't so forgetful,' an angry female voice said. 'Having to leave the party early! You know what that meeting with Sir James could mean to me. To *us*.'

'To *you*. Anyway, it was you who forgot the papers, not me.' The second, male voice gave a snort of derision. 'Don't worry – Sir James will still be there when we get back.'

Something about the female voice gave Larkin a start. He'd heard it before. It was a voice that had once meant something to him ... With an alcohol-fuelled sense of curiosity and effrontery, he ran to the bottom of the steps and jumped into the couple's path.

The three regarded each other in stunned, freeze-frame silence for a second or two, until the action resumed with Larkin's recognition of the woman.

Charlotte the bridge fighter.

Before he had time to reintroduce himself, a quick glance to his right clocked the fist of her heftily built companion as it powered towards Larkin's jaw.

4: Ghosts

The bell rang. And suddenly Larkin was in the ring, fighting. Just as abruptly the fighting stopped, but the bell kept on ringing; he opened his eyes. He'd expected to be laid out on the canvas, but he wasn't, he was in a bed. A strange one. He jumped up, immediately regretted it, and flopped back down. Whoever he'd been fighting had won.

The bell kept ringing. With shaking, fumbling fingers, he traced the noise to the bedside phone and picked it up.

'Hello?' Blearily.

'Mr Larkin?' A girl's voice, squeakily cheerful.

Larkin grunted.

'Call for you! Putting you throu-ough,' she sang.

The line was connected. Then a ghost's voice: 'You made an exhibition of yourself last night, didn't you?'

Charlotte.

'Great. Just what I need. I feel like shit and now you phone up to make it even worse.'

'Don't swear, Stephen. And if that's how you feel I'll go.'

'No you won't. You're too nosy.'

'Oh, am I now?'

And Larkin was left holding a dead phone.

'Boring conversation anyway,' he said to the empty room, just to have the last word. Cutting him off like that – Birch the bitch hadn't changed.

He lay back down on the bed and tried to fill in the gaps in his memory of the previous night. After a few seconds his booze-soaked synapses started to make connections – and with a groan he remembered the events that had left him feeling like Mike Tyson's punchbag.

'What the fuck did you do that for?' Larkin shouted from the bottom step of the courthouse, where he had found himself after clumsily twisting from the path of the blow hurled by Charlotte's beau. The man, who was built like a rugby-playing brick shithouse, made a second lunge towards him.

'Charles, stop it!' said Charlotte forcefully, placing a restraining hand on the Shithouse. He stopped dead and turned to her.

'Do you know him?' It was issued as a challenge.

'Yes. He's an old . . . friend of mine.'

Charles snorted and resumed his menacing surge towards Larkin.

'And I want to talk to him.' She placed herself directly in Charles's path and stared deep into his eyes. Charles relented, but unwillingly, like a scrap-crazed pit bull terrier denied the kill.

'Ungawa! Down, Lobo!' Larkin said faintly, clinging to the guide rail, but his feeble humour went unappreciated. He tried to help himself up but the sudden exertion on top of the alcohol made his head and stomach spin. With a final withering look at Charles, Charlotte walked down the steps and pulled Larkin to his feet.

'Are you all right?' she asked.

'Think so,' said Larkin grumpily. 'What's his fuckin' problem?'

'I expect he thought you were going to mug us.'

Larkin grunted, then made his eyes focus on Charlotte. She was older, of course, but in a pleasant, wholesome way; not battle scarred and haggard like himself, on whom the intervening years had taken a visible toll. Her blonde hair was now worn in a sensible bob; a discreet collection of lines around the corners of her eyes was the only tangible sign of any kind of maturation. She gave Larkin the same kind of scrutiny; Lord only knew what she made of him.

'You're looking well,' she said, without much conviction.

'I look like shite – but thanks anyway.'

They both grinned; Charles shuffled uncomfortably behind them.

'It's been a long time,' she said.

'And other cliches,' said Larkin.

Silence. Charles took that as his cue to intervene.

'Come on – we're going.'

Larkin rounded on him, trying to sound calm. 'Hey, mate, no need for that. We're just talking. We haven't seen each other in a while.'

'And you won't be seeing each other any more. We're leaving.' He grabbed Charlotte's arm. Charlotte shrugged him off; again he stood mute. That pleased Larkin enormously; he made a great show of addressing Charlotte in a manner appropriate for a former lover. He asked her the usual questions of intimate strangers: how was she, where was she living, what was she doing. And she answered him: fine, Jesmond, working as a solicitor in Newcastle.

Then a pause, difficult for both of them.

'You've done all right then,' said Larkin.

'I suppose so.' Then, awkwardly, 'I heard about what happened.'

'Yeah.'

'I'm sorry.'

'Yeah.'

Charlotte filled the silence this time. 'What brings you back here?'

'Work. Still a journalist.'

'I wouldn't have thought there would have been any stories up here to interest you. Not compared with London.'

'Me neither, but my editor thinks otherwise. This one involves Grimley, believe it or not. Apparently there was a gangland murder there, and I'm here to see if it gets any big—'

The Shithouse jumped in. 'I won't tell you again, Charlotte. We're going.'

Larkin's fuse finally burnt out. 'Look, mate, what's your fuckin' problem, eh?'

'Listen to me, you little nobody. You're her past. History. I'm her present, and unless she gets a move on and you crawl back into whichever hole you crawled out of, she won't have a future.'

'Is that such a bad thing?' Larkin turned to Charlotte. 'I can't say your taste in men has improved. Does he support Sunderland as well?'

'I've had enough of you, you drunken little shit.'

The booze, combined with Charles's arrogance, had returned Larkin to fighting fitness. 'Fuckin' try it, cock-sucker. Come on! I'm ready for you.'

Charlotte turned away. 'Stephen, don't be ridiculous.'

'It's not me, darlin', that's ridiculous. It's fuckin' needledick there. He's the one who started all this. All I was trying to do was—'

Charlotte never got to find out what Larkin was trying to do, because at that moment the Shithouse took a swing at Larkin and connected with the side of his jaw. The blow knocked the drunken Larkin off balance; while he was trying to regain it, the Shithouse threw another punch that landed square in Larkin's chest. This one lifted him off his feet, carried him through the air and plonked him on his back where he lay unmoving. But the Shithouse obviously hadn't heard that you didn't kick a man when he was down. He took a vicious swing at Larkin's ribcage with his foot, and was about to take another when Charlotte grabbed his arm.

'Stop it, for God's sake!'

Fortunately for Larkin, he stopped. He looked at Charlotte, smirking. 'That should settle him for a bit.'

Larkin was starting to come round; Charlotte bent over him. 'Are you all right?'

'Fuck do you think?'

'There's no need for language like that.'

'There's every fuckin' need.' He raised himself on his elbows. 'Come on,' he said to Charlotte, spitting blood with each syllable.

'Where?'

'Pilgrim Street nick. I'm going to report this bastard for assault. And you're going to back me up.'

'I can't!'

'Yes you can! You're a witness, you saw what he did. Come on.'

'No.'

The Shithouse started laughing. 'Tell him.'

Charlotte looked apologetically at Larkin. 'A wife – can't give evidence against her husband.'

Charles knelt over Larkin and pulled him up by the front of his jacket. Up close Larkin could see that Charles was fizzing with a manic energy; an artificially stimulated *ubermensch*, with pinwheeling pupils.

'Welcome home, sonny boy,' Charles said, and let Larkin's head fall back on to the pavement with a dull thud.

Charles stood up, pulled Charlotte away. The heavy-goods train that was thundering through Larkin's head blotted out any farewell speech that Charlotte may have made.

Larkin lay there for a while, summoning up the energy to move. He laughed painfully to himself. He'd had the fight – now all he needed was the fuck and the bag of chips and he'd have had a perfect Friday night in Newcastle.

After downing an Underberg and Bisodol hangover cocktail, Larkin slithered out of bed, leaving a slug-like trail of linen and underwear on the way to the bathroom. In the mirror he inspected his naked body for injury and found bruises blossoming up his left side, where Charles the Shithouse had kicked him. His jaw was discoloured and tender; the slight swelling lent him an heroic, Captain America look. He attempted to shower the drunkenness and discomfort from his body, then towelled off, combed his longish, dark hair out of his eyes and put on his leather and Levis armour. All the while MTV blared in the background as a kind of penance, reminding him (as if he needed reminding) that, since punk, everything had lost its meaning.

He arrived in the lobby – the beige seemed less opulent in daylight – to find a horde of shame-faced middle managers, regretting the previous evening spent behaving like a bunch of fifteen-year-olds on their first trip away from home. A damage limitation exercise was now being discussed among them, as they desperately tried to create bravado out of embarrassment. As he checked his key in at the desk, he met the singing telephone girl in person. She looked exactly as he'd imagined: blonde, rictus grin, enough perfume to knock down a truck. Or truck driver. What someone with no personality calls a personality girl.

He was serenaded with the fact that there was a message for him and handed a piece of folded hotel stationery.

When you're feeling in a better mood perhaps we might have lunch together. I have something to talk to you about. Heartbreak Soup. 1 PM.

Charlotte.

Larkin was impressed; the personality girl had joined-up writing. He smiled at her and she beamed back as if he'd just handed her a Pools cheque. He looked at his watch: eleven thirty. He was just walking out the door when he heard a familiar voice behind him.

'Larkin! Hey, man, wait up!'

He turned: Andy.

He caught up with Larkin. 'Hey, where you going? Jeez, what happened to your face?'

'What happened to yours?'

Andy felt his face reflexively. 'I don't know. What's wrong with it?'

24

Larkin pointed to Andy's neck. 'Good night, was it? Or did you meet a vampire?'

Andy realised. 'Oh, yeah! Those two chicks off the train. Great scene, man. Where did you go? There was one for you. When you disappeared I just had to have both of them meself. Couldn't disappoint them.' His mind slipped back. 'Wow . . . You should've been there. Missed a treat.'

Maybe I should have, thought Larkin. *Couldn't have been any worse than what happened.* 'What you doing today, then?'

'Dunno, man. Have a recce round your home town – where is it? Grimley? See if there's anything worth getting the old camera out for. That sort of thing.'

'Very conscientious of you.'

'Well, that's what I've planned. Whether it'll turn out that way is another matter. What you up to?'

'I'm off to meet someone for lunch.'

'Yeah? That was quick. What's her name?'

'None of your bloody business. I'll meet you back here later, OK? About five, six?'

'Make it that pub I was in last night with them two birds.' Andy stopped for a moment and pondered. 'What we meeting for then?'

'To do some background, what else?'

'Oh. I thought perhaps you wanted to get drunk.'

'I do, but we have to work.'

'OK, you miserable bastard.'

'I may be a miserable bastard, but at least I don't have to visit the clap clinic every fortnight.'

'You want to watch yourself, Larkin! We nearly had some witty repartee going there. Bit of effort, we could turn into a double act.'

'I fuckin' hope not.'

'There you go again. The wit and wisdom of—'

'Half-five. See you later.'

Larkin turned away. Behind him he heard: 'Think of some good one-liners for tonight, won't you?'

Even though he couldn't stand the guy, Larkin couldn't help smiling as he walked out.

5: Heartbreak Soup

Heartbreak Soup, 1 PM. Larkin sat surrounded by a smattering of Saturday strollers and folky bohos artfully slumped in corners. No Charlotte. He ordered chicken satay with gado gado and a South American beer, wondering why the places with the worst governments had the best food. Then he remembered Britain and changed his mind. He waited: no Charlotte. Quarter past. No Charlotte. His satay arrived and he ate it. He downed his beer. Still no Charlotte. The bill was paid. The strollers had moved on; the bohos were still making the world a safer place for freedom of expression. No Charlotte. He stood up to go and sighed. Why had he expected anything else?

He was making his way out of the door when he saw a figure hurrying towards him from the courthouse. Overcoat flapping, power-dressed business suit underneath, briefcase under one arm, blonde hair bobbing at just the right length. *Here we go*, thought Larkin. *Explanations, excuses – and strictly no apologies.*

But the first thing she did was apologise. Profusely and sincerely for having to work on a Saturday, then for having to work later than she wanted to, then for forcing Larkin to eat alone. She promised to make it up to him by taking him to the pub – would The Baltic be OK? – and buying him a pint. She really was sorry, she said, and smiled. And Larkin was speechless.

* * *

Charlotte got the drinks and ordered a prawn salad sandwich for her lunch and they sat down by the window without speaking. They looked at the courthouse; as Larkin had done, the night before. They looked out at the muddy Tyne. They looked around at the other people in the bar, and when there was nothing else to look at, they looked at each other. Their eyes briefly locked, then bounced away, as if repelled by a magnetic charge. Larkin chose that moment to take a long mouthful of beer; Charlotte became fascinated by the progress of a used condom down the river. They sat like that for several seconds, during which the Pyramids could have been constructed. Then, eventually, Charlotte spoke.

'When did you arrive up here?'

'Yesterday. I was looking round the old town last night.'

'And you met me.'

'Yeah.' Larkin touched his swollen jaw.

Charlotte looked sheepish. 'I've told Charles off about that. He won't be doing it again in a hurry.'

'Sure.' Larkin took another swig. 'Didn't think you would still be in Newcastle. I thought you'd have moved on.'

'I did for a while – but I came back.' She pulled a little face that contained the skeleton of a smile. 'Sometimes it's better to be a big fish in a small pond.'

'And a solicitor, eh?'

'That's right.'

'That must be tough up here. They don't take too kindly to intelligent women.'

She gave a little smile that started off as coy and ended up conspiratorial. 'It's not a problem – not if you know the right people.'

'Which you do.'

She laughed. 'I try.'

'And Charles?' said Larkin; he knew he'd have to mention him some time, so best get it over with. 'How did you meet him?'

28

She seemed guarded. 'Oh, very boring, I'm afraid. He's a solicitor as well, we work together.'

'Love among the briefs?' said Larkin, trying to be nonchalant.

'Something like that.' Charlotte had the decency to look embarrassed, but she collected herself sufficiently to give Larkin her broad killer smile, the one he'd never been able to resist. He decided, half-heartedly, to try.

'So you're still a journalist,' said Charlotte, finding small talk anything but easy. 'Work for anyone I'd know?'

'Oh . . . I doubt it.'

'We do get newspapers up here, you know. The stage-coach brings them every Wednesday.'

'Very funny. No, I mean it's not one that you've probably read. And if you had, you wouldn't want to admit it.'

'Come on – what is it?'

'I work for the *Daily World News.*'

She trawled her memory. 'I . . . don't think . . .'

'It's like the *Sunday Sport* but more downmarket. I create headlines: GOD DISCOVERED IN KIWI FRUIT! and ELVIS REINCARNATED AS SCOTTIE DOG! That was a particularly good one – we even had a photo of a Highland terrier with sunglasses and big sideburns. And my all-time favourite: I WAS GLORIA HUNNIFORD'S KINKY WATER-SPORTS SEX SLAVE! Thankfully we didn't have a picture to go with that one.' He stopped, sensing her lack of response. 'What? What's the matter?'

'Oh . . . nothing.' She paused. 'Do – do you enjoy it?'

He considered. 'No. But it pays the rent, gives me something to get up for in the morning.' She'd put him on the defensive. 'I still do other bits, just to keep my hand in. Proper stories, features, stuff like that. The odd investigative job.'

'I used to read all that. It was excellent.'

'Thanks.'

'D'you wish you still had your investigative job?'

Larkin's face became impassive. 'There's a lot of things I still wish I had.'

Charlotte caught the tone of his voice, the look on his face, and didn't press him further. Instead she looked at his near-empty glass. 'Another drink?'

'Yeah. Same again, thanks.' Sitting opposite Charlotte the successful solicitor he suddenly felt the need to justify himself. As she went to get up he put his hand on hers. 'It's crap. I *know* it's crap. But that's the way it has to be, because if I start to enjoy it I might start to forget what happened. And I don't want to.' He looked down, aware that he had opened up more in a few minutes with Charlotte than he had in years. With an effort he pulled himself back. 'Go and get those drinks.'

She went to the bar. When she returned they resumed their silence; it was the kind of moment when the conversation could have gone deeper, but Larkin felt he had exposed himself enough. So they sipped their drinks and behaved like civilised people.

Charlotte broke the silence.

'You seeing anyone at the moment?'

'Speaking as a married woman?'

'I'm just asking.'

'Well . . . I'm sort of with someone, but I'm not really involved. Haven't been since . . . well, you know.'

'Would I know this woman?'

'You're in an inquisitive mood!'

Charlotte grinned engagingly; Larkin continued. 'It's my editor. But she's only after me for my body.'

'Lucky her.' Charlotte had a teasing glint in her eye; Larkin knew he was in trouble.

'Sorry. Married women aren't my style.'

'Oh, you presumptuous thing, you! Can't a woman give a man a simple compliment? Why do you always have to bring sex into it?'

Their conversation was getting onto thin ice and Larkin didn't want to skate on it. He felt himself blush. 'Was there something special you wanted to say to me, Charlotte? I've got a feeling you didn't just summon me here for the pleasure of my company.'

She smiled weakly. Larkin noticed that she seemed

agitated; as if she had a secret and didn't know who to trust with it.

'Look . . . I did ask you here today for a reason. I want to ask you a favour.'

Same old Charlotte, thought Larkin. *Always getting her money's worth.*

But, almost as an afterthought, Charlotte added, 'And I've got some information for you. I wouldn't expect something for nothing.'

'What?'

'I'll tell you in a minute.'

'After you've asked the favour.'

'Yes.'

'What is it then?'

'Well, you've kind of answered it in a way, but I still have to ask. I wondered if you were interested in a spot of investigative work. I wouldn't ask if it wasn't important, but I'm at my wits' end. I don't know where to turn.'

'About what?' He knew he shouldn't have asked; he didn't really want to hear her answer.

She looked straight at him, with a lawyer's honest face. He knew he was getting into deep water. 'If I tell you, you'll want to do something about it. Are you prepared for that? If not, then I won't say another word.'

She was good; she was playing him well. 'Just tell me – then I'll decide.'

She looked sad, distressed; he felt honoured. He was getting the whole range for free. Well, on second thoughts, not for free – whatever she wanted was going to cost. He knew that from past experience.

'It all came to a head a couple of weeks ago. But it had been building up for ages.'

'What?'

'One of the legal secretaries in the firm, a friend of mine—'

'What about her? Been caught with her fingers in the petty cash?'

Charlotte stared at him. 'No. She died.'

31

He immediately regretted his flippancy; he tried to make up for it with a blast of sympathetic sincerity. 'That's terrible. How?'

'Well . . . the official verdict was suicide. But—'

'What?'

She tried to be as undramatic as she could. 'I think it was murder.'

Larkin fell silent.

'I'll tell you about it,' she said.

She explained that her friend, Mary, had been married to a cruel, abusive man, – ex-Army, ex-Security Consultant, ex-anything in a uniform – who had regularly beaten her up. When he had destroyed as much of her soul as he could, he left her for another woman. This resulted in Mary feeling completely worthless. Full of hate for herself. Charlotte paused, then continued.

'After a while she recovered. Started going out with the gang from the office, that sort of thing. That's when the two of us became friends. She would confide in me, tell me her secrets. It was like seeing a new person emerge. She still didn't have much self-confidence, though. A friend of a friend put her in touch with a counselling group – she was reluctant at first, but eventually she went. Did her the world of good. She discovered she wasn't the only one in her situation. It made her realise she deserved something more than she'd been getting.'

'Good for her,' said Larkin.

'Yes. The next thing that happened was she started going to a singles club. Didn't meet anyone special there, I don't think. Maybe she wasn't ready, maybe she didn't like any of them – I don't really know.'

'How old was she when she started doing this?'

'When she died she was forty-seven . . . She suddenly found this new boyfriend, – where from, I don't know. His name was Terry, she said he was twenty years younger than her and she fell in love with him. We couldn't believe it. Mary, of all people, had a toy boy.'

'What was he like?'

'Don't know. I never met him, none of us did. That was the peculiar thing about it. Mary wasn't the most gregarious of people at the best of times, but I thought I was close to her. I thought she trusted me. I asked her to introduce me to him, but she put me off, every time. We started to drift apart. She became more remote, started to behave – strangely. Secretive, almost furtive, as if she was doing something forbidden. Something that she enjoyed. Then she started to deteriorate; she began to look like she had when she'd been living with her husband, towards the end of her relationship. Finally,' she gave a courtroom pause, 'she killed herself.'

'How?'

'Shotgun.'

Larkin's mind went into flashback; a shiver slipped down his spine. He tried to concentrate on the present. 'Sounds like she just couldn't bear being a victim all over again.'

'I think there's more to it than that. She got through it once before, she could have done it again. She was a strong person, Stephen.'

'But if she'd staked all her future happiness on this Terry—'

'Look,' said Charlotte, 'I don't know what went on, but I know he killed her. She wouldn't do that to herself. Even if he didn't actually pull the trigger, morally he brought about her death.'

'But you could never prove that in a court of law.'

'You know I couldn't.'

'What did the police say about all this?'

'The usual. Tragic waste. That's all.'

'Didn't they find the fact that she supposedly shot herself a bit suspicious? Where would a legal secretary have got a shotgun from?'

'Mary told me once that her husband used to enjoy shooting – rabbits, birds, anything that moved. He was that kind of guy. The police did mention that he didn't hold a current firearms certificate, so they couldn't prove it was his. But he was in the army years ago, I'm sure he'd have known where to get hold of a gun on the cheap. When he left Mary it happened in such a hurry that he left most of his possessions behind. I suppose Mary just kept the gun. Perhaps it made her feel safer – a woman on her own – to have one in the house.'

'So why do you want me to find out if Terry did it? And if I do find out – what then?'

'I don't know. I just want justice to be done.'

Larkin drained his glass and sighed. 'This is crazy, you know that? You want me to look for a metaphysical murderer.'

'Stephen, she was my friend. I may have lost her before she died, but I still loved her. I just have to *do* something, that's all. Please. It . . . it would mean a lot to me.'

She touched his hand; Larkin looked at her, ghosts dancing behind his eyes as he gazed into hers, deep and dark enough to drown in. She held his gaze. '*Please.*'

He tried to postpone the inevitable. 'Have you been to a private detective about this?'

'No. I don't know any good ones that aren't connected with my company. I wanted to keep this as secret as possible.' Her eyes bored straight into him again. 'Stephen, I know it's painful, and I wouldn't ask you if I had any alternative, but you were the best. It's asking a lot, and I'm the last person you'd probably want to do a favour for – but it's important.'

He had known all along he'd say yes. What he didn't know was why. 'All right.'

Charlotte lit up. 'So you'll do it?'

'Yes. But I can't spend too much time on it. I've got a proper assignment as well.'

'That's no problem! And I'll pay you for your time, of course.'

'What about the hunky Charles? What will he say about all this?'

She hesitated, then went on. 'He needn't know. Anyway, he's away at the moment. Business.' The last bit was spat out with distaste; Larkin decided not to push it.

'Has she got an address, this Mary? And a surname?'

'Yes. I've written it down for you.' So she must have been very certain he'd accept. She rummaged in her handbag, producing a neat little business card. That was something else Larkin remembered about Charlotte; she had the neatest handbag of any woman he'd ever known. 'That's my card. The address is on the back. It's in Low Fell.'

Larkin took it, read the front. 'Nicholson Griffin Harwood And Howe?'

Charlotte smiled wryly. 'Bit of a mouthful, isn't it?'

Larkin pocketed the card. 'How do I get in?'

'Here's a key.' She handed it over.

'You carry this around with you?'

She reddened. 'No. I . . . said I'd clear up anything to do with her work. She used to take work home, so . . .'

'How about family?'

'Couple of brothers, I think. She hardly ever saw them. One lives over in Cumbria somewhere – the older one – and the other's in Darlington. Married, I think. They're supposed to be clearing the house out.'

'What about the policeman in charge of the investigation?'

'Moir. Detective Inspector Henry Moir.'

'I'll have to talk to him as well.'

A cloud passed over Charlotte's face. 'You can try, but I think you'll be wasting your time. He's not the most sympathetic of people.'

'OK. When do you want your first report?'

Her voice changed, grew warmer. 'When you've got something to tell me. Will you have something to tell me by, say, eight o'clock tonight? At Francesca's?'

Larkin grinned. 'Maybe.'

'Good.' Was she flirting with him – or was he imagining it?

'Oh, by the way. What was this information you said you had for me? You scratch my back, I'll scratch yours.'

She stiffened slightly; when she spoke it was with reluctance. 'The Wayne Edgell case?'

'Yeah?' said Larkin.

'We're representing Gary Fenwick.'

'Who's Gary Fenwick?'

'He's the man who's supposed to have murdered Wayne Edgell. I can see you haven't studied your background file yet.'

Larkin was stunned.

Charlotte grinned. 'Surprised?'

'A bit.' He recovered quickly, putting the information to work for him. 'Trade of information, then – you help me with my assignment, I'll put your mind at rest. Deal?'

'Deal! Got to rush now – see you at eight.'

They stared at each other. Larkin felt the thin ice begin to crack. He wondered what she was wearing beneath her business suit; that thought was enough to shift the North Pole.

'Look . . . the last time I saw you, we . . .'

She gently placed her lips on his, then removed them, in case he got ideas. 'Later,' she said, and disappeared through the door.

Larkin sat there in disbelief. Against all his better judgement he'd signed himself up as private investigator, for his now married ex-girlfriend, who seemed to be coming on to him – in addition to working on the murder of a childhood acquaintance, in his home town. *Welcome back, Larkin. You sad, confused bastard.*

6: Checking In, Checking Out

It was a stone bungalow; quiet, unassuming, homely, set back from Durham Road, situated in Low Fell which had once been a turn-of-the-century satellite community of Newcastle but was now no more than a section of main road with down-at-heel shops and pubs, a garage, and a Methodist church. It had been Mary Greene's idea of a decent place to live.

Larkin squeezed into the one remaining parking space near Mary's house – Mary's next-door neighbours seemed to be rebuilding their house from scratch, judging by the selection of skips and battered panel vans littering the road outside – locked his Saab rental car and approached the house of Mary Greene, née Torrington. He noticed next-door's net curtains twitching – perhaps it was a watchtower they were building, rather than an extension. He felt in his pocket for the keys, looked straight ahead, and walked up the garden path as if he had every right to be there.

As the tumblers of the lock clicked, a bilious dread overcame him. The last thing he wanted to be confronted with was the remains of a shotgun blast. His mind began to re-run the reel he had canned up for years; he tried to screen it out, to change channels, but it was no good. The sequence had started and he was transfixed. His heart beat faster; the blood pumped furiously round his body. Even with his eyes screwed tightly shut he couldn't block out the images.

Larkin forced his eyes open. Sophie and Joe wouldn't be there. This was a different house, a different city. He had nothing to fear.

The heavy door opened straight into the living room. Dark wooden beams running the length of the ceiling; a floral print three-piece suite; horse brasses, slightly tarnished; china figurines dusty with neglect. A print on the wall: Victorian children playing on swings. The relatives had done their looting; dust-free templates showed where they had recently helped themselves to ornaments of possible value, thinking Mary would no longer need them. As vultures think dead bodies no longer need flesh.

The room was further tainted by the careless remains of police incident investigation; sills stained with silver fingerprint dust, discarded cordoning-off tape left in clumps, the carpet worn down by many pairs of heavy boots. Thankfully most of the blood had been cleared away. Behind the door, a tea chest full of newspaper-wrapped objects stood waiting to be removed. Bit by bit, traces of Mary's life were seeping away, draining from her home. Yet a residue of cosiness, of vitality, still managed to cling, reluctant to let go.

Larkin put his mind into gear and focused on the job at hand. He stood in the centre of the living room, to work out her position when the shot had hit. From the angle at which the blood had dried into the carpet she must have been facing the mantelpiece. Staring at a photo of Terry, perhaps? He checked the mantelpiece for dust, searched for spaces where a photograph might have been. It was hard to tell if there was anything missing. He scanned the rest of the room. A shelf unit stood on the other side of the fireplace; it held a small selection of books and an elderly stack hi-fi system. He lifted the lid and saw there was still a record on the turntable: Elton John – an early one. Larkin had never liked him much but, not wanting to pass over a possible clue for the sake of musical snobbery, he plugged in the stereo and switched it on.

The needle crackled through the well-worn intro and then Elton began his ode to Marilyn Monroe, a woman more loved after death than in life. Larkin wondered whether Mary Greene had identified with the song, if she had harboured some romantic notion that she could buy into that legend. In reality he knew only too well that all that was left behind after a shotgun death was a bloody mess. He continued with his search.

The bedroom was neat and tidy, as if Mary had just straightened it up before going out to work. The furniture was pine: wardrobe, chest of drawers, dressing-table, bedside cabinet. More floral prints on the duvet and curtains, this time in autumnal shades. He scanned the room: no photographs. He moved on to the wardrobe, checking through coat and jacket pockets, unfolding the jumpers, trying to put them all back as he had found them. He took out her shoes, shook them upside-down, returned them. All he could tell was that, judging from the dress sizes, she had kept herself in trim, and that there had been a distinct variation in her style of dressing. Three-quarters of the garments were dull, conventional. Then there were the newer items, flashier outfits that a younger woman – or a woman trying to appear young? – might wear. Brighter colours, shinier fabrics.

Finally he turned his attention to the chest of drawers. The first drawer contained underwear; this followed the same pattern as the clothes in the wardrobe. Marks and Sparks three-packs, then new stuff. Only these looked as if they had come out of the Ann Summers catalogue: stockings, suspenders, basques, peep-hole bras, crotchless panties – the whole works. It was an odd mixture of obviously expensive silk and satin lingerie, and cheap and tacky mail-order. The next drawer revealed nothing but staid jumpers and blouses – more vestiges of the old Mary. But the contents of the bottom drawer brought Larkin up sharply. It held a porn wardrobe for all occasions. There were various uniforms; a baby-doll nightie; a schoolgirl's gymslip; and a sophisticated range of bondage gear. Leather-wear, spike-heeled boots, spike-heeled shoes – and spikes.

Was it all for Terry, Larkin wondered? Had he encouraged her, first with some mildly daring underwear, then gradually introduced her to what he really wanted?

Although he found it distasteful to be trawling through a dead woman's sex life, handling her clothes and accessories was curiously erotic. He felt he was discovering her intimate secrets, getting to know her, piecing together her life through her sexuality. He found himself getting an erection. With an effort he pushed his mind back into investigative mode and completed his methodical exploration of the room in which Mary revealed her innermost self.

The continual repetition of 'Candle In The Wind' was begining to irritate, so Larkin returned to the living room to switch off the stereo. And as he bent to unplug it he made another discovery: what looked like a diary, for this year, hidden away among the books on the shelf next to the hi-fi. Larkin thought it strange that a grown woman should have kept such a document; stranger still that the police should have ignored it. He had just sat down in a chair to take a closer look when he heard a key in the lock.

He froze. There was nowhere to run to. He shoved the book down the side of the chair and sat, his heart pounding, ready to brazen it out. The door opened. And in came a man in his well-preserved mid-forties, looking every bit as surprised as Larkin. Tall, fair, wearing a V-necked sweater with a striped shirt poking out from the collar, slacks and trainers, all co-ordinated in various shades of pastel that screamed 'weekend leisure'. The man spoke first.

'Who the hell are you?'

'Larkin. Stephen Larkin.' He casually crossed his legs as if he trespassed on a regular basis. 'And you are . . .?' The confident approach worked.

'Phillip Torrington. I've been here all morning – I've only been gone an hour. Did the estate agents send you?'

40

'No, they didn't. You're Mary's brother, right?'

Phillip Torrington was so amazed at the deduction that he blurted out an answer. 'Yes, I am!' Realising that Larkin posed no obvious threat, he seemed to find his courage. 'Are you going to tell me who you are, or do I have to call the police?'

'I've told you who I am. My name's Stephen Larkin and I'm here on behalf of the company your sister worked for. I'm investigating her death.'

'Why? Is there any reason to think it was suspicious?'

What's the matter, son? thought Larkin. *Afraid you won't get her money if it was?* 'No. It's just routine in cases like these.' The old lies were coming thick and fast.

'Which one sent you?'

'Charlotte Birch. Know her?'

Torrington sneered. 'Yes, I know her.'

'And I take it from your reaction you don't like her?'

'I've only met her once, but I admit I took an instant dislike to her. Arrogant. Snooty. She came up to me after the funeral, claimed to be Mary's friend.' He paused. 'I'd never heard of her.'

'Were you and Mary close?'

'I'm her brother.' As if that answered it.

'I know. But I asked, were you and Mary *close*?'

'I suppose—' He thought about it. 'No, not really. Not as close as we should have been. It's quite a distance away, Darlington. But still, we should have read the signs. Didn't notice anything wrong until it was too late.' He shook his head. 'After Robert – her husband – left her, we rallied round. But when she got back on her feet again we didn't think she needed us.'

Meaning you couldn't be bothered, thought Larkin. 'Did she ever mention a man she was seeing? A younger man, Terry?'

Torrington was suddenly wary. 'I . . . I don't know. As I said, I didn't see her that much.'

'You're married, that right?'

41

Torrington's jaw dropped, as if Larkin had unearthed something classified. 'Yes, that's right.'

'Any kids?'

'I've got a son,' he answered reluctantly.

Larkin thought briefly of his own son. 'What's his name?'

'Why? What d'you want to know about him for?'

'Just routine, as I said. I wouldn't be doing my job if I didn't ask.'

This reassurance of proper channels to be followed seemed to calm him somewhat. 'Danny. Daniel.'

'Thank you. Now, about Mary. When you last—'

Torrington interrupted. 'Look, Mr ... what did you say your name was?'

'Larkin.'

'Larkin. We weren't that close, as I've said, so I don't think I can be much help to you.' He moved towards the door.

'OK. I'll not keep you, Mr Torrington. Just one more thing – do you have a photo of Mary? Her employer couldn't supply me with one.'

Torrington glanced outside; Larkin picked up the hint. 'You've got one in your car? Could I have a look at it, please?'

'It'll take a couple of minutes. I had to park quite a way away, there weren't any spaces—'

'I think I could wait that long.'

Torrington realised he was in a no-win situation. Picking up the tea chest from behind the door, he went down the road to the car, reluctantly leaving Larkin in the house unsupervised. Larkin prayed he wouldn't do a runner.

Alone, Larkin shoved the diary inside his jacket and waited in the living room. Although he couldn't see it, he could imagine Torrington's car: the kind that a man who worked damned hard for the right to wear a suit during the week and leisure wear at the weekend would have. And woe betide anyone who tried to stand in his way.

A car horn sounded. Larkin looked out of the window; Torrington had pulled up just outside the bungalow in a Nissan Micra and was revving his engine, clearly ready for a quick getaway. The Micra surprised Larkin; perhaps Torrington had fallen on hard times. Or perhaps it was his wife's. Larkin hurried outside to meet him.

'Here you are,' Torrington said, reluctantly handing Larkin a brown, photographer's display wallet through the driver's window.

'D'you mind if I keep this?' asked Larkin.

'What for?' Torrington looked aghast.

'For investigative purposes. You'll get it back when I've finished with it.'

Torrington didn't object; he was clearly eager to end the interview. Larkin turned to go, then crouched down to the driver's window once more. 'By the way . . . Why did you have this?'

Torrington paused. 'A . . . a keepsake.'

'Don't you have any photos of Mary at home?'

If Torrington had been able to teleport, he would have done. 'Of course. I just . . . liked this one.'

'So you came all this way for one photo?'

Torrington was back on solid ground. 'Oh no. The tea chest too. And I had to do some shopping, down at the Metro Centre. Carol and I often pop over there.'

'Long way to travel just to shop. Must be, what, thirty-odd miles?'

'It's so convenient with everything under one roof. We make a day of it. A long way, but worth it.'

'But too far from Darlington to Low Fell to come and see Mary.'

Torrington didn't answer; Larkin took that as his cue to leave. 'Thank you very much for your time, Mr Torrington. If we need any more information we'll be in touch.' And he stepped back, enabling a worried-looking Torrington to engage first gear and pull away.

As he walked past the house next door, Larkin saw the nosy neighbour's nets twitch again. He blew the looker a kiss then waggled his tongue lasciviously; the

43

curtains whisked back into place. *Simple pleasures are often the best*, he thought.

Back in the car, Larkin opened the folder. It was a photo, taken at a table in a restaurant – perhaps at a birthday celebration; streamers and balloons were much in evidence. A young man: short hair, smart suit, gold jewellery, shark face. Terry! It had to be. And there was Mary. Radiant, happy. She looked much younger than Larkin had thought she would.

He put the photo back in the envelope and drove off.

The green-painted brickwork, the cast-iron radiators and the lino-covered floor made Larkin feel like he was on his way to the headmaster's office for a caning. Only the dog-eared posters about home security, stray dogs and duty rosters – and the fact that his escort was a ginger-haired constable who looked about twelve – reminded him he was in a police station.

He had managed to get past the desk sergeant by claiming to be an insurance investigator working on behalf of Nicholson Griffin Harwood and Howe; he had to speak to Detective Inspector Henry Moir about an urgent matter. After much to-ing and fro-ing he had eventually been allowed in.

They reached a door, half-paned with frosted glass; the constable stopped and knocked. Finding no one in, he went to search for Moir, leaving Larkin alone.

Larkin stood impatiently for a few minutes until a large shadow loomed up behind him and eclipsed the light in the corridor. He looked round.

Moir was a big bloke – not a man, a bloke – about six feet tall and the same width, but he carried his size with authority. He was wearing a suit that managed to fit where it touched – which wasn't in a lot of places. It had probably once been a pleasant shade of Coventry City blue, but years of neglect, sweat and police work had turned it a rather sinister shade of battleship grey. Ominous stains decorated the front. His shirt, too, had seen better days – perhaps when Harold Wilson was in power – and the ensemble was completed by a garish Jamaican sunsplash of a tie thrown round his neck. His hair was cut into a Sweeney Todd special.

'Inspector Moir?'

'Who are you?' A gruff Scottish accent.

'Larkin. Stephen Larkin. I'm working with Nicholson Griff—'

'You a reporter? 'Cos I don't talk to reporters.' He turned to enter his office, signalling that the interview was at an end.

'I'm working on behalf of a firm of solicitors dealing with an apparent suicide. I believe you were in charge of the case.'

'So?'

Larkin tried not to let his exasperation show. 'I'd like to ask you some questions.'

'Would you, now?'

Larkin wanted to hit the man. 'If it's not too much trouble,' he said through gritted teeth.

Moir turned, grinning, showing an intelligence and cunning that could easily have been missed. Larkin imagined lesser mortals had done so at their peril.

'Come in,' said Moir, and unlocked the door.

The room was no bigger than a broom closet; Moir had filled it to bursting point with a seemingly random assortment of files, paper, old coffee mugs, books and dirt. Despite the mess, Larkin would have betted that Moir knew exactly where to lay his hands on anything of importance.

Moir unearthed a chair from the chaos and pointed at it vaguely. 'Sit down.'

Larkin sat, dusting it surreptitiously first with the palm of his hand.

'So what was it you wanted to see me about, Mr Larkin?'

'It's about the death of Mary Torrington – rather, Mary Greene.'

Moir mentally grasped the file. 'Yes. And?'

45

'Well, I've been hired by her solicitor—'

'Who is?'

'Charlotte Birch.'

'Yes. Continue.'

'By Ms Birch. To investigate Mary Greene's death.'

'I've already done that. Why would you want to bother?'

'Because Ms Birch has reason to believe that Mary Greene didn't commit suicide.'

The idea seemed to amuse Moir. 'And why's that?'

Larkin took a deep breath. 'She believed that the man Mary Greene was involved with abused her to the point where she was emotionally and mentally destroyed. In that state she took her own life. So, morally, he's the murderer.'

Moir sighed heavily, as if he was weighed down by a burden even bigger than himself. 'Mr Larkin. When someone takes their own life, it is often hard to understand why. Those left behind to grieve sometimes feel a scapegoat must be found. It's a sad fact of life – but there it is.'

'Didn't you try to find her lover?'

'We informed her next of kin. Since she and her husband were divorced, that was her two brothers. Case closed.'

'Yes, but—'

'Where are you from?'

Larkin was stopped in his tracks. 'Sorry?'

'Where are you *from*?'

'Newcastle.'

'But you've lived away for a few years.'

'London.'

'Thought so. Your accent betrays you. Will you be staying long?'

Larkin felt like the accused. He was supposed to be asking the questions . . . 'Why? Are you the sheriff that every lone gunslinger has to report to?'

'I don't know. Are you a lone gunslinger, Mr Larkin?'

'Hardly.'

46

'Good. Then leave this alone. The case is closed. I expect you can see yourself out.' And Moir picked up a pen and began rifling through the papers on his desk. Larkin didn't move.

'*Goodbye*, Mr Larkin.'

Larkin stood up, left the room and strode angrily down the corridor. *What an arsehole*, he thought.

7: Tracings

Having left Moir's office full of rage and indignation, Larkin decided to go for a therapeutic drive. He had nowhere particular in mind, so he let the car choose the route, and eventually he found himself up on the Scotswood Road. Rather than head over the river and risk getting lost in Blaydon, he turned the car round at the abattoir and, aiming for the city, ventured into Scotswood itself.

He remembered the area as being bad – but nothing like as bad as this. No longer the jolly, holiday landmark depicted in a century-old folk song – although he doubted that place had ever existed – what he saw now was rotten to the core. It looked like the leftovers of a particularly wild party, a celebration that had been pissed on and burnt up by gatecrashers while the party's organisers had lain drunk, dreaming of glorious futures, while their proud creation was pummelled into rubble.

It was all the result of broken post-war promises and dodgy land deals, Larkin knew. A bright new day, a new deal, had been promised for the trusting inhabitants of Scotswood. So their terraced homes were torn down and the hapless owners relocated into vast concrete monoliths. This was the future, they were told. This was the way the world was heading. A teeming, optimistic generation had gone willingly, two by two, into the new Ark, happy with a view of the Tyne that stretched all to the way to the Team Valley Trading Estate. But then things started to fall apart: the lifts, the walls, the ceilings. Then came the rats, the fires, the burglaries, the muggings. Potential danger lurked in every poorly designed cranny. The people began to feel like prisoners, afraid to leave home, unable to move, abandoned. Like packs of wolves, gangs of ravening humans started to roam the estates. And Scotswood had become a crumbling high-rise hell, with tormented souls on every level. Abandon hope? They'd done that years ago. Now going to the shops for a pint of milk was considered an act of heroism.

Larkin drove slowly; he had no choice. Apart from the refuse, the everyday detritus of existence, the streets were strewn with sleeping policemen and chicanes, designed to stop the joyriders. Clearly the scheme had failed. He gazed round sadly as he drove. Concrete edifices that could never have been called homes looked like front-line barricades; some were burnt-out husks, some boarded up, some cemented over with breeze-blocks, as if, in a deranged quest for novelty, the council had employed as many different ways as they could of sealing up the buildings. Every now and then he came across a terraced street that had somehow escaped; or, more accurately, been granted a temporary stay of execution.

Yet for all this there were some small signs of human spirit amidst the despair. A Community Centre (a misnomer if ever there was one) advertised a children's daycare scheme; posters called for residents to form a City Challenge group, in order to force the council not to abandon them. Larkin knew they would have a struggle on their hands. Suddenly remembering his meeting with Andy, he gunned the car up a gear and drove back to his hotel. He needed a shower and a beer.

So there he was, in The Forth, on his second pint. When he'd last drunk there, years ago, it had been a desolate but comfortably run-down dive for whores and losers. Now it seemed desolate in a different way. Split-level, open-plan, concealed lighting, padded seats. On the CD jukebox Michael Bolton was getting himself all worked up over nothing in particular. In short, it had become just like any other brass-arsed city pub. It had no identity – or not one that Larkin wanted to share.

On entering, he had ordered his drink and taken a trip to the toilet, surprised to find it now at the top of a spiral staircase and newly tiled in gleaming grey and white. As he returned to the bar he overheard a customer chatting with the barmaid, enthusing at the speed with which the vicious Stanley-knife stabbing in the toilets a couple of nights ago had been cleared up. At Larkin's approach they both fell silent, keen not to spoil a stranger's impression of their local. Larkin took his beer to his seat, smiling to himself. *You can tart up the pub*, he thought – *but you can't change the people.*

He sat in contemplation. He tried not to spend too much time in reflection, but he had cut himself off from humanity to a point where he distrusted emotional involvement, found it painful even. His relationship with Lindsay provided him with sexual gratification, if nothing else, and his job put food in his mouth. But that was the present. He was still so bound up with the past that he didn't dare think about the future.

And then there was Charlotte. Her presence puzzled – if he was honest, frightened – him.

He was still deep in thought when Andy appeared.

'Oi! Where's my fuckin' pint, then?'

Larkin jerked out of his reverie.

'Don't matter, I'll get them.' His colleague looked at him. 'Still the same miserable face. What's the matter with you, then?'

Andy was framed by the fading light spilling in from the doorway. His mousy hair was scraped back into its inevitable ponytail; his beard was neatly trimmed; the earring in his left ear glittered; his Levi T-shirt and jeans were immaculately faded. Cat boots and Chipie suede bomber completed the ensemble. Every inch the South London wide boy. Larkin saw the smattering of early evening drinkers eye Andy with mistrust; through centuries of Northern in-breeding, they had instinctively rejected him. Everybody's pal, Andy Brennan, had become another outsider – just like Larkin.

Andy didn't notice their hostility, however, as he ordered drinks for himself and Larkin, his South London accent at full decibel. The barmaid eyed him like a laboratory specimen as he returned to Larkin with the drinks.

'Bit of a fuckin' borin' cow, ain't she? Don't they teach them manners up here?'

'They do, but only in relation to other Geordies. Southerners always get the cold shoulder.'

'And how far south d'you have to go to be considered a Southerner, then?'

'Durham, I think.'

Andy took a deep drink, nodding seriously. 'Yeah, figured. Why do they hate Southerners so much?'

'Well, traditionally it's because Tory landowners from London fuck us over so many times. But . . .'

'Yeah?'

'I think it's because they keep beating us at football.'

Andy laughed. 'Used to, you mean.'

'Yeah, right. More to it than that, though,' said Larkin pensively. 'When my dad used to go to work on a Monday – he was a mechanic at the Northern bus garage – if Newcastle had won over the weekend then he knew he was in for a good week. But if they lost it would be awful. That's what football means to people up here.'

'Yeah?' Andy paused and drank, then grimaced. 'I'm not surprised it means so much to them. The beer's shit.'

Larkin shook his head and tried to ignore him.

'So what's she like, then?'

'Who?' Larkin knew full well who.

'This bird you went to see. What's she like?'

'She's a lawyer. Involved in the Edgell case. I thought it would be helpful if I spoke to her.' He was trying to sound convincing, dismissive, but he couldn't help remembering Charlotte's breasts constrained by the lacy bra underneath a sheer cream silk blouse . . .

'And was it?'

'Sorry?' Charlotte was now tantalising in a leather basque straight from Mary's collection.

'Was it helpful?'

'It might be. I'm . . . we're having dinner together.'

Andy beamed, his eyes glinting. 'You sly bastard! Always the quiet ones you've got to watch out for, eh? Oh, well, bang goes my idea for the night's entertainment. I thought we could go on the pull, but if you're sorted I'll have to make other arrangements. That bird at the hotel was giving me the eye—'

To change the subject Larkin said, 'What did *you* find out?'

Andy jumped straight in, head-on. 'Got the name of that guy who killed Edgell. Gary Fenwick. Know him?'

Larkin ran it through his memory. 'I think Char – the lawyer mentioned it. Keep going.'

'Apparently, from what I could gather, Fenwick walked up to Edgell and just knifed him. Witnesses, the lot. It was about two in the mornin', just down an alley from a taxi rank outside a nightclub. In Grimley.' He paused and thought. 'Christ, I'm surprised they've *got* a nightclub in a shithole like that.'

'How did you learn all this?'

'Went to the library. They keep newspapers. Didn't you think of doing that, Mr Reporter? Anyway, I went out to Grimley.' He shuddered. 'Never seen a place more aptly named. I can see now what's made you such a sullen bastard.'

From the murderous look in Larkin's eyes, Andy realised he had said the wrong thing.

'Sorry. It was just a joke.' Larkin nodded almost imperceptibly; Andy took that as a cue to continue. 'Put it this way – it's a bit depressing. And that nightclub, it looks risky enough in the daytime – I bet it's fuckin' dangerous at night.' He paused and took a drink. Larkin knew the place. He held it a matter of personal pride that he had never set foot in it.

'Anyway, they closed it down after the stabbing. Looks

like something they should have done years ago. Took some snaps, though.'

He delved into the leather file he had brought with him. Larkin looked through the photos; they brought it all back. There were shots of the high street – in reality the *only* street. It looked deserted, even on a Saturday afternoon. The shops were more or less the same; maybe a few more video stores, another Chinese takeaway, the innovation of a kebab shop. It all looked much starker in black and white. Then the nightclub, an old Victorian Gothic building more suited to an asylum than a dance hall. The windows had been blacked out, the brickwork was stained and discoloured, and the gaudy neon sign announcing the legend CONNEXIONS had more than a few letters missing. The taxi rank was outside the main entrance and there was a maze of alleyways around the building, dark even in daylight. Larkin handed the photos back to Andy. They had made him even less keen to go back.

'Where's Fenwick now?' asked Larkin, trying to take his mind off the bleak images.

'On remand waiting for his trial. Open-and-shut case, apparently.'

'What about Edgell? Anything on him?'

'Yeah. Lived in London for a few years. Must have gone south to make his fortune.'

'Lot of it about,' said Larkin. 'Doesn't always work out, though.'

'Too right, mate. Streets of London aren't paved with gold.'

'No. They're paved with *Big Issue* sellers.'

Andy looked at Larkin. 'Yeah . . . Well, anyway, after a few years he came back up here, moved into his old man's flat in Grimley. His parents are divorced – mother went down under with some Australian, so to speak. Looks like our boy was setting things up for a big London firm to move in. Funny that. I'd have thought they'd be here already.'

54

'They are. But you know Northerners, how insular they are. Even their drugs dealers have to be local.'

'You want to watch yourself, mate. You're nearly developing a sense of humour.' Andy smiled; Larkin smiled; happy times. Andy continued, 'Anyway, Edgell Senior didn't mind his son bein' there. Helped himself to the profits and turned a blind eye. Proud of the fact that his son had made something of his life, even if it was short.' He took a drink and sighed. 'I dunno. Some people.'

'So what now?' asked Larkin. 'Gang war?'

'Looks like it. North against South.'

'So what else is new? At least it's not football.'

'Ha, fuckin' ha.' Andy took a drink. 'Did you know this Wayne Edgell, then?'

'Not really. I never hung out with him or anything. We were in the same class at school, that's all. About the only thing we had in common was the fact that we couldn't wait to get out of Grimley. Us and half the school.'

'What about the other half?'

'Oh, they were staying put. Grimley was where they were born and Grimley was where they would die.'

'Looks like the place has beaten them to it.'

'It used to be a prosperous mining community, Andy. North versus South. Remember that.'

Andy snorted. 'I can't figure you out. You say you couldn't wait to get away from this place, but you won't hear a word against it. What's the matter with you? If you liked it so much, why did you move away in the first place?'

Larkin looked around at the refurbished pub. It had changed almost beyond recognition – but maybe if he'd stayed here he wouldn't have noticed. Maybe he'd have gone along with it, embraced it, been part of it. Maybe things would have been different.

Maybe not.

'Dunno. I don't feel at home in London, I don't feel at home here.'

'And you want to? Fit in, I mean, either here or there?'

Larkin stood up. 'Who knows? Who fucking cares? Have a nice evening, Andy. I've got to go.'

Andy looked disgruntled. 'Yeah sure.' Then, just as Larkin was turning to go, 'This solicitor bird, how d'you know her? She your ex?'

Larkin sat down again. 'Yeah. I met her at university.'

'What, Newcastle?'

'Yeah.'

'You didn't travel far.'

'Neither did she.' Larkin got back up.

Andy's face was downcast; he didn't want to drink alone. He said, without much enthusiasm, 'Give her one for me, right?'

'Fuck off, Andy. See you later.' And Larkin strolled away.

Through the window Larkin saw Andy slumped, staring into his drink. For a moment, Larkin was seized with a pang of guilt. On his own, in a strange city – it couldn't be much fun. Then Andy rose, crossed to the bar. Larkin heard his London tones wafting through the doorway.

'Same again, darlin'.' Then, after a pause, ''Ere, anyone ever told you you look like Sandra Bullock? Yeah? Well, d'you want to know a story about her?'

8: Whining And Dining

London has Hampstead, Birmingham has Mosely, and Newcastle has Jesmond. A place consisting of charming Victorian houses, inhabited by the city's professionals, intellectuals, pseudo-intellectuals, the kind of people who profess concern about the rest of society but manage to stay a *Guardian*'s length away from it. The kind of place where the architects of Scotswood probably lived.

Larkin, on foot to clear the booze from his brain, walked up Osborne Road scrutinising the small hotels. He and Charlotte had booked into one once, for the thrill of an illicit night together, away from college, away from their parents. It had done nothing to help their deteriorating relationship. Their night of unbridled lust had ended in mutual bickering. Larkin had lost his erection and Charlotte had lost the urge. The next morning, they paid the bill and left without saying a word to each other. They had also, much to Larkin's regret, missed breakfast.

He put all that behind him as he rounded the corner. The restaurant was dimly lit, and looked warm and inviting. The name, Francesca's, was emblazoned above the door in fat, reassuring capital letters. A perfect playground for the chattering classes to discuss the world into infinity over a plate of *tortellini al pesto* and a carafe of Chianti.

There was a time when Larkin aspired to be one of them. A time when he had thought that dissecting

Rohmer's latest ironic epic, loudly debating Third World debt and affecting a middle-class liberal air represented a lifestyle to cherish. Now the very idea repelled him. His delusions had led him to university, but he had hated it so much that he left after two terms and took to wearing his regional roots, his working-class origins, like a badge. He started writing cocky, witty pieces about Newcastle's burgeoning punk scene, selling them to anyone who would take them. He began to take an interest in local affairs, making a nuisance of himself with councillors, exposing their sleaziness and ineptitude. Slowly, he made a name for himself as a journalist. When Larkin was offered the chance to use his talents in London and be much more handsomely rewarded, he took it. His father, a lifelong union man and staunch believer in working-class integrity, had been violently opposed. His father's last words to him before he left were still virulently ringing in his ears: 'Aye, there's nothin' wrong wi' wantin' to better yourself. Nothin' at all. It's when you start thinkin' you're better than us. Well, you're not. If all you want to be is like *them*, then you won't have bettered yourself at all. You'll have worsened yourself. And I won't want to bloody know you.' They hadn't spoken from that moment on. At the time, he had thought his father was talking shit, and told him so – but on reflection he wasn't so sure. Despite making a name for himself as an investigative reporter Larkin had eventually succumbed to the trappings of middle-class success: a town-house in Greenwich, an ex-model wife, a sports car, an enthusiastic interest in cocaine and alcohol. He had become the kind of person his writing had once held to ridicule – the kind his father had vainly warned him against. Recently he had been thinking of his father more and more; the things he had said, his beliefs, his values. He should have paid more attention to him. Too late now, though.

He stopped in front of the restaurant and found himself, yet again, inadvertently gazing into other people's lives through a plate-glass window, literally a spectator at the feast. But he was suddenly galvanised by the sight of Charlotte hurrying towards him.

'Sorry I'm a bit late,' she said, slightly out of breath, staggering Larkin by making two apologies in one day. 'I hope you haven't waited too long.'

He said he hadn't and looked her over. She was wearing a short, fawn-coloured skirt with sheer black tights (or stockings, Larkin couldn't tell, he forced himself not to dwell on the possibility), black suede heels, a plain black sweater with a single strand of pearls around her neck and a well-tailored, calf-length, black overcoat. With her golden hair and emerald green eyes she looked little short of a dream. Larkin was glad he'd had the foresight to wear his Armani suit and black silk shirt. He didn't want to disappoint. When her lips brushed his (lingering a beat longer than they should have) he resisted the temptation to grab her, rip off her overcoat, and declare his undying lust right there in the street. Instead he said, 'You look nice.'

'Thank you. You don't look so bad yourself.'

Their eyes locked.

'Shall we stand here all night, or would you prefer to eat?' she said.

Larkin weighed up the alternatives. 'Let's eat.'

'OK. After you, my sweet.' She stepped back to let him enter. There she was again – definitely flirting with him. What the hell was she playing at?

He stood aside to let some rich, satisfied diners, braying with self-conscious laughter, out of the door; resisted the urge to trip them up, and ushered Charlotte in.

They were greeted by a waitress with a frizzy pony-tail who led them past half a dozen disgruntled customers, still waiting to be seated, to a quiet little table in the corner.

'Preferential treatment?' asked Larkin quizzically.

'Old friends,' replied Charlotte.

Larkin scrutinised his surroundings. Red and white checked tablecloths; candles in old Chianti bottles caked with wax; mismatched modern prints hanging from bare brick walls; a haphazard collection of cutlery and crockery; a delicious smell of home-cooked Italian food coming from the kitchen. And service with a genuine smile.

It was all too much. The atmosphere and bonhomie seemed to be as carefully cooked as the food. The place appeared to have lost some of its spontaneity since his last visit – as if AUTENTICO ITALIANO PLC had been stamped across it in big black letters. Perhaps it had always been like that; perhaps it was Larkin's own spontaneity that was now missing.

They ordered a bottle of Chianti from the waitress. 'Let's get drunk,' Charlotte suggested saucily. He decided on paté to start, then a *quattro staggioni* pizza; Charlotte ordered parma ham and melon, with *gnocchi al fungi* and a side salad as a main course. They both ordered garlic bread. The waitress disappeared again; Larkin filled their wine glasses.

'Here's to ... what?' said Charlotte.

'I don't know. How about "Here's to the successful conclusion of a trial and a case"?'

She pouted appealingly. 'Oh, you stoic! Whatever happened to that hedonistic, irresponsible Larkin I used to know?'

'Oh, he's still around somewhere.'

'Well, I hope he puts in an appearance tonight. Maybe later?' She gave him a wide-eyed, teasing look that Larkin couldn't misinterpret. But he didn't feel able to return it. He dropped his gaze to his wine glass. 'Maybe,' he mumbled.

He felt like a piece of the parma ham that she'd soon have on the end of her fork, on its way to her mouth. He couldn't think of anything to say that wouldn't be misconstrued as a come-on. Out of desperation, he asked after her parents, and was told that Daddy had retired and Mummy was living a life of careful leisure on his pension.

Mummy? *Daddy*? She used to call them Mum and

Dad. Larkin could remember them vividly: determinedly clawing their way up from upper-working-class all the way to lower-middle-class – the difference being immeasurable. They'd put all their hopes, aspirations and ambitions into their only child, lived their lives vicariously through Charlotte. Her father had always made it quite clear that he thought Larkin was unworthy of their daughter's affection; but then, even the Angel Gabriel would have been considered an unfit suitor for Charlotte's hand. Larkin wondered what they thought of Charles.

He told Charlotte that his mother had died shortly after he'd moved to London; his dad, a couple of years after that. He hadn't gone to the funeral. Charlotte made no comment – she knew relations hadn't been good between Larkin and his parents.

They lapsed into silence again. After a vast expanse of polite, nervous smiles Charlotte spoke.

'So what have you been up to since we last met?'

He gave her a businesslike report of his progress, from his visit to Mary's home and his discovery of the diary, to his meeting with Andy. Charlotte listened with the face of a poker player. When he'd finished he took a big gulp of wine, almost feeling like a proper reporter again. 'So,' he said, playing with his paté, 'what d'you think?'

'Well, the parts about Edgell and Fenwick I already knew, of course. I'm afraid I don't really have any inside information.'

'Oh.' He couldn't help thinking he'd been had. So far, Charlotte hadn't told him anything he couldn't have found out for himself – and he'd been running round all day on her behalf. He smeared paté on a slice of toast. 'Fenwick's trial date – when's that?'

'Hasn't been set yet.' A genteel sip of wine, then she continued. 'He's on remand at the moment, in Durham. He's been in front of the magistrates but we're still waiting for him to go through committal. He could be there for anything up to eighteen months.'

'And you're his solicitor.'

'The firm is representing him. Not me personally.'

They finished their starters and the waitress took their plates. Noticing they'd all but finished the wine, she asked if they wanted another bottle. Yes, they said, and off she went, giving Charlotte a sly wink which Larkin pretended not to notice.

'Who's paying?' he asked suddenly.

'I thought we'd go dutch.'

'No, I mean who's paying you to be Fenwick's solicitor? That murderous nobody couldn't stump up the money – so who is it?'

She stiffened slightly and used the arrival of the wine as an excuse to delay her answer. Eventually she spoke. 'I . . . I don't know. All I know is, he has the money. Like I said, I'm not even his solicitor—'

'Who is, then?'

A hesitation. 'Charles.'

'Really?'

'Why do you find that so interesting?'

'I just do.'

'Well . . . that's all there is to it,' she said. Larkin leaned forward.

'Look, Charlotte, we both know there's some really heavy shit going on with this case. Drugs, gangsters, the lot. So either Fenwick did the deed in a brave attempt to rid the streets of an evil drug dealer – which I rather doubt – or it was a professional hit. If that's the case, then either it went wrong or he was expendable. What d'you reckon?'

Charlotte fixed her eyes on the dancing light in her wine glass. 'I really couldn't comment. As far as I'm concerned he's a client who is entitled to legal representation – just like any other.'

'What does he say about it?'

'Nothing. Yet.'

Another silence enveloped them; it seemed accentuated by the vacuous babble of their fellow diners. Larkin took a mouthful of wine and threw caution to the winds.

'Y'know, it's funny.'

'What is?'

'What we've come to. Here you are, being paid to protect a murderer – and here I am, trying to get you to dish the dirt on him.'

'And that's funny?'

'Ironic, maybe. A good example of how idealism adapts to the lure of the wage packet.'

Charlotte opened her mouth to protest, but Larkin continued. 'I always had you pegged to be a politician or a writer. Something like that.'

'Why?'

'Because you were a leader, an opinion-former. That's where your talents seemed to lie.'

'But I read Law, Stephen. I trained for a career in the law.'

'I know. I just thought—'

Charlotte's face reddened and her voice developed an edge. 'You might have had the luxury of dreams. I had *goals*. I wanted to do something with my life, not waste it on fantasies that had no chance of coming true. And I have done something.' She paused and took a deep breath before continuing. 'And if I have to come into contact with people like Fenwick, then so be it. This is the real world. Not some utopian vision. I've worked bloody hard and I've achieved something and no one's going to take that away.'

Larkin leaned forward. 'Yeah? Don't be too sure. *I* worked hard, I achieved something – and some bastard took that away.'

Charlotte was going to speak, but the look on Larkin's face discouraged her. She sat motionless, withdrawn. Larkin felt like getting up and walking out. Or bursting into tears.

The waitress chose that moment to arrive with the main courses, which defused the tension.

'Hey,' said Larkin, wearing the flimsiest of smiles, 'that was almost an argument. Just like old times, eh?'

From the look she gave him he couldn't tell whether

63

she wanted to kiss him or kill him. 'It wasn't all like that. We had good times as well,' she said reproachfully.

They concentrated on eating for a while. Eventually Charlotte summoned up her courage.

'Do you miss your wife?'

Larkin took a long time to answer, searching for the right words. 'Yes. All the time. And my son.'

Another awkward silence; then Charlotte said, 'Did you ever think about me?'

Larkin stared at her, holding her gaze, his eyes unflinching.

'I'm sorry . . .' Charlotte began.

'Yes, I thought about you. I thought about you a hell of a lot. You were everything to me once.'

He hadn't wanted to say it, but there it was. The statement hung there, like the coyote in the Roadrunner cartoon, suspended in mid-air after running off a cliff, prior to meeting a sticky end on the valley floor.

Charlotte steered the conversation back to safer ground. 'What's your impression of Mary?'

'I think – I feel sorry for her. *Felt* sorry for her. I mean . . .' He was struggling to make his thoughts coherent. 'She . . . this singles club she went to – what kind was it?'

'I don't know. Just a lonely-hearts club. The Rainbow Club, it was called.'

'It wasn't one of those "Can travel, no timewasters" affairs was it? A sex-contacts kind of thing?'

Charlotte looked shocked. 'Course not! At least, I shouldn't think so. I can't imagine Mary . . . Why?'

'Well, it's just the stuff I found in the bottom drawer – all that tacky Frederick's of Hollywood stuff. It seemed so . . . out of character.'

'You're saying she seemed too nice to go in for kinky sex? Come on, haven't you ever done anything like that? I bet you have.' She smiled. 'I *know* you have.'

'That's not what I meant,' said Larkin, his face reddening. 'I just got the feeling something was out of place there, that's all.' He swallowed a big lump of pizza, dripping with stringy mozzarella, tomatoes and olives, and washed it down with a slug of wine. He tried to keep his mind on business. 'Do you know if she went in for any of that with her husband?'

'I wouldn't have thought so.'

'Reckon it's worth talking to him?'

'I doubt it. Anyway, he's long gone by now. Last I heard he'd taken early retirement and was running a pub in Somerset or somewhere.'

Gradually they began to feel more at ease. They let the conversation drift and meander as they ate: books, music, how Newcastle had changed. Larkin asked Charlotte about her job.

'We're only a small firm,' Charlotte said, 'but we've come a long way in quite a short space of time.'

'How did you manage that?'

'Well, apart from being completely brilliant whizzkids, we did a couple of jobs for Sir James Lascelles. He was very impressed with us and asked us to handle his affairs. He knows we're small but ambitious – he likes that.'

'Who's Sir James Lascelles?'

Charlotte gave him an incredulous look, as if he'd failed to identify the Princess of Wales. '*Who's Sir James Lascelles*? You don't know who he is?'

'If I did I wouldn't have asked.'

'He's hugely important. Very influential. And not just in Newcastle.'

Larkin's ears pricked up. 'How big is he, then?'

'*Very*. There's not much happens that he doesn't know about.'

'Really? Might he know who stumped up the money for Gary Fenwick?'

Charlotte's face was a locked door. 'I'm not even going to answer that.'

'Why not? It's a legitimate question. If he knows, I'll need to talk to him.'

Charlotte looked upset. 'He won't, and you can't – and that's the end of it.'

'I thought you—'

'Just change the subject, OK? Talk about something else. He's done a lot for us – he's a good man.'

'OK. Speaking of good men, how's Charles?'

Charlotte's face remained closed. 'He's fine. Still away.'

'Right.' Larkin tried to affect a casual manner. 'So, you met him through work?'

'He was a partner in the firm. He took a shine to me. What did I have to lose? He was young and dynamic, he was . . .' She looked at Larkin to gauge his reaction before continuing, but he had temporarily borrowed her poker face. 'He was good-looking, and he was going places. A powerful combination.'

'And you've been happy?'

Charlotte wore the poker face this time. 'I've been . . . contented.' Then a look at him. 'Yes, I've been happy.'

'Good. That's all that matters.'

The waitress chose that moment to beam herself over to ask if everything was all right, remove their dishes and offer the dessert menu. While they were scanning it, Charlotte suddenly sat upright, a whimsical expression playing about her mouth.

'Remember this?'

Larkin listened. 'Forest Fire' by Lloyd Cole And The Commotions. He did remember.

'Lloyd Cole.'

'An "Our Tune" for us, if ever there was one!'

'Yeah. I love this bit—' Larkin sang along, professing with Lloyd Cole his belief in love, or indeed anything that would get him what he wanted, get him off his knees. Charlotte joined in the chorus; by the end of the song they were smiling widely at each other.

'It's great to see you again, Stephen.'

'It's great to see you, too.' He knew he was committing himself by saying it.

'I thought I'd never see you again.'

'And that bothered you?'

'Yes!'

Larkin laughed. 'Why? Last time we were together you tried to push me off the Swing Bridge.'

'Oh, that was then. This is now.'

'And now you're a married woman.'

She gave him a smile that he couldn't quite read – and then the waitress arrived and they both ordered cassata and cappucino. Larkin, felt uncomfortable, tried to defuse the situation.

'Good album, that Lloyd Cole one. "Rattlesnakes"? Not a bad track on it.'

'I know. I've still got it.'

'So have I.'

'I even went out and bought it on CD.' She paused; their ice cream arrived. 'There's a song on it that always reminds me of you.'

'Which one?'

' "Are You Ready To Be Heartbroken". Remember it? That's how I've always thought of you.'

'As someone who's doomed to be eternally disappointed?'

She gave her unreadable smile again and they focused on their ice cream.

'You've changed, you know,' said Larkin.

'Of course I have,' Charlotte replied. 'Nobody stays the same. You either go forwards or backwards.'

'And which way have you gone?'

'Forwards, I hope.' She looked straight into his eyes. 'You've changed too.'

'For the better?'

Charlotte smiled. 'You've just changed. It's going to be fun getting to know you again.'

Larkin felt he should say something meaningful, but he couldn't think what. Instead he adopted an expression that he hoped was darkly inscrutable. He hoped it didn't make him look like he had indigestion.

They drank their coffee, paid the bill, grabbed their coats; the waitress's knowing smile followed them out to the street.

Outside the air was sharp and the night was clear.

Larkin was feeling light-headed, a combination of booze and Charlotte. He offered to walk her home and she accepted. She slid her arm through his and snuggled close.

They covered the short distance without speaking. Then Charlotte said, 'Here we are.' They had stopped in front of a big, imposing Edwardian house. Charlotte had clearly landed on her feet in one way at least.

They turned to each other at the gate: time for the ice to break. Larkin didn't know who made the first move. All he knew was that their mouths were suddenly together, hungry. Tongues, in and out, Charlotte's body up close to his. He could feel her breasts pressing against him, her pelvis grinding into him. No doubt she could feel his erection growing. His hands were all over her, all over the body he'd thought he'd never feel again, never respond to, never make love to. He felt her breasts, her nipples hard through her sweater. His hands moved down to her waist, over the curve of her hips, and slid between her thighs, making her gasp. His fingers were as avid as their mouths, devouring her. Her perfume might have changed; her dress sense had become more conservative; but her body still felt exactly the same. Eventually she pulled away from him, her lips swollen, parted, sexy.

'Let's go inside.' She pulled at him; he didn't move. 'It's all right! Charles isn't here. Come on. We've got a lot of catching up to do.'

He couldn't think straight. This was what he wanted most in the world, right here and now, and he recognised that. But he wanted it too much, and that scared him. It wasn't the sex, it was the involvement; he had wrapped so many layers around himself that his emotions had become mummified. In the last day or so Charlotte had found a loose piece of bandage and started to pull, spinning him round, unravelling him. If he allowed it, she would leave him naked and dizzy. Desire and despair were mixed, fighting for possession of his soul, but she wanted an answer.

'No.' A cracked whisper.

She stopped. 'What?'

'I can't.'

'Why not?'

'I ... it's what I want. *You're* what I want, I just haven't ... I can't do it. Not with someone I ... care about.'

'It'll be all right. We'll make it all right.'

He started to move away, back to something he could handle, something he could control.

'I'll call you. Sorry. Thanks for a ... a lovely evening. I'll see you soon. I really am sorry.' And he hurried away, leaving Charlotte standing alone.

He walked through the streets of Newcastle like a sleep-walker. Back at the hotel he went straight up to his room, telling himself over and over that he'd done the right thing. He tried to relax. But he couldn't stop thinking about Charlotte. He got out his bottle of whisky and a glass, turned on the TV and flicked idly through the hotel's cable channels. Finding the porn station, he stared at it dumbly, watching writhing flesh lovelessly simulate passion. Charlotte. *Charlotte* ... He turned the sound down and put a tape in the machine: Roy Orbison. He lay back on the bed, letting Roy tell him that only in dreams could he find true love. The flickering images washed over him and the sour alcohol ran round his body. When the tears finally came, he was too drunk to notice.

9: A Little Light Reading

It was the dream again. It began as always, with a clear, blue sky. He'd done his two early morning lines, left for work, realised he'd forgotten something, driven back to his Georgian town-house in the Porsche. He could see Sophie holding little Joe, standing on the front step. A car pulled up ahead of him. Ralph Sickert got out and crossed towards them, carrying a double-barrelled shotgun. Heavy black clouds rolled over the blue sky. He saw the smile on Sophie's face turn to a look of confusion as Sickert raised the gun and aimed it at her. Larkin told himself it was going to be different this time; he'd shout out, he'd get the gun, he'd take the shot. But the dream never changed. His legs turned to lead and he watched as, in sickening, cinematic slow-motion, Sickert pulled the trigger. A huge, reverberating, industrial roar; Sophie's front exploded in a blossoming fractal flower of red. Little Joe, drenched in so much of his mother's blood he looked as if he'd just emerged from the womb, began a slow, air-raid siren wail. Another roar – and Joe's head was gone.

The heavens opened with a torrential downpour as Larkin heard a deep bull howl and realised it was his own. He was too late. Sickert turned round. And with swift dream logic, he metamorphosised into Charlotte. Something had happened! This wasn't the normal route for the nightmare to take. Naked, she held the shotgun

71

in her hands, reloaded both barrels and looked at him. She smiled gently and spoke.

'I've released you, my darling. Now there's only us.'

He stood transfixed, staring, the rain sheeting between them. She continued.

'I love you, Stephen. I'm going to save you. I'm going to make you live again.'

And with that she gave him a lascivious grin, sighted him with the rifle and pulled the trigger.

Larkin shot awake. He looked around, disorientated. The TV was showing static, the tape had finished hours ago, and the whisky bottle was empty. He realised where he was and looked at his watch: six-thirty. He was lying on the bed, fully clothed, feeling terrible. Kicking off his shoes, he scraped off his trousers and shirt and climbed into bed. Although he felt barely alive, he was disgusted to realise that the dream had given him an erection. He put the light off and tried to will himself back to sleep.

He lay completely still, slipping between awareness and unconsciousness. He felt the sun rise weakly, the day begin. He was vaguely aware of the phone ringing once, twice. Whoever it was, he didn't want to speak to them.

Eventually he managed to drag himself to the bathroom where he shitted, pissed and puked. He felt better after that, relishing the feeling of complete emptiness. He was a blank slate, with the illusion of a chance to start again. Needing to occupy his mind, he rummaged around until he found Mary's diary, got back into bed, wrapped the bedclothes around him and began to read.

The diary was a cheap, page-a-day one: blue-ruled, spiral-bound. He flicked through it. The script – three or four months' worth, he reckoned – almost filled it. After a while Mary had ignored the printed dates, as if she hadn't been able to include what she needed to say within the space allotted to a single day. This diary looked more like a confessional than a record of events. The handwriting was neat and concise, almost like printing. He started with the first entry, back in July. Mary, very precisely, told the reader who she was, how old she was and the fact that she was single after the departure of her husband Robert. She talked a little of her job as a legal secretary, saying she was happy with it. She mentioned the Rainbow Club, saying she didn't think it was really her sort of thing. Then the admissions started:

The main reason I stopped keeping a diary after I got married was because my life came to a standstill and there was nothing to write about. But that's all changed now. I've got a new man! I met him two nights ago at a party given for the firm by Sir James Lascelles. The moment his eyes met mine he came over and we talked. He was very charming and witty and we got on very well. I am ashamed to admit that I was a little tipsy and started to flirt with him. Not like me! He seemed to be responding to me. Well, I was overwhelmed when that happened.

I spent the whole evening chatting to Terry and it was lovely. When it was time to go he asked for my phone number. I gave it to him and thought that was that, he was pulling my leg and I'd never see him again.

I thought I'd made a fool of myself but when I got home from work the next day the phone rang and it was Terry. He wanted to know if he could take me out to dinner! Well, what could I say? Of course I said 'Yes', and he took me to the Blue Sky Chinese Restaurant on Pilgrim Street. We had a lovely time. He was very kind and gentlemanly. He paid the bill, then took me home. As he dropped me off in the car I took my courage in my hands and leaned across and kissed him. I know it was forward of me, but I just meant to give him a peck. Really to show my gratitude. He responded by giving me the most passionate kiss I had ever had! I asked him in for coffee and although I was very nervous and I think he was too I asked him if he wanted to stay the night and he said he wanted to, but didn't want to give me the wrong impression.

Larkin turned the page to the second entry.

This morning I felt awful. I felt I was a slut for asking Terry to stay and I thought I'd never see him again. I talked myself into accepting it, I thought, what would a man like that want with me?

Then came a space. Then, a couple of lines later, the writing grew a little less precise:

He's just phoned to say he's coming round and wants to take me out again!

Larkin read on. Descriptions of restaurants where they had eaten, little anecdotes, jokes they had shared. The secrets of a woman who was, cautiously, falling in love. And then there was the sex. Terry may not have been the type of boy who went all the way on a first date, but he certainly made up for it later. Her descriptions were quite explicit: all the different positions they'd tried; her introduction to oral sex – which she'd thoroughly enjoyed; an intimate analysis of each and every occasion. Her orgasms were tallied in each day's margin with little ticks. It read like a teenager's awakening to the pleasure she could have with her own body.

There was another theme running through the diary: God. When she met Terry she had apparently been a regular church-goer, finding solace and fellowship among the congregation after Robert had left her. She mentioned discussing religion with Charlotte, which surprised Larkin; from his experience, it would be like discussing the virtues of chastity with the Marquis de Sade. It had given a stability, an order to her life. From what Larkin could tell, she now expected Terry to fulfil these needs. But the sex had been a problem; she still thought it sinful to get so much enjoyment from it. After every carefully detailed bout of lovemaking in the diary came an equally carefully detailed bout of self-condemnation. Larkin thought it strange that a Methodist like Mary should be nurturing such a healthy crop of Catholic guilt. Perhaps it was endemic to all religion. She had eventually convinced herself that it wasn't immoral, but Larkin had his doubts as to the depth of her conviction. As she had written:

God wants us all to be happy. That's what I believe. And Terry is making me happy. Perhaps God sent Terry? I like to think so. I know there's the sex thing – out of wedlock and all that – but if He wants us to be really happy, like it says in the Bible, then He'll look on that kindly and forgive me. Won't He?

When Larkin read that, he sensed danger. The impression he had gained of Terry was that of a perfect gentleman; perhaps too perfect. A bland, handsome cipher, straight out of *GQ* magazine.

Terry didn't appear to have discussed his job with her. Yet he always seemed to have money and insisted on paying for everything. Not only that, but he took her shopping, bought her expensive clothes, their descriptions matching the items Larkin had found in the wardrobe. And then there was the fancy lingerie, that they had both taken pleasure in. No mention of the tackier stuff, though. Not yet.

The next month or so was blissfully happy for Mary. The diary became an itinerary of pleasant shopping trips including a full list of purchases; meals out together – complete with menus and restaurant reviews – and passionate sex with all its variations.

I know I'm not seeing my friends as much as I used to. Even Charlotte. I'm aware that I'm not writing as much in my diary, but that's because I'm doing more living.

I know it's a terrible thing to say, but I'm even pleased about not relying so much on God. For the first time ever, I'm actually starting to believe that my life will have a happy ending.

Then the mood began to change. Terry suddenly developed violent mood swings: one minute the perfect gentleman, the next snapping and cantankerous. He became verbally abusive. The black moods would be short but intense, and afterwards there would be a brief apology, blaming his behaviour on 'pressures of work'. Mary accepted the apologies at first and attempted to make light of the situation. Clearly she thought it was a temporary phase and that things would soon be back to normal.

Larkin read on. Sex became rougher for Mary, with Terry caring less about her responses, her feelings. It wasn't lovemaking anymore, she said – he seemed to be using her as no more than a masturbation aid. This, Larkin discovered, was where the tacky underwear came in:

He came round again tonight. Unannounced. I was making the tea. He flung this package at me and told me to put it on. More fool me, I did. It was some ridiculous split-crotch creation. I was embarrassed, to say the least.

Terry was sitting in an armchair, drinking beer. He ordered me to – do things. I feel so humiliated, writing this down, but I actually did what he asked me. I wriggled around, touched myself, pushed the sex aid things that he'd bought for me inside myself, and all the while I had to look like I was enjoying it.

He played with himself, came, then looked at me with contempt. He couldn't meet my gaze. He got up, and left. I just sat there with all this awful stuff on, crying my eyes out. I'm pathetic, shameful. I hate him. But he'll turn up again, I know he will, and I'll let him in, because next time it might be different. Please let it be different.

The old Terry didn't return. He became rougher; sometimes he tied her down and masturbated over her breasts, or in her mouth, forcing his penis down her throat until she thought she would choke. On one occasion, she wrote, she was so scared she actually wet herself:

I couldn't help it. I thought it would stop, repel him. Instead it had the opposite effect, turning him on, allowing him to feed on my fear, my tears.

Not content with that, he screamed out a list of indignities he intended to put me through. I couldn't even begin to list them.

Larkin could imagine, but he tried not to dwell on it. The wounded litany of the perpetual victim was repeated page after page. Her questions were cliches, but under the circumstances they were the only ones she could have asked.

Why me? What's wrong with me? What have I done wrong? Is God punishing me for abandoning Him? He's a jealous God as well as a God of Love, isn't that right? 'Thou shalt have no other God than me.' If I've offended You, God, then I'm sorry. I won't do it again. You're a forgiving God. Can't You make things right for me? Can't You forgive me?

The handwriting became sprawling, incoherent; she was losing control.

All my hopes were pinned on Terry, to build me a new life. But the Terry I love has gone. I've got nothing left. Nothing to live for. I'm a vain, stupid woman. Why did I think I could ever be anything else?

I walk round Newcastle and the Metro Centre, I see couples arm in arm, laughing and smiling. I want to run up to them and shout, 'You've no right to this happiness! It's not fair!' I want to kick and gouge and pummel them. But somehow I don't.

Eventually she had had too much. She hadn't simply snapped – she had shattered into a thousand tiny shards.

After one particularly unpleasant visit from Terry, ending with him leaving 'to teach someone on the wrong side a lesson', as he put it, she found she couldn't take any more. Her final diary entry described playing the Elton John single, preparing to die. Whoever found her body would hear the song, find the diary and know that Terry had killed her.

Larkin closed the diary and sat back. Experiencing the disintegration of a woman's life, even vicariously, had left him feeling numb. He sighed and rubbed his eyes. He couldn't just leave it. He knew he'd have to do something, make some kind of reparation. He flicked through the diary, wondering where to start. Robert? No, long gone. The Rainbow Club? Worth a look. Sir James Lascelles. Was it more than coincidence that he'd heard his name twice in two days? Then there was Terry: his sexual proclivities, his mood swings. Drugs, perhaps? Psychosis? And what did he mean by 'teaching someone on the wrong side a lesson'?

Despite the warmth of the bedclothes, Larkin froze. Fuck. Check the dates. The final entry in Mary's diary: September. Four weeks ago. He got out of bed, reeling slightly, his hangover in remission, grabbed jeans, a T-shirt and went to Andy's room. He pounded on the door for what seemed like a couple of centuries, his heart throbbing in his ribcage.

Eventually Andy came to the door, looking as bleary-eyed as Larkin, his eyes bloodshot and black-ringed, hair dishevelled.

Andy groaned. 'Shit, man, you look terrible. As bad as I feel. Fuck happened to you?'

Larkin barged past him. 'I need some info, Andy.'

'Hey – wait a minute—'

Larkin was in the room. In bed was the barmaid from The Forth, the colour draining from her cheeks as she grabbed for the bedclothes.

'Hello. Nice to see you again. Andy, I need all the stuff you got yesterday on the Edgell killing.'

78

'What, now?'

'Yes, now. Where is it?'

Andy sauntered over to the desk, tugging at his bathrobe for decency's sake. He flicked through a pile of photocopies, handed a bundle to Larkin.

'There you go, mate.'

'Ta. See you later.'

And with that he dashed out, leaving Andy almost lost for words.

'Don't mention it . . .'

Larkin returned to his room to leaf through the stack of papers. When he found what he was looking for, he sat back as though he'd been walloped in the face with a wrecking ball.

The same date . . . As Fenwick was pulled away from Edgell's body he had been shouting something. *'I was just teaching the bastard a lesson. He shouldn't have been on the wrong side . . .'*

Larkin was trembling. Was it all just a massive coincidence? Or was 'Terry' really Gary Fenwick?

10: Mary's Prayer

The rain was Sunday afternoon rain; non-committal, clammy and cold. Reminding the world that, on a Sunday, the city is the most depressing place on Earth. And the loneliest.

There was a time, in his youth, when a walk through a city of rain would have kindled a sense of romantic melancholy in Larkin. Not any more. He had been caught in too many downpours for that. He was wandering because he had nothing else to do. The Rainbow Club was due for a visit, but that wasn't until later; Sir James Lascelles, too, but he hadn't worked out how to approach him yet. There was someone else he had to talk to – but that was for the evening. So he walked.

His route had taken him up Dean Street, the Bigg Market, and onto Clayton Street. Cut-price, cheap-jack shops selling crap that nobody needed; everything a pound, unbeatable offers. Amusement arcades, packed with customers poor enough to start with and getting poorer by the minute. He walked past the second-hand record shop (closed), the dodgy jewellers. The bingo: twenty-four-hour fluorescent lights showering the area with fake money and neon stars, simultaneously colourful and depressing.

Over the traffic lights, past the end of Pink Lane. He turned left along the bottom of Westgate Road; finding nothing but closed motorbike dealers and rip-off second-hand clothing stores, he went in the opposite direction, past the Central station, into Mosely Street. He wandered down towards the quayside. It was the same route he'd taken on his first night back; the bleak daylight added nothing to it. The acid rain merely made the grey water greyer.

He had hoped that his stroll would instil some order into his mind, but all he had succeeded in doing was wearing down his shoe leather on the old unloveable streets, and allowing his past to reach out and grab him. His memories were so firmly ingrained in the stone and air of the place that he felt he was travelling through a city of ghosts.

He went back up the Side; the cobbled road and looming buildings made him feel like a character in someone else's movie. He walked past the men's toilets. A couple of young men in white jeans walked in; one of them eyeballed Larkin, gave him a little wave. Larkin shook his head. If they wanted to play Russian roulette in a toilet cubicle, then let them. Bugger all else to do on a bleak Sunday afternoon.

He walked past The Empress – a dodgy pub if ever there was one – and up by the side of the Cathedral. As he was rounding the corner, he saw Charlotte, wearing her black overcoat and a determined look. He instinctively ducked into a recess in the stone wall as she crossed the road heading straight towards him. At the last moment she veered to the left, out of his vision. He left it a beat, then tentatively looked round the corner. Gone. He breathed a little sigh of relief. Somehow he didn't want their next meeting to be one of chance. Her sudden disappearance intrigued him, though; since she was no longer on the street she must have gone into the Cathedral. Telling himself he was curious, nothing else, he entered.

The last time he'd set foot in a church had been at Sophie and Joe's funeral. Larkin's faith in God, like everything else, had lapsed dramatically since then. He looked around. The usual high, vaulted roof, death-and-glory stained-glass windows, the air damp and chill. On an ancient table were piles of musty red prayer books. Leaflets hanging from a pinboard exhorted worshippers to Praise! and Rejoice! and explained where to find God in the inner city. Posters for a church disco billed it as a 'Rave 'n' Save!'. A slogan written in Gothic script – 'TRUST IN THE LORD AND YOUR FELLOW MAN' – sat above a heavily padlocked wooden donation box, chained to the wall, Larkin shook his head.

Dotted around the pews, a few souls were praying for salvation and accepting their destiny. Heads bowed, their lips mouthed silent words of supplication. No one seemed to be Praising! or Rejoicing!

It was in a pew that Larkin found Charlotte, shoulders slumped. He was disconcerted; of all the things he'd taken her for, a lost soul wasn't one of them. Thinking an element of surprise would give him the edge, he sat down. Her eyes were screwed shut, her body hunched forward. As his weight hit the pew she glanced up; she didn't seem recognise him. He spoke.

'Didn't think this would be your kind of place.'

She gave a double-take that would have been wonderfully comic it hadn't been for the expression on her face. Larkin couldn't tell if she was angry, shocked or suffering a heart attack. She took control of herself with a great effort and settled for being embarrassed.

'Have you been following me?' Her embarrassment was followed by outrage.

'No. I was just walking and I saw you come down the Bigg Market.' Silence. 'I called out,' he lied, 'but you didn't hear.'

She didn't reply. *So much for being in charge of the situation*, Larkin thought.

'Look . . . if it's about last night,' he said, 'then I'm sorry. I haven't . . . It was a shock. Everything happening at once, that's all.'

'That's all right. I shouldn't have rushed you.' She spoke like a bad actor, reading her lines in monotone. She certainly didn't sound as if she meant it.

'So what are you doing here?'

She sighed, obviously not wanting to answer. 'None of your business.'

'Just interested.'

'I don't have to explain myself to you. And I don't like you spying on me, either.'

'Bye, Charlotte.' Larkin made to go. If he stayed they'd only argue; he'd forgotten how infuriating she could be. She grabbed his arm.

'No – don't.'

She looked up at him, relaxed her grip. He slowly sat down. There was a long pause, during which Charlotte seemed to have something spiky stuck in her throat.

'Sorry,' she eventually vomited out.

Larkin nodded. She'd definitely broken the world record, as far as apologies went. He sat back; it was up to her now.

'Have you read the diary yet?' she blurted out.

'Yes.'

'And?'

'Not a barrel of laughs.'

'I didn't think it would be. What about Terry? Any clues?'

Larkin took a deep breath. 'Well ... I thought Terry might have been Gary Fenwick.'

Her stony expression became incredulous. 'Impossible ...'

'Yes, I know that now, I checked some cuttings. But I do think they knew each other.'

'How?'

'Don't know yet. But I'll keep looking.'

'Good. Thank you.' Charlotte sat back, her face impassive.

Larkin watched one sad old wretch leave her seat, genuflect, then shuffle out to be replaced by another.

'You never did tell me what you were doing in here.'

She cast her eyes down, mumbled something at the hymn book in front of her.

'Sorry?'

'Mary. I started thinking about her. I got a bit upset.'

She took a deep breath. 'So ... I ... came for a walk. And came in here. Just to let her know I was thinking of her. And to say a prayer for Mary.'

The confession seemed to be painful for her to make.

'Like the song.'

'What?'

' "Mary's Prayer". By that Scottish group, what was it? – Danny Wilson. Good song.'

She looked at him like he'd just exposed himself. 'Don't be flippant.'

He thought of the diary. 'I didn't mean to be.'

They fell silent.

'I've got to go.' Charlotte stood up, then turned towards him. She said, as if at gunpoint, 'Look, Charles will be away for a few more days. There's a little drinks party on tomorrow night. Would ... would you like to go?' The monotone was back.

'Well ...'

'Will you?'

'Yeah. OK. I've got to cover Edgell's funeral tomorrow, though.'

'That's all right. I'll leave a message for you at your hotel.' It seemed as if she'd suddenly run out of things to say. 'I've got to go. Bye.'

And she was off, without even a backward glance at the altar. Larkin sat back and let out a sigh, glad that the awkwardness of seeing her again was over.

He got up, walked to the door and was about to exit, when he remembered the chained donation box. He paused, put his hand in his pocket, and tossed some loose change into the box. He looked up at the agonised figure, the face a mask of purity and suffering, the hands springing fresh blood, and dug into his pocket once more. He came up with a fiver, stuffed it through the slot, looked the crucifixion window in the eye, saw the misery of being human, and departed.

As he passed the Central station, Larkin had the irrational feeling he was being followed. He turned

85

round quickly; no one on the pavement seemed to be paying him the slightest bit of attention. But suddenly, a white saloon car that had been crawling along the kerb shot out, did a U-turn and was away. Had that been his shadow? He looked after the car; he didn't recognise it, couldn't place the make, hadn't even noticed the registration number. Reprimanding himself for his creeping paranoia, he kept walking.

He reached the traffic lights at Marlborough Crescent bus station, waited for green, and stepped into the road. Immediately the white car appeared as if from nowhere. And this time it was gunning straight for him. Larkin stood still, transfixed. He couldn't quite grasp the reality of what was happening. With a monumental effort, he put himself into motion and lurched to the left. The car swerved. To the right. The car swerved. Forcing himself to wait until the last possible minute, he ran for the side of the road. He leapt onto the pavement, narrowly missing the front of the car, and lay there, spread-eagled and winded. The car pulled out to avoid careering into the railings next to the traffic lights then roared away.

A small group of people began to cluster round Larkin's prone body. He heard their voices coming and going, as if he were tuning in a transistor radio.

'All right, pet?'

'Drive like maniacs, don't thuh?'

'Kids, man.'

'Aye, the *Chronicle* said so.'

' – was a Lancia, an' all.'

' – smart, them. Ee, are you all right, pet?'

He blinked. Looming into his face was a rotund woman of about sixty with a furrowed brow.

'Yeah, I—'

He gingerly struggled to his feet. He was at least eighteen inches taller than her.

'Kids! Bloody kids. Bloody joyriders. Dreadful, in't it? And the parents. I blame them. They just let them run wild.'

86

He stopped her tirade before she brought back the birch.

'Did anyone get the number?'

Several shaken heads. People were drifting away, disappointed, now that Larkin was standing. The ghouls were retreating.

'It was definitely a Lancia,' said one man before walking off.

'Thanks.'

'Are you sure you're all right?' the munchkin asked, genuinely concerned.

'Yeah, thanks. I'm fine.'

He started to walk away, unsteadily, his heart pounding. *Joyriders*? Someone had just tried to kill him.

11: The Broken Doll

The hall was cavernous and dark. Fringed, fake-candled wall lamps waited to be lit and the maroon and black velveteen flock wallpaper seemed to absorb what little light there was. Lining the walls were plush velvet booths, giving the illusion of shabby intimacy. Chairs were stacked on tables; a woman wearing a cotton print dress and a lacquered hair-do was struggling to get them down. At the other end of the hall a hefty, balding man in a short-sleeved, polyester-mix shirt and tie combo was making heavy weather of opening up the bar. He was clunking crates of Britvic around so heavily that it was a wonder he wasn't surrounded by a pool of tomato juice and broken glass. In the cathedral-like expanse of the hall, the bar was the altar: just right for a Sunday night.

Larkin was still pretty shaken after the incident with the Lancia. He badly wanted a drink, but had denied himself; he knew that just one wouldn't have been enough. Instead he had walked round until he found the Rainbow Club. He looked dishevelled from the hangover and battered from the pavement, but he was still going strong. Thinking his brand of charm would work better on the woman than the man, he approached her.

'Excuse me?'

'Yes?' Her head sprang round brightly. She had round eyes, a wide mouth and was so cheerful that she must have had a natural Prozac gland in her body.

'I'm terribly sorry to trouble you, but I wonder if you

could help me.' Larkin looked round innocently. 'This is the Rainbow Club, isn't it?'

'Well, it will be in a few hours. Frank – that's my husband—' she pointed to the barman, who was now wrestling with a knife and a lemon as if in preparation for a bizarre communion, 'he and I run the club.' She appraised Larkin. 'Are you seeking membership?' She sounded doubtful, clearly thinking he wouldn't help to raise the tone of her clientele.

'No, no. It's . . . business.'

She didn't hide her scepticism; the charm wasn't working. He'd have to work fast to gain her trust. No hesitation, or she'd think he was lying. He drew Mary's photo out of his inner pocket. 'Do you know this woman?'

She looked at the photo. 'Yes. She used to come here.' She gave Larkin a quizzical look. 'Could I ask who you are, please?' She spoke with one of those sing-song Geordie accents that some women affect to make them sound middle-class.

'I'm working for her solicitor. We're trying to trace that man.' He tapped Terry's face.

'Oh. Is he her son?' she asked.

'No, he's her—' *Killer*, thought Larkin. 'Boyfriend. We think.'

'We're a club for middle-aged, divorced, separated or bereaved people. We provide a place where they can come together, share a common interest. Meet others in the same boat, help regain a bit of self-confidence. We treat them as our friends.'

'I'm sure,' said Larkin.

She looked at the photo again. 'I haven't seen him in here.'

'We think she may have met him after she stopped coming here. We're just checking. Can you remember anything about her?'

The woman suddenly froze. 'I read about this. She killed herself, didn't she?' Her eyes grew to the size of dinner plates.

'Yes, I'm afraid she did.'

'Is there a problem?'

'No, no. She didn't make a will, you see,' he was winging it now, 'so we're just making enquiries. Just routine.'

'There won't be any bad publicity for the club, will there? Only we've got our reputation to consider.'

Yes, thought Larkin; *you treat them all as friends.* 'None at all.'

She subsided. 'Well, I'm afraid I can't be much help. I didn't get to know her very well, you see. She only came a few times – and when she did, she didn't seem to be enjoying herself very much.'

'Can you tell me what kind of person she seemed on first acquaintance? If there was anyone in particular she gravitated towards, that sort of thing.'

'What can I say? She seemed pleasant enough, but she didn't make friends with anyone special.' The woman thought for a moment. 'She didn't seem to have much confidence when she first arrived, but by the time she stopped coming she seemed to have a lot more.' She beamed beatifically, like a born-again Christian. 'Perhaps the club did that!'

'Perhaps,' agreed Larkin. Realising he was down a dead end, he wanted to leave, but the woman had decided to talk.

'That's how I met Frank, you know.' She gestured again to the martyred barman, this time struggling so intently to wipe the bar down that he was in danger of removing the formica veneer. She was still giving her testimony: 'Two ships that passed in the night!' She came back to the present. 'That's all I can tell you about . . . what was her name?'

'Mary.'

'Of course. Mary. Yes, very sad. Tragic. Perhaps if she'd stuck with the club it might not have happened.'

'Perhaps,' he said again. 'What about the young man in the picture?'

'I'm sure I've never seen him here. We tend not to let

the younger ones in. We suspect their motives – their sincerity.'

'How d'you mean?'

The woman's sunny mask slipped for a moment. 'People who come here have usually suffered something in their lives. They're a bit vulnerable. And there's always someone waiting to pounce. Usually you can spot them, but sometimes you can't. It's best not to take any chances. I know an opportunist when I see one.'

'And d'you think he,' Larkin pointed to Terry, 'could be one?'

The woman looked at the photo again. 'Could be.'

'Well, thanks again,' said Larkin.

'Don't mention it.' She gave a mock sigh, the mask back in place. 'Well, back to the grindstone. No rest for the wicked.'

'Time and tide wait for no man,' said Larkin. He could out-cliche her any day of the week. 'I'll see myself out.'

He walked to the door leaving the two ships, that had collided in the night and formed a safe harbour for others, alone. He took one last look around the gloomy hall, imagining how it would appear later; the lonely people dotted round the tables, just like the lost souls at the Cathedral.

The long-suffering Frank was about his sacred duty, hands raised, appealing to the optics. Larkin walked out. He didn't leave a donation. There wasn't a box.

The Broken Doll occupied the same place it always had. And judging by the people that Larkin saw walking in and out, it served the same customers. Depending on your point of view, it was either a place where the unwaged detritus of society got arseholed at the tax-payers' expense; or a place where the genuinely disenfranchised could meet like-minded souls. The truth was probably somewhere in the middle. The only thing Larkin knew for definite was that if he wanted infor-mation, this was the place to come.

If Larkin had stayed in Newcastle he would probably

have ended up as a regular. The Broken Doll had been his favourite pub: the Bigg Market was, intellectually speaking, beneath him, The Trent House too pretentious, The Strawberry too laid back. It was here also that, unless he was very much mistaken, he would find The Prof.

No one knew The Prof's real name. When asked he'd come up with something different every time. When he worked, which wasn't very often, his wage-slips were made out to 'The Prof' – Larkin had seen them. He claimed 'The' was his Christian name and 'Prof' was his surname and no one had ever proved otherwise.

His age was another mystery; he could have been anywhere between twenty-eight and forty-five. He never admitted to the same age twice and claimed numerous and varied birthdays. He had once said to Larkin, without a trace of a smile, that he was three hundred and sixty-five – quite young for a Time Lord.

Most people regarded him as a bit of a joke but this was to underestimate him totally. He was one of the best read and most erudite people Larkin had ever encountered, as well-versed in the sciences as in the arts. He had been employed in both areas – not for very long, though. His near-genius meant that he was easily bored. The Prof was also one of the biggest users of recreational drugs Larkin knew. If something was happening on the drug scene in Newcastle, The Prof would know about it.

Larkin entered The Broken Doll. It was like stepping back into his past. A thrash metal band occupied the miniscule stage area, ranting about what was wrong with society: same song, different singer. The tobacco-coloured walls were covered with xeroxed posters for gigs, featuring unknown bands, the floor was haphazardly covered in threadbare lino. An unhealthy mix of bikers, anarchos, drop-outs, and untouchables huddled on wobbly chairs round rickety tables; a small number of nervous sightseeing students were being ritually ignored. The book-learned and the street-learned had nothing in common.

Larkin walked slowly down the steps to the bar. The

music was at pain level, but none of the drinkers seemed to notice. It wasn't the kind of place where you could reserve seats, but there at the bar, on his usual stool, sat The Prof, painstakingly rolling himself a cigarette. Larkin sidled up to him. The Prof's clothes were worn like a uniform; DMs, faded Levis, faded Madman Comics T-shirt, bike jacket, crew-cut, red braces; his little, round granny specs denoting his intellectual status. The barmaid, a short girl with a Gothic white face and a slack mouth, widened her eyes; clearly it would be uncool actually to ask Larkin what he wanted. He realised he hadn't eaten or drunk a thing all day – apart from a medical couple of gallons of water before he left the hotel that morning. He pointed to the Becks pump, manoeuvred himself to The Prof's side and tapped him on the shoulder. The Prof turned round, his expression quizzical, the elaborately rolled cigarette left unfinished. Larkin beamed at him.

It took The Prof a few seconds to recognise Larkin, but when he did his face lit up.

'Good Lord! Stephen. Stephen Larkin.' Still the same deeply modulated baritone: a combination of perfect enunciation and a broad Geordie accent. He pumped Larkin's hand enthusiastically.

'Hi, Prof. Good to see you again.'

'Well, well! A blast from the past. What brings you round these parts, stranger?'

'Mainly business – but I have to have some time off.'

'So you came here? Wise choice. Wise choice.'

The barmaid chose that moment to arrive with Larkin's pint; despite his protestations, The Prof insisted on paying for it. Larkin took a few sips and, social niceties out of the way, they began to fill each other in on the intervening years.

Larkin told The Prof he was still a journalist, for a paper he was too ashamed to name. The Prof's career had obviously been a lot less clear-cut: 'This and that. Sometimes flourishing, sometimes surviving.' Larkin left it at that. He knew it was as much as he would get from him.

'I heard what happened to you,' said The Prof.

Larkin fell silent.

'A few words were said in your honour that night. You should have had some strong psychic energy around you.'

'Much appreciated. I suppose you'll say that's what I deserved for being a capitalist bastard.'

'Stephen, you should know me better. There's an old Navajo proverb: "Before you judge me, walk a mile in my moccasins". Drink up.'

They drank. The Prof told Larkin what had become of their old gang. Who was in prison; a girl they knew who had stabbed her two-timing boyfriend when she found out he was married. Who'd changed; 'Dave split the band up. Never went anywhere. He's running an agency for freelance journalists now. Give him a call.' Who had died; 'Remember Jack? Overdose. That old horse habit? Well, he just did too much. And when they cut him open, they found he was HIV positive. Devil and the deep blue sea.'

Larkin sat back. Listening to The Prof, he began to realise that the past was exactly that. Things had moved on, out of reach: people, places, the city itself. The only constants seemed to be this pub and The Prof.

'They're thinking of knocking this place down and building a flyover, you know,' said The Prof.

There you go, thought Larkin. Just The Prof left.

The band finished their set with a sonic barrage that threatened to mutate into a solid wall. A couple of people clapped. The silence that followed was deafening.

'Hey, Prof.' Larkin tried for casual; the knowing glint in The Prof's eye made him realise that he had failed.

'You *do* want something.'

'Just your help. It won't cost you anything.'

He mulled it over. 'How may I be of assistance?'

Just then the jukebox burst into life with a noise like a bone-china dinner service being thrown into a stainless-steel sink. It made the hairs on the back of Larkin's neck stand up, his stomach lurch: 'Do Anything You Wanna Do' by Eddie And The Hot Rods. The first few power chords kicked in, and then the voice: a charmless growl, fired with the eternal optimism of youth.

'This song . . .' Larkin began, 'it was *my* song.'

'It was lots of people's,' said The Prof. 'Forget The Pistols, forget The Clash – this song more than any other from the punk era defined the spirit of a generation.'

And on it thrashed, a blueprint for cocky individualism. 'It was such a positive era,' The Prof continued. 'Such a positive time, a time when we could be anything, do anything we wanted. Hedonism plus idealism; the perfect equation.' The Prof sighed. 'You can take the temperature of a society from its popular culture. You wouldn't get a record like that being made today. Now we live in a regressive society. No idealism – just hedonism. A state of decay. What bands there are sound like they wish they'd been going thirty years ago. The cult of the DJ has replaced the musician. The creative act is now no more than recycling, repackaging someone else's creativity. That's how we experience the world now. By sampling it, not living it.'

Larkin nodded. All he'd said was that he liked the song.

'Anthem for doomed youth,' mused the bar-room philosopher *par excellence*. 'The eighties were a bad decade for anyone with integrity.'

Larkin stayed silent. The Prof looked at him. 'The Government's fault, of course. There's an old Chinese proverb: "When a fish dies, it dies from the brain down".' He took a meditative swig of his pint.

The song finished, to be replaced by 'Teenage Kicks' by The Undertones; someone had taste, thought Larkin. He grinned, knocked back his pint, and almost forgot that someone had tried to kill him earlier.

'You know, Prof – good company, good beer, blinding music – this could be heaven.'

'Not heaven – but a haven, at least, and that's something to be thankful for.'

Larkin smiled. 'Just like old times.'

The Prof sat back in his chair and looked serious. 'You wanted my help, I believe.'

Larkin dragged himself back to the present. 'Drugs.'

'You want me to score some for you?'

'No, no. Haven't touched them for years. No coke, no speed, nothing. Not even a spliff. No, what I need is information. And I thought you would be the best person for the job.'

He raised his eyebrows. 'I'll try.'

'You still experimenting?'

'I'm still on the journey of self-exploration in which consciousness-altering substances play a part, yes. It's a noble calling, shamanism, and I'm following a long and worthy tradition. De Quincey, Byron, Shelley – all the way down to Kerouac, Leary, and Burroughs. A lot to live up to. So what would you like to know?'

'A bit of background, really. I'm covering Wayne Edgell's funeral for the paper. I just want to know more about the state of the market up here.'

The Prof cleared his throat, preparing to give a lecture. 'Look around. What d'you see?'

'People in a bar.'

'Notice anything?'

'They all need a wash?'

'Look closely. Most of the younger ones are on fruit juice or water. They're just waiting to slip a few Es, stand in a field all night and dehydrate. It's the sad old farts like us who are doing most of the drinking.'

'Your point being?'

'My point being, hard drugs are not a counter-culture thing anymore. Everyone's off on one. Indie has gone mainstream. There's a demand. And where there's a demand, there's a supply.

'It used to be the usual gangs, the criminal families, running things. That's all changed. Crack is easy to make, easy to supply, and highly addictive. You can get hold of a batch of Es anywhere. Everyone's having a go. And competition's fierce. It's big business. The new bunch have corporate structures with quarterly profit projections, demigraphs – the lot. They have target areas, to increase their market share. Pushers have infiltrated schools: start them young. Hedonism plus capitalism minus idealism doesn't add up.'

'I know all this, Prof. But how does it apply locally?'

The Prof took a swig of his beer and continued. 'Globally it's a pyramid.'

Larkin butted in. 'I know *globally*. How about locally?'

The Prof looked hurt, disappointed that his specialist knowledge was being rebuffed. 'Impatience,' he said, and shook his head in admonition. Then he relented. 'Put simply, someone wants to be Mr Big. They want everyone under their control. It's not so much a battle as a hostile takeover bid. Then there's also the Londoners wanting a share. Very nasty.'

Larkin took the battered photograph of Terry and Mary out of his pocket. 'Recognise him?'

The Prof squinted hard at the picture. He held it up to the light, up to his face, put his glasses on his head and squinted at it some more. Eventually he handed it back to Larkin.

'No joy?'

'No. He's never been in here. Too classy for him.'

'So. You got any names for me?'

'I'm not entirely sure. I had heard that there was a strange bunch involved. Real hard trouble. Some kind of weirdo sadists.'

Larkin looked at him. 'Really?'

'Yes. Proceed with extreme caution.'

'I will. And if you should happen to hear something?'

The Prof smiled. 'Then I'll let you know.'

'Thank you.'

They both looked at each other. Larkin felt he should say something meaningful, but The Prof beat him to it.

'Look Stephen,' he began, 'even though we haven't seen each other for years, I'd still like to think of myself as your friend. You're dealing with some dangerous people out there. Please – be careful.'

Larkin assured him that he would. With nothing left to say to each other, they made their goodbyes.

'It's great to see you again, Prof. You restore my faith in humanity.'

'Your faith's intact. You just don't know how to look for it.'

They shook hands. Larkin left The Prof the name of his hotel – 'That pre-fab on the quayside' – and went out into the night, leaving The Prof to contemplate his place in the universe.

Larkin walked through the dimly lit backstreets, over the pockmarked tarmac. These were the kind of streets where dealers dealt, where couples of either sex and any combination consummated something that could never resemble love.

His feet took him behind Marlborough Crescent bus station. Suddenly he caught a sudden, shadowy movement from the corner of his eye. Remembering the events of earlier that day, he instinctively ducked into a garage doorway. He heard a pounding, hi-energy, disco beat, remembered that The Hole In The Wall, a gay pub, was right in front of him. That calmed him a little. Probably some customers had come round the back for a snog. Still, something stopped him moving.

A shadow came round the corner; Larkin could just about make out a youngish-looking man. He was well-dressed and, to Larkin's concealed eye, vaguely familiar. He was trying to work out where he'd seen the young man before when another shadow came round the corner and stood in the light. Larkin's heart flipped over. It was Charles.

Larkin stayed stock-still, hoping that the disco music would drown his ragged breathing. The last thing he wanted was another run-in with the Shithouse. But what the hell was Charles doing frequenting a gay pub?

As Larkin watched, Charles, dressed in a loose-fitting

99

suit that was shapelessly expensive, was joined by another man: tall, clad in motorbike boots, leather jeans and, despite the chill in the air, a white vest. The cold made it quite obvious that his nipples were pierced, with rings inserted through them. The two men shook hands. Pierced Nipples held his left hand out to Charles, who bent in close. Left nostril: sniff. Right nostril: sniff. Then again. He straightened up, blanking for a few seconds as the cocaine jolted his body – the freezing heat that Larkin remembered so well – then shook his head, his lips curling at the side. The two men started talking, but the throb of the music hid their words. Another man joined them. Dressed in a similar uniform of leathers, he was holding his arm by the crook of its elbow, flexing it rhythmically. He lolled against the wall, mute, a gay bodyguard. Heroin, post-fix. These guys weren't fussy, thought Larkin, transfixed and terrified.

Formalities concluded, Charles and Pierced Nipples proceeded to have a very businesslike chat. Then, after what seemed like hours, they went their separate ways: Charles to the right, towards the main street and the bus station; the vicious-looking mute ambling off to the left. But Pierced Nipples came straight towards Larkin.

Larkin froze, tried to stop breathing. As Pierced Nipples reached Larkin's hiding-place, there was a muffled call from down the road; he turned and hurried towards it. Then he was gone. He had been close enough for Larkin to smell his Armani aftershave, study his razor-cut hair, feel the cruelty that emanated in waves from the man. Larkin counted to two hundred, then ran as hard as he could in the direction he had just come from.

Andy was performing his camera ablutions when Larkin knocked frantically on his door. He opened it and Larkin tumbled in to the room.

'What the fuck's the matter with you?'

Larkin was panting, trying to get his breath. It was the most exercise he'd had since he was sixteen.

Andy moved over to the fridge and got out two beers; he popped one and handed it to Larkin, who gulped a long draught then flopped back on the bed.

'So?' demanded Andy.

Larkin didn't move.

'Fuck's sake, what's the matter?'

'It's . . . it's . . .' Larkin sat up. He looked at Andy, his heart still pounding.

'Are you gonna tell me, or what? Here's me, stuck in fuckin' chickentown, to quote John Cooper Clarke – and there's you, runnin' all over the fuckin' place! Not even showin' me where I can get a proper drink, or pick up a decent piece of skirt. And now you burst in here like all the hounds of hell are after you, crash on my bed and keep stumm. What the fuck's wrong with you? You're a right fuckin' nutter, you know that?'

'I never knew you liked John Cooper Clarke,' Larkin gasped.

'Lot about me you don't know.'

Larkin took a deep breath. 'Can I trust you with something? I mean, *really* trust you?'

'What is it? A matter of life an' death, or summink?'

Larkin managed a weak laugh. 'Yeah. Yeah, it's exactly that.'

'Is this goin' to be an epic?'

'Yeah.'

'Well, get another couple of beers out. Reckon it'll be a long night.'

12: Home Is A Long Way Away

'This duck goes into a chemist, right? An' he goes up to the bloke behind the counter, an' he says, "You got any lip balm?" And the guy gives him some. Then the duck goes, "Er..."' at this point Andy patted his pockets, 'and says, "Look, I can't find my wallet.' Andy pointed to his face. 'Could you just put it on my bill?"'

Larkin smiled: Andy, meanwhile, was convulsed by a near-apoplectic fit of laughter.

'D'you like it?'

'Yeah! It's a good one, that.'

'Why aren't you laughing, then?'

'Because I don't like people who laugh at their own jokes. Reminds me of Tony Blackburn.'

There was a silence, then Andy guffawed. 'You're quite funny, you know that?'

'Yeah. Sure.'

Andy had kept up the barrage of jokes all the way from Newcastle. Larkin had told him everything the night before, and in doing so had gained an ally. Probably. With Andy you could never be sure.

Larkin had had a bad night. He had dreamed of coffins and Lancias, of being carried up the aisle of the Cathedral in a coffin while Charlotte, Andy, The Prof and Mary said prayers over his body. He had woken up in a cold sweat at about five o'clock, and hadn't been able to get back to sleep again.

They went past Alledene New Town – another failed

experiment in sixties anthropology – and turned off towards Grimley. A new bypass system made the place look even more neglected and unapproachable. They went down the slip road and into Grimley itself. As Larkin had suspected when he saw it from the train, it hadn't altered much. A few new buildings here and there, old pubs newly painted, corner shops that had changed hands. Hardly anyone about. All it needed was for some tumbleweeds to blow across the street and it would resemble a ghost town in a Western. They drove on until they reached the Catholic church, where a gaggle of people were standing outside.

'They're starting early,' said Andy.

They pulled off the road and parked along a street of old stone cottages. They got out, Andy with his cameras over his shoulder, Larkin with his portable cassette recorder and notebook. They locked the car, headed down to the main street. The police were already erecting barricades and diversion signs beside the war memorial, as if they were preparing for a state visit.

Larkin went over to a talk to one of the coppers. He took a bit of warming up but, after some skilful persuasion on Larkin's part, he wouldn't stop once he got going.

First of all, to warm things up, Larkin elicited the policeman's views on law and order, which were discussed in great and reactionary detail. Then, subtly, Larkin commented on the elaborateness of the funeral arrangements, asked if the poor old taxpayer was, as always, footing the bill. The policeman looked round to check if he could be overhead and then dropped his voice conspiratorially.

'Well, it's backhanders all round, isn't it? That, and the funny handshakes, I suppose. I mean, how are we supposed to operate like this?' He pointed to Larkin's cassette. 'Is that . . .'

'Don't worry. You're not being recorded,' he lied.

'We've been told to say nowt. But someone has to speak up.'

Larkin smiled. 'You're a rarity, you know that?'

The policeman became suspicious again. 'How's that?'

'An honest policeman. Not a lot of them about.'

'Oh, there are. There's lots of our blokes hate this sort of thing. Treatin' that cunt like a fuckin' hero.'

Larkin was about to leave him when he continued.

'I mean, like, we caught this other un piss-easy – and now we have to make him out as the bad guy! Makes you laugh, dunnit? Or makes you sick.'

Larkin thanked the policeman for his time, and left him alone with his unhappy lot.

The funeral wasn't for another couple of hours so they found their way to the nearest pub, an old, crumbling, Victorian edifice called Stephenson's Rocket. By the look of the place Stephenson might have still been in there: a spit-and-sawdust pub, if they'd had any sawdust. Bare boards, bare walls, and a thick patina of greasy dust covering everything, including the manager. They ordered two pints, which came complete with filthy glasses. The barman was wearing a stained shirt and thick Dr Cyclops glasses which lent him the air of a child murderer. Perhaps he was. He seemed glad of the custom and tried to start a conversation. To avoid this they took their drinks, sat in a run-down booth and talked in quiet voices, in case the vibrations cracked the plaster.

'So, how does it feel to be back?'

'How do you think?'

'Yeah. I see your point.' Andy looked around. 'Are all the pubs like this?'

'No! Some of them are real shitholes.'

They both laughed.

'No, seriously there's the scampi-in-a-basket kind, as well.'

'Grimley doesn't look big enough.'

'Oh, just about.'

Andy looked round. 'I can't see you growing up here.'

'Everybody has to grow up somewhere.'

'Yeah, suppose.'

Larkin asked Andy where he was from. He reddened a shade.

'Oh, Hampshire. My dad was a gentleman farmer.' As he talked his accent cleared slightly. 'Sent me off to boarding school, university and that – hated it, so I dropped out and got a job as a roadie with a heavy metal band. Took some photos of them, decided there was money to be made, and off I went.'

'I figured that all this Sarf London wideboy bit was just smoke.'

'You become the mask you choose to present,' said Andy, no trace of an accent. 'I mean, who'd have employed me if I'd told them that I was some rich farm boy?'

'True.'

Relaxing a little more, they downed the rest of their pints in unison.

The funeral procession had reached and entered the church by the time Larkin and Andy decided to emerge from the pub. The streets were now like a scene from a fifties thriller; chock-a-block with onlookers, well-wishers and the usual funeral ghouls, there for the spectacle.

Larkin and Andy made their way through the crowds up to the church. Lining the pavement in front of the stone wall of the church was what looked like a bouncers' convention. They were dressed like movie gangsters; sober suits, sunglasses despite the non-existent sun, white shirts, black ties, chunky gold knuckle-duster rings. They were impassive, anonymous mannequins modelling the latest in designer mourner-wear. There was space around them; they exuded a palpable aura of menace.

'Where they from, then?' asked Andy.

'London, I reckon,' said Larkin.

'All this fuss just to pay their last respects to their little soldier.'

'And to show off a bit.'

Andy snapped away; Larkin talked into his cassette. Other reporters, presumably from the local press, had been sent along to do the same. A plate-glass carriage hearse, drawn by two white horses and festooned with flowers, appeared from a side street by the Catholic Men's Club, followed by two flat carts, both horse-drawn and piled high with flowers. Bringing up the rear were three black stretch limos. They drew up to the entrance of the church, where the porch doors opened and out stepped the funeral party.

A man was led out first, supported by another suit.

'That'll be the father,' said Andy, snapping away.

The flow continued, with carefully orchestrated wailing from the women, and suitably downcast looks of regret from the men. Then the coffin emerged – all glass, revealing Edgell lying on satin cushions with orchids rimming his face. He was dressed in a dark grey lounge suit; his face looked at peace, probably more so than when he was alive.

The movie gangsters, doubling as pallbearers, took the coffin and loaded it into the hearse. Then, with the streets cleared and the traffic halted, the horses moved off. They headed down the main street, past the war memorial, and turned right down Hawksley Lane.

'Where they off to now?' asked Andy.

'Either the crem or the graveyard. Doesn't make much difference, really.'

'You reckon? They'll have their work cut out getting all that glass to melt.'

They followed the procession all the way to the crematorium. It was a long walk, down roads thronged with crowds; the whole town seemed to be there. Shops were closed, offices shut down; clearly an official day of mourning had been declared. A cacophony of cameras clicked away.

'Look at all these people!' Andy said, staring around him. 'You'd think it was the Lord Mayor's Show.'

'It's the most exciting thing that's happened in Grimley for years,' said Larkin. 'You don't get many

107

gangsters round here. It's like the Krays all over again. But I reckon it's fear as well. Shock. If a murder like that can happen here, they don't know who'll be next for the knife.' He looked round at the streets, the bleak faces of the onlookers. 'Just wait. Soon everyone'll be saying what a tragedy it is. What a great bloke Edgell was. How kind he was to his granny. No one'll dare come out and say he was a vicious, psychotic little thug who deserved everything he got.'

They walked on a little further, along a street where rows of terraced houses snaked off on either side, dark-bricked and anonymous. Larkin pulled at Andy's sleeve as they passed the top of one street, indistinguishable from the others.

'You see down there, third on the left?'

Andy looked: third on the left or twenty-third on the left, he couldn't tell them apart. 'Yeah,' he said.

'That's the house I grew up in,' said Larkin.

'Yeah? Happy memories?'

Larkin looked. The house now had a new front door, a mock-Georgian job, to give the house a little originality. Unfortunately it had been cloned up and down the street.

He shrugged. 'The usual.' A swirling mixture of emotions were fighting for dominance. He couldn't decide how he felt, but he knew, as he looked at the house, that Grimley wasn't his home any more. Not now. He put it out of his mind; he had a job to do.

They moved on. With sudden clarity, last night's dream came back to Larkin and he realised what it meant. The coffin they were following, like the one in the dream, was symbolic; he was burying his old innocent self, his past. Grimley, his childhood refuge, was in reality as corrupt and violent as anywhere else. He had no one to turn to but himself.

They eventually reached the gates of the crematorium, to find their way barred by a Missing Link. Andy took a couple of token shots, but couldn't really get close enough to make them worthwhile.

'Hey, you wanna go round the side, see if we can get in that way?'

'You think there's any point?' asked Larkin.

'If I can get a picture, yeah.'

'With this lot on guard?'

Andy looked around. The suits were standing motionless, dormant Rottweilers, waiting for the Pavlovian command. 'Yeah . . . maybe you're right.'

They walked back the way they had come, the crowds now dwindling. The British Legion had a sign up: OPEN ALL DAY TO GENUINE FRIENDS OF WAYNE EDGELL. MEN ONLY.

'Where do the women go then?' asked Andy.

'Same place they've always gone round here. Back home.'

They decided to push their luck.

The decor was just as Larkin remembered it: early Gothic crossed with MFI. They went up to the bar and got their drinks.

'Are you friends?' said the barman.

'Known each other for years,' replied Larkin.

The barman smiled politely. 'Of Wayne's.'

'As a matter of fact I was at school with him.'

'OK – what would you like?'

They ordered. All drinks on the house.

They had just got seated when the Missing Link's twin brother, Piltdown Man to the other one's Bromsgrove, came up to them and did a bit of towering.

'Excuse me, gentlemen,' he said, going slowly, as if speech were a novelty, 'are you mourners? Genuine friends of Wayne?'

'Yeah we are, actually,' said Larkin.

'It's just that you look like gentleman of the press to me.' His brow was creased with the effort of completing a whole sentence; he was really pushing the boat out.

'That too,' said Larkin, thinking that if he swung at him, the brain-to-muscle ratio on the Missing Link was in inverse proportion to his steroid-boosted size. 'I went

109

to school with Wayne, I grew up here. I just wanted to pay my last respects.'

The Link mulled this one over. 'You may finish your drinks, and then leave.'

'We may, may we? That's most magnanimous of you.'

The Link leaned in close to Larkin, his breath as fetid as a garlic-eating pit bull terrier's. When he spoke it was in a growling whisper. 'Listen – just drink up and leave, and I won't break your fuckin' arms. Right?'

'Oh, but the atmosphere is so convivial!'

'Right. That's it, you smart-arsed cunt.'

And with that the Link took a swing at Larkin. He was surprisingly quick, but Larkin was quicker. Both he and Andy jumped out of the way, sending chairs, table and drinks flying. The Link turned round, sighted Larkin by the bar. He made a lunge for him but Larkin anticipated it and swerved out of the way at the last minute, leaving the Link winded on the edge of the bar. Larkin grabbed a soda syphon from between the peanuts and squirted him full in the face. This stopped him in his tracks. Larkin took the opportunity to swing the syphon at his head; it connected, but he didn't go down. Larkin persisted, swung it again. And again. The Link was beginning to crumple when Andy rushed forward with a pool cue and walloped him in the balls. The steroids couldn't have shrivelled them completely because, once the signal got through to his brain, he doubled over.

'Is he dead?' asked Andy.

'Was he ever alive?' retorted Larkin. He bent down to check his pulse. 'Sadly, he'll live.' He stood up again. 'Well, we'd better be on our way.'

The barman was gaping at them; Larkin turned to him. 'You saw what happened. My friend and I were enjoying a nice drink, paying our quiet respects to my old schoolmate, when this brute set upon us. Self-defence. Tell the big boys that when they arrive.' The barman looked terrified; Larkin bent in close. 'Just because there's more of them than there are of us, doesn't make them right. Remember that.' He started to walk out. 'And you serve a crap pint as well. No wonder it's free.'

And that was it, straight back to Newcastle. Laughing all the way with the kind of hysterical laughter that bravado and fear creates. Larkin was driving; The Clash blared out.

'Fuckin' 'ell, what a laugh! I don't think I've ever had an assignment like this one.' And Andy collapsed into giggles.

'Me neither,' said Larkin truthfully.

Andy dug into his case, on the back seat, and pulled out a hip flask. He unscrewed the top, took a long swig, and handed it to Larkin. 'Happy homecoming!'

'Cheers!' Larkin took the flask and tipped it into his mouth. They kept it up all the way back to the hotel.

There was no message from Charlotte. Andy went to send his film by express post; Larkin wrote his articles on his laptop. There were two; one for the tabloid he worked for, one to sell, freelance, to the Sunday supplements. He'd been working on that one already, an ironic, elegaic account of his homecoming and the funeral. A real load of crap, in other words. It took him about an hour and a half then he faxed them. Finally he gave his editor a reluctant duty call.

He told her he'd be staying in Newcastle for a few days because he thought he'd found a good story. Lindsay accused him of seeing another woman; Larkin didn't confirm or deny it.

There was a muffled noise at the other end, then Lindsay was back on the phone. 'We've got your fax. Well done. You can still write when you want to.' There was a pause; Larkin heard her light a Silk Cut. 'Well, hurry home soon, darling. I'm missing your dick.' And with that she rang off.

Larkin stood there holding the dead phone, wondering why he'd bothered. And where the fuck was home, anyway?

* * *

The same tired old shit, thought Larkin, as he watched Prince gyrating on MTV. He switched the set off, bored. For something to do, he had another flick through his pile of background information on Edgell and Fenwick; nothing grabbed him. He looked at the photo of Mary again. Behind her there was a whole load of people; he tried to make some of them out, but it was impossible – they were out of focus. There was one man closer to Mary's table who did look familiar, though. He went scurrying through his pile of paper and came up with a matching face. Sir James Lascelles. He was pictured in the cutting presenting a cheque to a local hospital's renal unit, surrounded by nurses, looking as if the health of his serfs depended on their squire's benevolence. Larkin checked the photo. There he was at the party, doing a Gatsby, looking on while his guests availed themselves of his generous hospitality. Perhaps it was time he paid a visit to kindly old Sir James. The newspaper article named his company as Golden Crest. He got the number and address – Crest Towers – from Directory Enquiries and made the call.

He had no luck until he mentioned the law firm that Charlotte worked for; immediately he was connected to Sir James's private secretary. He was going to blag it, pretend to be from *Hello* magazine, but he sensed he wouldn't get far. Instead he said, 'I'm a friend of Charlotte Birch's.'

He was put on hold. After what seemed like an eternity, made even longer by having to listen to 'Greensleeves' played on a stylophone (*ha*, thought Larkin, *money can't buy you taste*), the secretary came back on the line. 'Sir James will see you at four thirty. Today.'

Larkin sat back, stunned. He hadn't thought it was going to work. It was three thirty already. He grabbed his jacket and made for the door. This was either the best move he'd ever made – or the worst.

13: Welcome, Mr Bond

'Larkin. Stephen Larkin. I've got an appointment with Sir James at four thirty.'

Although he hadn't had time to smarten himself up, he didn't think he warranted the frosty greeting he was getting from the receptionist at Crest Towers. She was all in black, with cropped hair and an expression that would have done Heinrich Himmler proud. Her very presence made the temperature drop a few degrees. She hadn't believed him when he'd told her he had an appointment with Sir James.

'Why don't you check?' said Larkin, getting irritated.

She reluctantly punched something into her terminal. Larkin looked round; the reception area was minimalist to the point of severity. Situated just off Mosely Street, Crest Towers was a vast, black edifice, casting a towering shadow over the whole city. No one could see in; and, as Larkin was discovering, no one could *get* in. The building was either a monument to endeavour, risk and progress – or an ugly, characterless eyesore. Larkin knew which one he'd pick.

The receptionist looked up. On discovering that Larkin did have a bona fide appointment, her in-built thermometer plummeted still further. Probably her idea of a good night out was going to the abattoir to watch the cattle being slaughtered; she might even help to beat them with a stick first.

'The lift is over there. Don't move or touch anything once you're inside.'

'Why? Is there an ejector seat?'

She fixed him with a death-ray stare.

Larkin smiled. 'I bet that beneath that tough, hard exterior, you've got a heart of pure marshmallow.'

Her ice-chip eyes followed him all the way to the lift.

The doors whispered open; Larkin saw a desk with a man sitting behind it. He stepped out and the doors hissed shut behind him.

The lift was a stainless-steel canister attached to the side of the building. It silently descended, leaving Larkin to his fate. The room was glass, circular, dizzyingly far from the ground, with a three hundred and sixty degree view of the city. At the other end – if a circular room could have ends – was a huge, antique mahogany desk, unadorned with anything resembling work, and inset with tiny TV screens. The desk also carried a hi-tech phone, but nothing else. No family photos. Nothing to indicate a life outside Crest Towers. Behind the desk sat Sir James Lascelles. Larkin sized him up; his photos had flattered him. He was squat, with a rubbery, slimy face, a deficit in the hair department and a bloated body wrapped in an expensive suit. He had the sleek, oddly attractive look that money and power lends to ugly men: a handsome frog, perched on a lily pad.

Sir James smiled as if he had a long tongue and Larkin was the fly.

'Good afternoon, Mr Larkin. I believe you wanted to see me.'

Lascelles' composure made Larkin feel like James Bond walking into Blofeld's lair. Next he would be told the villain's master plan, then placed in a trap that he had to escape from armed with only a comb and a wristwatch. Larkin checked for the presence of a tank of pirhana fish, a trap door, or a fluffy white cat, and then crossed the floor towards Sir James.

Just because he makes more money than God, thought

Larkin, *don't let him intimidate you.* 'Yeah. Hello.' He looked around. 'Nice view you've got here.'

Sir James smiled smugly. 'It is rather, isn't it?'

'Bet it gets a bit boring after a while.'

'You think so?'

Larkin shrugged.

'Mr Larkin, look around you. I am rebuilding this city to my personal design. Everywhere I look I see a project of mine – a shopping complex, a hotel, a cinema. Urban renewal. Everywhere I look, I look on my work.'

'And tremble?'

The predatory smile widened. 'I see you are well-read, Mr Larkin. I admire education in a man.' He sighed elaborately. 'Alas, I am not educated.' He sat back, smiled corpulently. 'But self-improvement takes many forms.'

Larkin took that as his cue to speak. 'Wouldn't you say – the higher you are, the harder you fall?'

Lascelles smiled again; it wasn't pleasant. 'I won't be falling. This was a decayed city, blighted by unemployment, poverty, bad housing – but I've changed all that. I've employed hundreds – thousands, perhaps – housed families, whole communities, improved the quality of life for the whole region. In short, I have become the saviour of the North East. I have become The Grand Architect.'

A monumental bore, more like, Larkin thought. All the self-made men he'd ever met wanted to do nothing but talk about themselves. It was like being stuck in a room full of actors. He decided to see how far he could go.

'So you've got a vision. But haven't they tried that vision thing round before?'

'I take it you are referring to Mr Dan Smith and his unwise choice of associates. Yes, they did have a vision of how this city should be.'

'And to do the same thing they did, you have to resort to the same methods. And end up in the same mess? Doesn't that worry you?'

Lascelles smiled indulgently. 'No. I won't make the mistakes they made.'

'So all these grateful people you've given work to, allowing them to build your grand designs . . .'

'Yes?'

'Can they afford to live in them? Shop in them?'

A flicker of anger crossed Lascelles' face and was gone.

'Your kind are quick to mock the accomplishments of others. But was it not ever thus? In a society, there will always be those at the top and those at the bottom. I do what I can to help. Would that everyone would do the same!'

Larkin had taken an instant dislike to the man. Anyone so rich and successful had to be bent. The thrill he'd felt at being granted an audience was quickly dissipating; all he wanted to do now was ask his questions and leave. But Lascelles was in full flow.

'Do you know something?'

'A few things,' said Larkin. 'What in particular?'

'I'm now the biggest property developer in the North East. Bigger than John Hall, even.'

'Really.' Larkin took a stroll around the room. 'Is this all you do all day? Sit here at your uncluttered desk and look out at Newcastle? Not much of a life, is it? Not much different from being on the dole.'

Another smile. 'Ah, you misunderstand me. I look out here on *my* city. I see what progress I am making, or is being made on my behalf.' He looked directly at Larkin. 'There is very little goes on down there that I don't know about – or won't find out about?'

'Then you're just the man I want to talk to. Do you know Mary Greene?'

'Should I?'

'You might know her as Mary Torrington?'

'The names are not familiar. Am I being interrogated, may I ask?'

'It's just that I'm doing a little investigating into a

suspicious death. And your name has popped up a couple of times from independent sources.'

'And you think I am responsible for this death?'

'No.'

'What then? Do you think I know who the guilty party is?'

'As you said, nothing goes on in this town that you don't know about.'

He sat back, stung: one-nil to Larkin.

'*Touché*, Mr Larkin, *touché*. I'm afraid I don't know anything about this woman.'

'What about Gary Fenwick?'

'Gary Fenwick?'

'Oh, I should imagine you've heard of him, Sir James. I'm sure you read the papers.'

He made a theatrical show of remembering. 'Ah, yes. Wasn't he involved in a . . . a death, Mr Larkin? Is this the case you're asking about? I thought it was all very clear-cut.'

'It is. But he may have been involved in the death of Mary Torrington as well.'

'What an anti-social fellow! But isn't he locked away? No longer a menace to society?'

'You should know. It's your pet law firm that's handling the case.'

'Oh, I'd hardly call them that, Mr Larkin. I just happen to know a few of its partners and associates.'

'Including Charlotte Birch?'

'Ah, the lovely Ms Birch. Or Mrs Twigge, to be exact.'

'*Twigge*?' Larkin couldn't hide his surprise and amusement.

'Didn't she tell you her married name, Mr Larkin? I imagine not. She keeps her maiden name for professional purposes.' He sighed again, repositioning himself. Sir James continued. 'You said on the phone that you are a friend of hers?'

'I am. And I'm looking into the death of Mary Torrington on her behalf. You *must* remember her, Sir James. You were photographed with her.'

117

That caught Lascelles off balance, but he clung on to his composure.

'Yeah,' said Larkin. 'Got it here . . .' He dug into his pocket, handed the photo over.

Lascelles took it, but didn't respond. Larkin decided to help him along a bit. 'Look, there you are in the background. You do photograph well, don't you? I'd hardly have recognised you in the flesh. And look, there's Mary, sitting at the table. Recognise her now?'

Lascelles said nothing.

'And who's her companion? I don't suppose you know him, do you?' Larkin tried to sound offhand.

Sir James looked up, the edges of his mouth twitching in a smile – or a grimace. 'No, I don't. Are you insinuating that I'm personally acquainted with everyone who comes to my parties? That's a lot of people.'

'I'm just asking for your help in my enquiries. A public-minded citizen like yourself – only too happy to help, I'd have thought.'

Sir James sat back. He returned the photo to Larkin. A look of amusement played over his face as he regained full control of the situation. 'Are you attempting to blackmail me in some way, Mr Larkin? I only ask because this office has every bugging and counter-bugging device known to man. Threats don't work in here.'

Larkin had the distinct impression he was being toyed with. 'I wasn't threatening you! I was just asking you a few simple questions.'

'Which I'm afraid I am unable to answer.'

'Anyway,' said Larkin before he could shut his mouth, 'if you ever want a good firm of solicitors, I can recommend one. Nicholson Griffin Harwood and Howe. They'll take anybody.'

At the touch of a button on Sir James's desk, the lift hovered into view once more.

'I think this conversation has run its course,' said Lascelles amiably.

Larkin crossed to the lift. Then he stopped, and turned.

'One more thing. Ever heard of Wayne Edgell?'

'Only from the papers.'

'And – just one last thing – you wouldn't happen to know who's paying Gary Fenwick's solicitor's bill? It's just that Charlotte, bless her, won't tell me, and I thought that you—'

'Goodbye, Mr Larkin.'

And Larkin knew that was all he would be getting.

The Hitler Youth receptionist was still at her post. Larkin winked at her as he walked past but he may as well have been invisible for all the notice she took.

He walked out through the main entrance. Then he saw something that made his blood freeze: Pierced Nipples, walking directly towards him.

Larkin stared at him. He was wearing his leather trousers, a leather jacket with thin lapels and a white linen, collarless shirt buttoned up to the neck. He headed straight for Larkin with a determined stride – and past him, into Crest Towers.

Curiouser and curiouser, thought Larkin. Pierced Nipples and Sir James? And what about Charlotte – where did she fit into all this? And Charles. Fenwick. Terry. Edgell. And Mary. Poor Mary. So what was all this – conspiracy or coincidence? Larkin was sure of only one thing.

Give it up. Stop this 'investigation' right now. He was in way over his head. If there was something illegal going on, then it was a job for the police, not a solitary journalist. He wanted nothing more to do with it. He felt a pang of conscience over Mary – but it was something else he would have to live with. The whole thing had got too big. *Finito*. He would tell Charlotte tonight.

As he walked back to his hotel, rehearsing how he was going to break the news, he noticed something he hadn't seen before: just how many boards there were dotted

119

around, advertising Sir James's company. What he owned, what he was developing. It made Larkin feel queasy.

When he got back to the hotel there was a message for him, from Charlotte. A time, and an address in Jesmond. He steeled himself for what he had to do. He knew she'd go apeshit.

He knocked on the door of Andy's room.

'Oh, 'allo, mate. Come in.'

Larkin followed him. The room was virtually spotless; Andy's bags and equipment were piled up on the bed.

'What's up?'

'I'm off, mate. You coming, or what?'

'Erm ... no, not yet. There's a few things I have to take care of tonight.'

'Oh, her again. You still on this case?'

'No. That's what I've got to take care of. I'm going to see her tonight, tell her it's all off. Tell her I'm going back to London and that's that.'

'Couldn't you just phone her and get the train back with me? We'd have a laugh.'

He saw the look in Larkin's eye.

'No. Don't suppose you could, really.'

There was an awkward silence between them.

'Well, look,' said Andy, 'I didn't think I would – but I've had a great time up here. All things considered. You're all right, you are. It's been – different, but good.'

'You're all right too,' said Larkin.

They both stood like a pair of embarrassed teenagers, grinning like idiots.

'Well, look, mate, I've got to go. You know my number. Give me a bell back in the smoke and we can go for a couple of bevvies or something. Yeah?'

'Sounds good to me. As long as there's not a funeral going on at the time!'

'Yeah, well.' Andy stuck out his hand. 'Cheers, mate.'

Larkin shook it. 'Cheers.'

And he shut the door on the nearest thing he'd had to a friend in ages.

14: Ennui And Action

The house was exactly as he had thought it would be; a rambling, Victorian monolith which the owners had tried to keep 'in period', a euphemism for opening an account at Laura Ashley. Huge sofas squatted in the large rooms; the curtains were the floor-length kind climbed by Emily Brontë heroines when they were having a bad day. A profusion of rugs littered the floor; heavily framed Klimt and Mucha prints adorned the walls. The music was even worse than the decor – Dire Straits – and, in short, the whole thing was just as horrendous as Larkin had expected it to be. And the guests didn't provide any compensation – the result of what happens when cousins marry, they were fake as a game show host's smile, and with about as much appeal.

And Charlotte had yet to turn up. He had hoped she would be there when he arrived, since she had invited him in the first place – but, knowing her as he did of old, he had half-expected her to be late as well. The hostess, a grinning, skeletal bimbo, had felt obliged to talk to him, but after a few minutes of stilted conversation she had wandered off, forcing him to mingle. Glass of chardonnay in hand, Larkin was cornered by one bore after another; after twenty minutes or so, he decided he could stand no more. He grabbed a bottle of red and sought sanctuary in the garden.

Larkin sat alone on the stone steps, the bottle nearly

empty. He would give Charlotte another ten minutes and then he'd leave. Maybe he could catch Andy, and they could get the train together. He wanted to get out of Newcastle for good.

He drained the bottle, looked at his watch. A couple more minutes... So this was how their relationship would finish: open-ended, unresolved. It was fitting; his life had never featured big Hollywood endings, all the loose ends neatly tied up. He was just getting ready to go, when the French windows opened. A brief blast of 'Walk Of Life' wafted through, against a background of banal conversation and hysterical laughter – and a figure emerged.

At first he thought it was Charlotte. As he looked more closely, he realised his mistake. The woman was in her mid to late twenties, with long dark hair; she was pretty but had a determined set to her jaw. She looked strong, capable, and very pissed off. She started slightly when she saw Larkin.

'Sorry. I didn't know there was someone out here.' Her broad Geordie accent was clear and unaffected; she sounded like she was used to making herself understood.

'That's OK. Don't worry. I was just leaving anyway.'

'Me too.' She heaved an enormous sigh.

'Not enjoying yourself?' Larkin asked.

She looked back into the house. 'Bunch of fucking wankers, the lot of them.'

'You're right there. Why did you come? You don't look like the type to be at a party like this.'

'Had to see someone. Hasn't turned up, though.'

'I know how you feel. Same here. But I can't say I'm sorry. If she'd turned up I would have had to stay even longer.'

'True.'

'What's your name?' Larkin asked. She looked at him suspiciously. 'I'm not being crass, honest. I just like to know who I'm talking to, and you're probably the only person here I'd want to have a conversation with.'

124

She smiled, loosening the set of her face. Nice smile, thought Larkin.

'My name's Jane. Jane Howell. What's yours?'

'Stephen Larkin.' There was a pause. 'So, Jane, what brings you here?'

'The bastard who never turned up, that's what. I'm part of a collective, a community project in Scotswood. The bloke from the council who's supposed to be giving us an urban renewal grant has been avoiding us. I found out he would be here tonight so I got myself an invite. Must have heard I was comin'.' She suddenly looked at Larkin, shocked. 'You're not part of . . .'

'No. I'm nothing to do with any of them in there. Where did you say the project was?'

'We've formed a Credit Union, we're tryin' to get some City Challenge money – and look at that lot.' She gestured back to the house. 'They haven't a fuckin' clue! None of them. They're all right, aren't they? They sit there in their fancy suits, with their five-figure salaries, in their posh houses – not that I'd turn a house like this one down if I was offered it.'

Larkin had taken an instant liking to her: no bullshit.

'So who are you waiting for?' she asked.

'Oh . . . an old friend. I've been doing a bit of work for her and I just wanted to tell her that I was packing it in.'

'Oh. Why? I mean, it's no business of mine, you don't have to tell me—'

'No, I'd like to. I was – looking into something for her. I'm a journalist. But it got . . . complicated. I don't want to be part of it any more.'

'Oh, right.'

'I feel like I'm getting too involved and I can't handle it.'

'So chuck it.'

'Yeah . . . I don't like walking away from something I haven't finished.'

'So stay with it.'

'Are you, by any chance, the kind of person who sees everything in black and white?'

She laughed. 'Uh-huh.'

'Just my bloody luck, eh?' He laughed as well. She let the laugh subside and looked at him seriously.

'Well, the choice is yours. You have to do what makes you happiest.'

'I know.'

They sat there in companionable silence for a while. Then Larkin said, 'So what are *you* going to do now? About the guy you've come to see?'

'I don't know. I'll catch him eventually.' She frowned. 'You know, if you could make people like this live in the kind of place we have to put up with, just for a month, bring a bairn up single-handedly – if they had to do all that, there would be no inner-city mess, no poverty, no crime. I bet you.'

'You're probably right.'

'Aye. I am.'

Larkin sat back. He was enjoying himself for the first time that evening. Perhaps he wouldn't leave yet.

'What are you goin' to do, then?'

'Dunno. I've missed my train back to London.'

'You live in *London*?' she said incredulously.

'Yeah. Something wrong with that?'

'Don't know how you can stick it. I mean, here's bad enough – but London? No chance.'

'At least the parties are better.'

She grinned.

'Look,' Larkin said, 'if we're staying for a while, shall I go and get us some more wine? It's free, and why not abuse their hospitality?'

'Aye! We'll make a night of it.'

Larkin returned bearing two full bottles and they sat together, ignoring the increasing cold, for the next couple of hours.

Jane told Larkin about her daughter, Alison, who was being babysat by a neighbour – another member of the collective. About Alison's father, who had had run off and left Jane as soon as he found out she was pregnant, leaving her to bring the baby up alone.

She explained the work of the collective, the council's indifference to the fears of the residents, its lack of admiration for the way in which they were trying to create a sense of community, a feeling of hope in the face of all the odds.

And Larkin told her the reason for his visit up North. About the funeral, and Charlotte. He didn't go into details about Mary; and he didn't mention Sophie and Joe. His confidence didn't extend that far.

He liked her. He liked her a lot. He thought of staying in Newcastle just so he could see her again. He felt close to her, but that could have been because as the night got colder, they'd huddled together. Now they were touching, but neither made a move.

Eventually she said she had to make tracks, and stood up to phone for a taxi. The wariness in her face was well and truly gone by now. 'Look . . . I'm not very good at this. I know I've only just met you, and that, but . . .' She took in a big breath. 'Will you be staying around? Or will you be going back to London?'

He had opened his mouth to answer when he realised he hadn't a clue what he was going to say. He knew that, at this moment, he didn't want to return; but if he was realistic, to stay because of someone he'd just met at a party was pretty ridiculous. And, hadn't he decided that wherever his future lay, it wasn't in this city?

And then there was Charlotte. What had happened to her?

'Look, I'd better be going,' said Jane. 'You do what you think's best.'

Jane's voice drew his thoughts back; he saw from her expression that she had taken his silence as a rejection. She gave him a smile that was somewhere between sad and defiant and turned to leave.

'Erm . . .'

She turned again, eyes lit up. 'Yes?'

'Have you . . . Can I have your phone number?'

The light faded slightly. 'Sure,' she said, rummaged through her bag for a pen, scribbled something on a scrap of paper and handed it over.

'That's home. The top one's the office. If I'm not at one, I'm usually at the other.'

He took it, put it in his jacket pocket. 'If I'm around, maybe we could go for a drink or something.'

'Sure.' She spoke like she was going through the motions.

'No, really—'

'I said, sure.' She smiled brightly, suddenly uncomfortable. 'Well . . . goodbye. Nice to have met you.'

There was a moment's hesitation; neither of them knew whether it would be right to kiss the other. Jane broke it. 'I hope you find what you're looking for.' And she disappeared through the French windows.

Larkin stood still. She hadn't believed him when he said he'd call her. Which was a shame, because he'd meant every word of it.

When he got back to the hotel, a young guy with wide hips, seventies-style framed glasses and a nylon tie, currently making the difficult transition between pimply youth and assistant manager material, was there to greet him. He handed Larkin a note he'd taken of an earlier phone message; Larkin studied it. It was from The Prof, telling Larkin he'd discovered something important, giving an address in Benwell, telling him to come alone.

Larkin left the hotel immediately. It seemed his stay-or-go dilemma had been temporarily sorted. It also seemed like he might be walking straight into a trap.

128

15: Bait

It wasn't the most grim and foreboding house he'd ever had to enter – but it was close. It sat in a street of similarly ramshackle, heavily vandalised terraced houses, all earmarked for demolition. Benwell was second only to Scotswood when it came to urban decay. The pall of despair hanging over the place was almost tangible.

Larkin had paid the cab driver off at the West Road and walked down onto Woodcross Lane; a sign at the top of the street announced: ANOTHER NEW LUXURY HOUSING DEVELOPMENT FROM GOLDEN CREST. MAKING HOUSES HOMES. An artist's impression of an impossibly happy young couple illustrated this concept; a characterless new housing estate formed the backdrop.

The house looked deserted. He decided to check out the back; round the corner, up the alley. He walked past the overturned bins, repelled by the feasting rats, his feet dodging weeks of discarded rubbish. He moved slowly, looking for light in the house, any sign of human activity. Nothing. Perhaps The Prof was in there ... Perhaps not. The feeling that he'd been set up intensified.

He circled back to the front of the house and stopped, scared to enter, but knowing he had to. In an attempt to weight the odds in his favour, he snapped a length of rusting metal from the house's ancient fence; it wouldn't offer much in the way of protection, but it was at least reassuring.

Taking a deep breath, he walked purposefully towards the door. The lock seemed to have been missing for some time; the door opened with barely a push.

The first thing Larkin noticed was the smell – like someone, or something, had died. The whole building stank of rotting remains – animal or human, he didn't know, and didn't want to. In the hall the wallpaper was tattered and mildewed; scraps of old carpet dotted the floor. He pushed open the door on his right: the front room. He tried the light. To his surprise the bare bulb lit up.

The room's most recent occupants seemed to have been squatters and junkies on their last port of call. The debris of spent lives was scattered all around. An old mattress, stained and sodden with damp; a couple of crates; old beer cans and fag-ends; rusty syringes containing a residue of a dark liquid, old spoons, discoloured tinfoil, a few old shoelaces. Bin-bags covered the window. On the walls were posters and pages ripped from magazines: hard-core porn. Women taking two men at a time, women with animals, women being anally violated by screwdrivers and other tools, expressions of agony that didn't looked feigned. The S&M pictures made Larkin want to throw up. A man had a nail hammered through his penis, safety pins holding his foreskin back, while another man took him from behind.

The other downstairs rooms yielded much the same. The kitchen was home to a couple of startled rats and a family of cockroaches feasting on bits of mould. But no sign of The Prof.

He was shaking now. His instinct screamed at him to get out while he still could, but curiosity drove him on. Next stop, the stairs. Larkin gripped the rickety bannister and started up.

The boards creaked with every step. At least, he hoped it was the stairs; if not, it was the rats, scampering secretly around him in this halfway house to hell. They would be under the floorboards, in dark recesses, infesting the whole structure: a house with living, rodent walls. He hoped that was the most he'd have to worry about.

He reached the top of the stairs. There were three doors leading off the landing, one at the back and two at the front. None of them looked particularly promising. One of them, however, was slightly ajar; he could just make out a faint sliver of light from underneath the doorframe. His scrotum shrivelled up and his heart went into overdrive as he slowly pushed at the door.

As it creaked open on worn hinges, he saw that the light was coming from two candles at the far end of the room. They were both lit, but would have been impossible to see from the street; thick black-out curtains were taped to the window. The candlesticks flanked a stained, damp mattress. And lying there, bruised, battered, and naked, was The Prof.

Larkin rushed over to him. The Prof moved slightly and expelled a gasp of air. He was alive – but only just. Larkin examined him. It was a thorough, sadistic job. Apart from the bruises and red blotches, frightening evidence of internal bleeding, someone had tried to erase the tips of the fingers on his right hand with what looked like a cheese grater. His shoulders showed deep, straight weals; one of his nipples was missing, leaving a bloody hole. His penis had a razored gash in it; the toenails of both his big toes were gone. There was vomit all down The Prof's chest, and Larkin felt like adding to it.

Larkin put down his makeshift weapon, slid his hands underneath The Prof's body and tried, gently, to lever him off the mattress. Then he heard a sudden commotion behind him. He saw a black blur, felt a dull pain, sensed an exploding yellow firework of light and colour, before everything went black.

As his consciousness dribbled back, Larkin felt cold. Very slowly he realised he had been stripped to the waist and tied to a chair. He was in the same room; a quick glance sideways revealed The Prof, still lying on his mattress. Larkin's head pounded; he felt nauseous. He strained to get his hands free, but only succeeded in tightening the knots.

His struggles must have alerted his captors, because at that moment the door opened and in walked Pierced Nipples, wearing his leather jeans and motorbike boots. He was bare-chested, showing off his nipple rings – two razor blades hanging from silver chains. The welcoming smile on his face scared Larkin all the more. He walked into the room, light, compact, his steroid muscles rippling, and spoke.

'You're back with us! Good. It's no fun when they pass out, like your friend there.' He nodded towards the prone body of The Prof.

'If you don't do something, he's going to die,' said Larkin.

'We all will, one day.' Pierced Nipples turned his head to the door. 'Boys? Are you ready to join us?'

Into the room stepped the biker Larkin had seen round the back of The Hole In The Wall, and his twin brother. They were nonchalant. Thug B took a biro casing out of his pocket and put it into his mouth. He pulled out a rectangular piece of tinfoil and smoothed it out; from a plastic bag in his other pocket he shook a small handful of white powder and scattered it on the foil. Thug A took out a cheap lighter, played the flame underneath the foil; Thug B sucked the vapour into his mouth and held it there, till his eyes narrowed and his mouth puckered like he was sucking a barbed-wire lemon. Eventually he breathed out with a feral grimace. Pierced Nipples crossed towards Larkin.

'Mr Larkin. You've been making a bit of a nuisance of yourself. Interfering, with my business, sending your lackeys round to spy on my staff. We can't have that, can we?' He spoke in perfect standard English, like he was reading the news.

Larkin tried to swallow. 'So what are you going to do to me? What you did to *him*?' He looked at The Prof.

'That thought had crossed my mind.' He gave a little

giggle. 'But no. That was just to fill in the time until *you* turned up.'

'Look,' began Larkin, trying to keep a note of desperation from creeping into his voice, 'if you must know, I was going to call it all off. Finish it. Go back to London.'

'Of course you were.'

'I *was*! Look, I couldn't care less what you're doing – it's not my problem. Why don't you just let me go? I'll get on the train and that'll be the end of it. Yeah?'

Pierced Nipples sighed. 'Oh, Mr Larkin, I wasn't born yesterday. Yes, by all means leave Newcastle. Go to London, go to bloody Timbuktu for all I care. If you can.'

'What d'you mean?'

'An example must be made. A warning to others.' He spoke to Thug A. 'Robin? Come and show Mr Larkin how you take your medicine.'

Despite the threat of a painful and imminent death, Larkin was amused. '*Robin*?'

'Yes. Batman,' Pierced Nipples indicated the other thug, 'must have his boy wonder. I myself am Superman. But only in the Nietzschean sense, of course.'

Robin brought a chair over. He sat down opposite Larkin, rolled up his sleeve, took out a leather thong and tied it round his left bicep; Larkin could see the faint tracks in his arm. At the other end of the room, Batman was busy with a spoon, some powder and his lighter, preparing a syringe.

Pierced Nipples strutted round in front of Larkin, flexing his ego. 'Are you admiring my body? Do you find it attractive? You think I must be queer, is that it?' He smiled; it wasn't pleasant. 'Sex, death, fear and pain. That's all there is. And power, of course. Does that make me queer?' He gave a glance in the direction of Batman and Robin. 'If you're lucky my two friends may fancy you too, Stephen. Give you a bit of special loving.'

Batman came towards him with the full syringe.

'Blood,' said Pierced Nipples, 'and needles. So exciting.

133

But so dangerous, these days. And these boys being so impulsive, I doubt they take proper precautions.'

Batman stuck the needle into Robin's arm; he pushed the plunger, pulled it back, pushed, pulled it back. Larkin could visualise the drug creep round Robin's system, poisoning him like a cancer. Robin's head pitched forward and he sat in his chair, immobile, as Batman lovingly pulled out the needle. The syringe was still about a third full.

Pierced Nipples continued. 'Bad blood mingling, comingling. How did Shakespeare put it? "Many thousands have the disease and feel it not."' He smiled at Larkin. 'You look too clean, Stephen. Want to get dirty?'

He took the needle from Batman and held it at the tip of Larkin's nose. Larkin stared at it, in cross-eyed terror. Pierced Nipples went on.

'Now, in the unlikely event that my boys have no nasty infections, you've nothing to worry about. But on the other hand . . .' Batman pressed down on a vein in Larkin's arm, making it stand proud. 'How do you rate your chances, Stephen?'

Fear made Larkin defenceless. He knew he had no control over whether, or how, he lived or died; the needle focused him, enabled him to see how every bad move he'd made in his life had led him to this spot. He felt his legs become wet and realised he'd pissed himself. One push of the plunger and his barren, uncertain future would become significantly shorter.

Suddenly, he wanted to live. He promised the God he'd lost his faith in that he would stop living in the past, make a future for himself – if only he was allowed one. The needle came closer. Pierced Nipples towered over him; freaky eyes bored straight into his pain. Larkin could see the erection in his leather trousers as Pierced Nipples touched himself, moaning softly.

The cold of the needle touched Larkin's arm. This was it. He began provisions for his fate, tried to accept a slow, premature death.

Larkin grimaced against the expected entry of the

needle, but nothing came. He looked up. Pierced Nipples was standing, legs apart, on a high that no chemical could induce. His eyes fixed Larkin's and he licked his lips lingeringly. 'Now, what to do with you.' He began to pace the room. 'Should I kill you? Probably not. That would only lend you credibility. Should I hurt you so much you become an example to others? Possibly. Should I make you disappear? Perhaps.' He sighed theatrically. 'So many options! So many options. What's a poor boy to do?'

Suddenly he stopped pacing. 'I have it! We'll start from a fixed point, and improvise a little. My boys are naturally creative – but they do get carried away sometimes. So best keep an open mind.' Pierced Nipples held the syringe in his hand. With a smile he pressed the plunger and squirted it all over Larkin's naked chest; Larkin squirmed as the liquid hit.

Pierced Nipples bent close to his ear. 'If you get out of here alive and, in the future, I hear you've so much as breathed the same air as me, believe me, you'll never breathe again.' He stood up and motioned for Batman to untie Larkin. Batman did so, pulling Larkin to his feet and pinning his arms behind his back. Pierced Nipples produced a switchblade from his back pocket.

'One slash of your chest, let the juices mingle – and that'll be that. Crude, but effective.' He brought the knife up to Larkin's chest. Larkin didn't move. He tried to hold his breath, keep his chest still, so that the cold, sharp steel wouldn't puncture his flesh. Pierced Nipples pushed the knife closer, then suddenly snatched it away with a mirthless laugh. 'Hand,' he barked at Robin; Robin firmly held out Larkin's right hand. Pierced Nipples took the knife and inscribed a little cross on the palm.

'X marks the spot,' he said, as Larkin flinched from the pain. 'Now!' In unison, Batman and Robin kicked out at Larkin's legs and he fell to the floor on his back, winded. From out of a dim, recessed corner Pierced Nipples appeared with a heavy metal clawhammer and an evil-looking six-inch nail. Robin held Larkin's hand flat, palm upwards, while Pierced Nipples positioned the nail over the bloody X. He looked at Larkin and smiled. 'Showtime,' he said, and brought the hammer down.

16: Come Away, Death

Black.

Walls, floor and ceiling seeped together into an all-enveloping liquid darkness. Larkin was back on the chair; tied, helpless. There was no sound, no light.

Suddenly, Pierced Nipples' face loomed in front of him, a garish light distorting his features into a hideous grin. He stepped back and from out of nowhere appeared the syringe. It was bigger than Larkin had remembered it, older and rustier. Pierced Nipples brandished it, light glancing off the barrel; Larkin recoiled. Pierced Nipples stopped his advance.

'Don't want it? Then you needn't have it.'

Larkin breathed a sigh of relief.

'Don't want to waste it, though.' Pierced Nipples' eyes gave off a glint as warm as gun oil. 'I know someone who'd appreciate it.'

Larkin's son Joe appeared at Pierced Nipples' side. He looked exactly as he had the last time Larkin had seen him alive. He stood there mute, expressionless, eyes cast down.

Pierced Nipples turned to face Joe. He pointed the needle at him; Joe didn't flinch.

'Feeling helpless?' Pierced Nipples asked Larkin.

'Get off him!' Larkin screamed. He struggled against his ropes; they became tighter. 'Leave him alone!'

'Someone's got to have it.'

'Then make it *me*!' shouted Larkin.

'Too late,' said Pierced Nipples, and pressed the plunger. There was a booming roar as the liquid leapt from the needle and splattered over the boy's chest. It seeped into his clothes, burning them away, and Joe screamed as the liquid turned to acid and began to scorch his flesh.

Larkin watched, horror-struck, as the acid ate its way through the boy's body, skin, muscle, organs, until there was a gaping hole from front to back, ragged and bloody.

He screamed.

Black.

Larkin woke with a start. He sat bolt upright in bed and looked around.

Sunlight streaked through the curtains, the room was summer-warm; and Larkin felt safe. He looked at the sleeping form beside him: his wife, Sophie. He touched her gently, trying to wake her up.

'Time to get up, love. Time to go.'

A voice came from the other side of the bed. 'It's not time for you. Not yet. Just me.'

She turned over and Larkin saw where the shotgun had done its work. He shut his eyes but it was too late. He screamed.

Black.

'Three choices, really.'

'Not as many as that,' said Larkin.

'How many, then?'

'Two, I reckon.'

Larkin looked round. He was in a pub, unfamiliar; but all the same, he was somehow no stranger to the place. Larkin looked at his drinking companion. Dressed casually, with a face that seemed to be constantly changing. Larkin had the uncanny feeling he knew him, though he realised that was impossible.

The man nodded and moved over to the jukebox while Larkin ordered two pints. By the time they arrived the man had returned, and The Clash's 'Should I Stay Or Should I Go' was echoing round the place.

'You were saying?' said the man. 'Two choices.'

'Yeah.'

'So what'll it be?'

Larkin shrugged. 'I'm happy here.'

'You can't stay here forever.'

'Suppose not.'

'What if all this disappeared?' The man gestured with his hand. And suddenly they were alone in a dark, silent void. 'What if there was nothing?' said the man. 'What if this? What if that? *What if? What if?*'

The man's features coalesced into a giant pair of lips. They blew Larkin a grotesque parody of a kiss. And then—

Black.

Flashlight, then black. Flashlight, then black. Suddenly, light. Continuous, blinding. He was hit by a wave of agony, from a toxic sea. He was back. He knew he was alive, because this was how he defined living. He was in pain.

17: Born Again

The vague, grey blur became a retina-searing burst of white. Figures milled about in space, some of them familiar, some of them not. Voices spoke, distant, indistinct. Pain coursed through his body, red-hot at first, becoming numb. The white turned to grey. And darkness returned.

Grey, white, black. How long he was adrift in limbo he didn't know. Eventually shapes became distinct, voices audible, surroundings clear. His senses slowly began to regain their vocabulary.

'He's back.' The man who spoke was slightly rumpled with receding, dark hair, a garish check shirt that clashed with a bright red tie, and a stomach that had spent too long in the staff canteen. 'How are you feeling?'

Larkin tried, experimentally, to speak. Whatever he had said the doctor nodded at, so it must have been the right thing.

'Of course you hurt,' said the doctor. 'That means you're alive.'

'How long . . .?' It was as much as his cracked voice could manage.

'How long have you been out? A week, more or less.'

Larkin couldn't believe it.

'Whoever did this to you meant business. It was a professional job. If your friend hadn't found you when he did, they'd have finished you off.'

'What friend?' Larkin sounded like a stroke victim.

'All in good time. This is what you've got: ribs – four broken, two cracked. They'll heal, given time and rest. Hand. Well, it'll mend, but you'll always have that scar. You may never have full use again, I'm afraid.'

Larkin stared at the heavily bandaged lump on the end of his right arm. He shuddered, suddenly back in the room. A scar. A reminder. He'd leave the bandage on for as long as possible, to avoid seeing what was underneath.

The doctor consulted his clipboard. 'Some internal injuries – again, nothing that won't heal given time. Your left kidney took quite a hammering, as did both your kneecaps.'

'Will I ever be able to play football again?'

'Could you before?'

'No.'

'We have a comedian on our hands, do we?' The doctor sighed. 'I'd say you're going to be ninety per cent there. Eventually. We thought we were going to lose you for a while, but you kept fighting. You must have a strong lust for life.'

'Yeah. I must.' He moved his head a little, awareness flooding back now. 'So who's my friend?'

'The one who got you out of there? Andy Brennan. You owe him a pint.'

'What about the other guy that was in there with me?'

The doctor's face darkened. 'He's . . . stable.'

'And what does that mean?'

'It means he's not getting any worse.'

'But he's not getting any better either.'

The doctor tried to change the subject. 'Just concentrate on getting yourself well – we'll take care of him.'

'Shit. It's my fault. I got him into it.'

'I wouldn't be too harsh on yourself. We didn't give *you* much hope when you first came in.'

Larkin fell silent as something came back to him.

'Doctor?'

'Yes?'

'Did I . . . I don't know . . . die?'

'You mean, did your heart stop?'

'Yeah.'

'It was touch and go for a while. But we pulled you back. What makes you ask?'

'I just had some . . . trippy dreams. That's all.'

The doctor smiled. 'Sometimes people have what they call epiphanies. We don't know what they are. You know the kind of things, dead relatives, benign deities, dark tunnels, bright lights. I don't how to explain them. It could be your subconscious, you could just be dreaming, your mind fighting like your body is, or maybe, I don't know, maybe it's God. Who knows?'

Larkin remained silent.

The doctor smiled. 'Don't let it worry you now. You're back. Get some rest. I'll look in on you later.'

'Thanks . . .'

And Larkin, feeling a slight sense of peace, slipped into a dreamless sleep.

They told Larkin they thought The Prof was slipping into a massive, shock-induced coma. They had given him seventy-two hours to fall into PVS – a persistent vegetative state. He'd had thirty-six of them. Even if he did come round, they thought he might have some lasting brain damage. That really made Larkin feel better.

A visit from Inspector Moir didn't exactly do wonders for his recovery either. Moir sat at the far end of the bed, with a told-you-so expression on his face and a barrage of questions. Larkin was in no mood for them, so he maintained the pretence that he couldn't move and could barely talk. In the end Moir left, exasperated but vowing to return. Larkin could hardly wait.

The next time he woke up, Charlotte and Andy were there. And Andy told Larkin how he came to find him: 'The train was cancelled. Derailment at Doncaster – vandals on the track.' He'd gone back to the hotel, found The Prof's note, and followed on, not wanting to miss

143

the fun. His arrival at the house had caused Larkin's aggressors to flee; horrified by what he saw, Andy had quickly called an ambulance.

'Cheers, mate.' Larkin didn't trust himself to say anything more effusive.

'Don't mention it. The police turned up as well. They've posted a guard on your mate's bed.'

'There was one on mine too. Is he still around?'

'Naw – they've given you up as a lost cause.'

Then Charlotte spoke. Or tried to speak. She got as far as apologising for missing the party before she broke down in tears. Andy put a comforting arm around her; Larkin felt helpless, impotent.

'Charlotte, don't blame yourself. I'm doing enough of that for both of us, believe me.'

'What have you got to blame yourself for?' she sobbed.

'The Prof. It's my fault he was there. If he dies, it'll be on my conscience. It shouldn't be on yours.'

Then she was hugging him. It hurt a little, but he didn't mind. They stayed that way for a while, Andy surprisingly tactful, looking anywhere but at the two of them. Once the tears had subsided, she disengaged.

'Look, Stephen, I've been talking with the doctors, and with Andy, and – well, how would you like to move into my place for a bit?'

'What about Charles?'

Her face darkened. 'Charles has . . . He's disappeared.'

'*Disappeared*? Why would he do that?'

'I don't know,' said Charlotte. 'The only thing Andy and I can think of is that he was somehow mixed up in all of this.' She looked shamefaced.

'It's a strong possibility, yes. Last time I saw him he was with the guy who did this to me.' Larkin raised his right hand slightly; Charlotte looked away. 'Any idea where he's gone?'

'None,' replied Charlotte. 'And, to be honest, I won't be sorry if he doesn't come back. But I think it settles it. Would you like to stay? I'll try my best to be the

144

perfect hostess.' She was smiling, but it was a fragile smile that could crack at any moment.

Larkin returned it. 'Best offer I've had for ages.'

She looked at her watch. 'I've got to be back at work. I'll see you soon.' She gave Larkin an unforced, delightful grin. 'You don't know how glad I am to see you again!' And she kissed him, full on the lips, while Andy minutely examined the bowl of fruit at Larkin's bedside. And then she was off.

'You should have seen your little machine when she did that! Off the scale, it was.'

'Ha, ha. Hey, Andy?'

'What?'

Larkin smiled. 'You saved my life.' He felt more ready now for the 'thirtysomething' bit. But Andy's reaction was typically British.

'Oh, fuck off, you melodramatic bastard!'

'You know what?'

'What?'

'I've had . . . I don't know how to put it. I've . . . being that close to death,' he shivered, 'it makes you think.'

Andy looked at him. 'Couldn't have put it better meself.'

'I just feel like I've been–' he almost said 'born again', but thought better of it – 'given a second chance.'

'Oh yeah? To do what?'

'Lots of things. But the first thing is, get the bastards who did this to The Prof and me.'

'Pleased to hear it. Count me in. You'll be interested in these, an' all.'

He fished into his case and brought out an envelope full of photos. 'Here we are – Truprint's finest. Have a gander.'

Larkin looked. There were photos for the tabloids and the qualities. He had to hand it to Andy, he knew his stuff. The procession, the coffin, the church; the atmosphere of the whole day, captured on film. Except the fight in the British Legion, of course.

145

'Look at that one there.' It was the crowd outside the church.

'Yeah? So what?'

Andy sighed impatiently. 'Look closer!'

'What am I looking *for*, exactly?'

'You'll recognise it when you see it.'

He did. Standing on the pavement, half-hidden by the crowds, were Terry and Charles. Larkin's blood ran cold; his stomach lurched.

'Fuck me . . .'

'No thanks, mate. What d'you reckon? Spooky, eh?'

Larkin looked at the photo again and pointed to a soberly dressed middle-aged man. 'Who's this guy they're both talking to? One of the suits?'

'Looks like it. He's in with the London crowd on one of the other photos.'

'Does Charlotte know about these?'

'Credit me with some fuckin' sense! "Awright, love – want to see some photos of your missin' husband doin' some dodgy drugs deal with some dangerous bastard from London?" Do me a favour.'

'So what next?' asked Larkin.

'Already got it sussed,' said Andy, pleased with himself. 'There's a place opposite your bird's house – little hotel. I've got a room there. Keep an eye on you, in case Charlie boy makes a return. Then I can save your life twice.'

'You'll not be quick enough.'

'You reckon? I scored some speed to keep me awake. Don't worry. When d'you think you'll be able to move?'

'Couple of days, I should think. Fill me full of pain-killers and point me to the door. Then it's Charlotte, here I come.'

Andy put the pictures away. 'What about this Charlotte? You think she's on the level?'

'You mean, do I think she's involved in any of this? No, I don't. I must admit the thought did cross my mind, but why would she be doing all this if she wants me out

146

of the way? Anyway, she's my ex-girlfriend. I've known her for years. Ex-girlfriends don't try to kill you.'

'Mine do.'

'With good reason, probably . . . Changing the subject – sort of – have you heard from Lindsay?'

'Yeah,' said Andy. 'It was her that ordered me to keep an eye on you.'

'Not like her to be concerned for my health.'

'She's not. She just reckons you're on to something and she wants to make sure you're well enough to write it.'

Larkin thought for a minute. 'You know, I've tried for years not to get involved. With anyone or anything. But nearly dying like that . . . I dunno.' He sighed. The painkillers were making him more voluble than he'd intended; he felt slightly foolish. 'If I've had some kind of reprieve, or something, then I'm going to try not to balls it up this time.'

Andy looked at him. 'What's happened to you? You've gone from Mr Misery to Mr Pretentious.'

'Don't worry – the old me'll be back soon. What goes around comes around.'

'Eh?'

'It's a karmic thing,' he said with a grin, knowing what effect his words would have.

'Karmic?' Andy stood up and paced the room. '*Karmic*?' He shook his head in disbelief. 'That's all I need! Nursemaid to a fuckin' hippy!'

18: Ghost Laying

Larkin was prodded and poked, tested and goaded. Over the days, his condition slowly improved. He was told he would be kept in hospital for a couple of weeks, although they were very pleased with his physical progress.

He still wouldn't talk to anyone about what had gone on in that room; he didn't feel able, yet, to confront it. His doctor, Dr Baker, often popped by to see him; Larkin enjoyed their conversations, but got the impression that the man fancied himself as an amateur therapist. Perhaps the hospital had adopted a holistic approach to healing and he was just doing his job.

On one such visit, Baker tried again to draw Larkin out.

'Look,' said Larkin, 'I know you mean well – but I'm just not ready to talk about it.'

'Fair enough. All in good time.'

Larkin paused. 'Can I ask you a question?' he said.

'You can.'

'Have you ever seen anyone die from drugs?'

Baker sat at the corner of the bed. 'I presume we're not talking about an overdose of valium here.'

'No. I'm talking about crack, heroin – that sort of thing.'

'We've dealt with a number of fatalities through heroin.'

'What were they like?'

Baker sighed as if he had the weight of the world

on his shoulders. 'Not pleasant. Heroin – diamorphine sulphate, if you want to be accurate – can best be viewed as a very strong painkiller. It blots out the symptoms, the pain of living. I don't mean to be melodramatic. But that's the effect it has. Once it gets a hold, your life's like a tap that gets turned on so the contents drain away. You could sit in a room for a year or more, doing nothing. Not speaking, or eating, or washing – just staring at your shoes, numb, until the next fix. That's all you think about. Taken too purely, it can send your heart and blood pressure fatally off the scale. But it's the rubbish it's cut with that usually kills you. The profit motive gives pushers *carte blanche* to add anything to it to make it go further. Could be Vim – could be baking powder. Or rat poison. You just don't know.'

'And crack?'

'It's not the drug that's addictive, it's the high. It's quick, intense. And it grips you. Fast. Coming down's the hard part. Some people use heroin for that. It's the beginning of a journey down a very slippery road. Even your old favourite, powdered cocaine,' Baker looked straight at Larkin – could he read minds as well as trying to psychoanalyse them? – 'that can get you. It's like adrenaline. Too much causes arrhythmia of the heart. If it's too pure, it kills you, usually by asphyixiation on your own vomit. As for Ecstasy – who knows? Far too early to tell.' He looked at Larkin again. 'I take it that whoever did this to you was involved in the drugs trade?'

'I think so.'

'Then you're lucky to be alive.'

Larkin sighed. 'So you keep telling me.'

He went for walks, stumping around on his crutches, agonisingly slow, an inch a minute, pain coursing through his muscles. Round the other wards, down the halls, his crutches leaving deep indentations on the lino, his muted grunts echoing round the General's sterile corridors.

He reached the room where the prone figure of The

Prof was lying, wired up to machines that registered the fact that he wasn't yet a corpse.

Larkin looked at him. Was this how it ended? Larkin on crutches; his old friend on a life-support machine, stuck in limbo. The villains who had done this to them were out there somewhere, part of the black economy. If they were caught, sentenced, others just like them would have taken their place by the time they'd been put into their cells. Even inside they'd keep on working. The laws of supply and demand were the only ones which had any relevance to them.

So what did Larkin think he could achieve? Revenge? Retribution? Yes. For The Prof, and for himself. And for Mary. As he looked at The Prof, tried to ignore the hot tears that pricked behind his eyes, he knew that soon he would have to turn his self-destructive rage into something more positive. And take action.

When his couple of weeks were up, Larkin was deemed well enough to be received into Charlotte's tender care. He said his goodbyes and was transferred, via wheelchair and ambulance, to Charlotte's bed. As he was being helped through her house, he noticed how firmly it was stamped with Charlotte's personality. There seemed to be nothing of Charles here.

The ambulancemen were ready to leave. Charlotte plumped up his pillows like Florence Nightingale and went to close the front door after them.

He looked round the bedroom. Bare, honey-coloured floorboards; linen and calico drapes; earthenware pots filled with hazel twigs and dried flowers. State-of-the-art TV and CD player. The pine furniture was expensively stripped and distressed. It had an oddly, calming effect.

Larkin looked out of the window to the little guest house opposite. *Andy's sitting in there*, he thought. *He's probably watching right now.*

Charlotte returned, a cock-eyed smile on her face.

'What's the matter with you?'

'Nothing.'

'What's that look for, then?'

'I'm just thinking – I've got to undress you and put you to bed properly . . .'

'You don't have to do it now.'

'Oh, I do.'

And with that she came over to the bed and began to gently tease his T-shirt from his body.

'You know,' she said playfully, 'I've been wanting to do this to you ever since I met you again. Never thought it would be in these circumstances, though.' She put her hand on his neck and began, slowly, to stroke him. She shifted her body closer to his. Her other hand moved over his chest and down to his Levis. His arousal was visible; she looked at him and smiled voluptuously.

'No.' His voice was feeble, unconvincing.

'Why not?'

'It's not that I don't want to . . . God knows it's not. It's just – I don't think my body could take it yet.'

She looked at him quizzically.

'Honestly,' he said.

He felt her hand firmly grasp his dick. 'I could always . . .'

'No,' he said quickly, 'the shock would kill me.'

She sat up, looking embarrassed. 'I'm sorry. My timing seems to be dreadful at the moment.'

He smiled reassuringly at her, his erection ready to burst, and said with an effort, 'It's fine. There's no rush. We've got plenty of time.'

'Yes,' she said, nuzzling down on the bed beside him, careful not to knock his bruises. 'We've got all the time in the world.'

Saturday became Sunday. Then Monday, Tuesday, Wednesday . . . all the way back to Saturday again. Larkin could feel the strength returning to his body with every day that passed.

Since their abortive attempt at lovemaking on the first Saturday, there had been a distance between the two of them. No ice; just a slight frost. They talked, ate together;

Charlotte wasn't a born hostess, but by cooking, cleaning and taking days off work, she was doing her best. That was the problem; they were both making too much of an effort. They were polite, friendly – but when it came down to it, they were two old lovers, back together and sharing a bed.

It was Charlotte who resolved the situation, as she walked into the bedroom on the second Saturday afternoon.

'Stephen, I'm sick of this.'

He put down his paperback copy of Scott Fitzgerald's *Tender Is The Night.* 'What?'

'You know what I mean.' Her cock-eyed smile was back. 'We've been circling round each other for a whole week now – and I'm tired of it.' She knelt at the end of the bed.

'And?'

'The doctor said I had to keep you calm and relaxed at first. No sudden shocks. But I think all that's gone on for long enough now, don't you? I think you're ready for a few surprises.'

'Erm . . .'

She pulled back the duvet, started to undo his pyjama bottoms.

'I mean, look at these,' she said as she went about her task. 'You've been wearing these all week! So I've had to be equally modest – and I hate wearing anything in bed.' She pulled them off; his erection was rising rapidly. 'Come on! I know you can move around a little bit . . .'

'It hurts,' he said pathetically, levering himself off the bed while Charlotte slid her hands gently down his body.

'I'll kiss it better.' And she began moving her lips lightly over his stomach.

He jerked slightly. 'What's the matter?' she said. 'Does it really hurt that much?'

'No,' he said. 'It's just . . . do you mind shutting the curtains?'

She looked at him. 'No one can see in. Since when were you so shy?'

'Please?'

She crossed the room and drew the curtains. He looked at her body, stretching, silhouetted against the daylight. She was perfect. She returned to Larkin and took off her cardigan, revealing a cream lace bra. She sat next to him.

'I've looked after you for a week now. Call me selfish, but I want something in return. I think you're well enough to give it to me, don't you?'

'Possibly,' said Larkin. 'Only time will tell.'

Slowly, she slipped off her shoes, knowing that Larkin was watching her, relishing the effect she was having on him. Her eyes never left his as, with great deliberation, she took off her bra. She had kept herself in good shape; her breasts were full and firm, her stomach tight. Hauling himself up, he reached forward and stroked her breasts with his good hand. The move cost him some pain, but it was worth it. She moaned slightly, her nipples hardening under his fingers. Her head tilted and she moved towards him, her breasts covering his face. He started to kiss her body, her shoulders, her neck, her breasts, taking each nipple in his mouth in turn, sucking, licking, biting. Charlotte's gasps of pleasure confirmed that her enjoyment was as overwhelming as his own.

Suddenly she wriggled free and stood up. Unbuttoning her jeans, she pulled them down over her hips, to reveal a pair of black panties which she peeled off in similar fashion. At last she was naked. And she gloried in the knowledge that she was driving him wild.

Once more taking the initiative, Charlotte climbed back onto the bed and straddled him. She took his dick in her hands, rhythmically slipping the foreskin up and down, pressing it against her clitoris, her eyes closed in sensory delight. Aware of Larkin's readiness, she opened her legs wider and took him inside her. She rocked backwards and forwards, drawing him deeper with every stroke. Her hand slid down and she started to tease herself, without breaking her rhythm, her muscles still holding Larkin tight. Her orgasm began to build as her other hand played over her body, exploring her breasts, running through her hair, over her stomach. Larkin was fascinated – and highly aroused – by Charlotte's total absorption in her own body, by her single-minded sexuality.

She came, tumultously. The waves of her climax went on and on. Eventually she came back to earth; but Larkin was still unfulfilled. As she climbed off him he thought that was that; but he was wrong. Curling up on the bed, she began to suck him, powerfully, demanding a response with her lips and tongue. It wasn't long before he felt his own climax approaching.

Charlotte sensed the change and, with almost military precision, finished the job with her hand. And he came, experiencing pleasure and pain in almost equal proportions. *Funny*, he thought to himself, *now I can't even come without Charlotte taking charge.*

The whole episode had a bizarre, unreal quality – like a hospital fantasy come to life. Afterwards she got up and cleaned herself clinically with a tissue. She hung her clothes up neatly and lay close beside him, a look of cat-like contentment on her face.

'How was that?'

All his doubts about her had been shoved to the back of his mind; everything was postcoitally right with the world. 'Fine. *Very* fine.'

'Didn't hurt you?'

'It was worth getting hurt for.'

'Good. I did promise the doctor I'd look after you.'

'You're doing that, all right.'

It was late afternoon now, getting dark, and neither of them had moved. After making love, Larkin had nodded off; he came round to find Charlotte awake, staring fixedly ahead, her thoughts unfathomable. He moved his head to look at her; after a couple of seconds' delay, she turned to him, suddenly aware of his presence. She gave him an ambiguous smile, kissed him on the forehead and got up. She was still naked; Larkin wanted nothing more in life, at that moment, than to watch her body more. He was starting to want her again by the time she left the room.

She returned a few minutes later, carrying a tray holding a chrome cafetiere, a milk jug and two mugs. Also a CD. She put the tray down, crossed over to the CD player and put it on, bringing the remote back to bed with her. She poured Larkin a cup of coffee.

'Milk, no sugar.'

She smiled again. 'I thought I remembered.'

Wincing, he sat up and she handed him the coffee.

'Thanks.' He sipped it: hot and bitter. Her hostess skills were improving. She pointed the remote and the song started. 'Are You Ready To Be Heartbroken' – Lloyd Cole And The Commotions. Charlotte smiled. 'Told you I bought this on CD.'

'To remind you of me?'

She smiled ruefully, as if she were being forced to make a shameful admission. 'Partly. Also to remind me of how it was back then. It's a part of my life on that album. I'm not a naturally acquisitive person – but songs, books – films, even – make better records than any diary. They tell you much more about your life, where you were, what you were doing. You hear a song again, see a film, and you're there. In the past. Sometimes it's good to look back. It was easier to be happy, then.'

Larkin listened to the music. Charlotte was right; nostalgia did make life less complicated.

The song came to an end. 'So, Charlotte,' Larkin said, 'does it still remind you of me?'

'Always.'

She pointed the remote at the player. The jangly, jaunty guitar of 'Perfect Skin' kicked in. Their reflective mood was punctured by the faster tempo; they returned to the present. Charlotte turned on her side, propping her head up with her hand, her breasts hanging gorgeously loose. She looked at Larkin.

'Stephen . . . d'you think . . . What I'm saying is . . .'

156

'D'you think there's a chance for you and me again? Is that it?'

'Yes.'

He sighed. 'I don't know. Here we are, in bed – and here you are, married, so . . .'

'Stephen . . . there's something about my marriage I haven't told you. It's Charles. He's . . . well, it's not a real marriage. It's more of a business arrangement. When you saw Charles behind The Hole In The Wall the other night – chances are he'd been in there. He's gay.'

Larkin nodded. 'I guessed that. So why the marriage? Surely, in this day and age, being gay doesn't matter so much.'

'It doesn't, no. To be honest, it was for me as much as him. Over the last few years, all I've done is career, career, career. Nothing else.' She offered Larkin a little smile. 'I know you've always thought I was ambitious – too much so, you once said – but it's paid off. I've got a position in the company that I never dreamed possible a few years ago. Trouble is, there's still a stigma attached to single career women. Up here, anyway. Some of our clients are really reactionary. Dyed-in-the-wool traditional Northerners, businessmen who still wouldn't dream of employing a woman as anything more than a secretary. If you're single as well as being a working woman, they tend to look very suspiciously at you. They see you as something unnatural. I was starting to find that some clients didn't want me to represent them. It was as if I wasn't safe, somehow. My professional life is much simpler as Mrs Twigge than it ever was as Ms Birch. So it was better for my career prospects if I got married. Charles was unattached – we were always getting sat next to each other at functions and dinner parties. The two odd halves. So we came up with this arrangement. Half the house is mine, half his. We keep ourselves, and that works just fine. If he wants to bring anyone home, that's fine – the same goes for me.'

Larkin was letting all this sink in. 'So if he doesn't

157

care about you and who you see, why did he take a swing at me that first night?'

She reddened slightly. 'That's because ... he's an arsehole when he wants to be. I didn't say I liked him, I said I married him.' She paused and stared hard at him, assessing his reaction. 'Do you have any comment to make about that?'

'Well ... I thought Charles might be gay, after I saw him outside The Hole In The Wall with his little friends. Though presumably, since he's lying low, they're professional as well as personal associates. But I just never pictured you making a marriage of convenience. It just seems a bit—'

'Sordid?'

'Something like that.'

'I suppose it looks that way. But our arrangement doesn't rule out the possibility of my meeting someone and – falling in love. If that were to happen, we would divorce like any normal couple, divide our things painlessly according to our pre-nuptial agreement, and go our separate ways.'

'So what about lovers?'

'You're pushing it, aren't you?' She smiled, a brittle smile.

'Invalid's prerogative,' said Larkin. Actually, he wasn't sure whether he really wanted to know.

'One or two.'

'Anything serious?'

She took a long time answering. 'No ... you couldn't call them that.'

'Oh.' He decided not to pursue the subject. They lay there quietly, sipping coffee, listening to the CD.

'Are you concerned about Charles?' Larkin asked eventually.

'Well, it's not unusual for him to stay away this long – but yes, I am worried.'

'Have you thought of calling the police? Reporting him missing?'

'I've thought about it, but what could I say? "Sorry

158

to trouble you, officer, but my husband has disappeared. I shouldn't worry, though, he's probably shagging some guy senseless – or getting stoned. Or hiding from you, because his friends have half-beaten a friend of mine to death.'''

'So you know about his—'

'His drug habit?' She sounded scornful. 'Of course. You can't live with someone, even if it's not a proper relationship, and hide something like that. Anyway, how did you find out? Was it just because of the company he keeps?'

'When I saw him at The Hole In The Wall . . . he was doing a line of cocaine.'

Charlotte scoffed. 'Right out there, in the street? He must have been desperate. He's finding it hard to keep it a secret, if you must know. He's in trouble at work, making mistakes, screwing clients around. It was bound to happen sooner or later. You can't sweep a coke habit of that magnitude under the carpet forever.'

The fact that Charles was clearly such a loser meant Larkin could afford to be generous. 'Perhaps that's why he's gone missing. We should give him the benefit of the doubt – after all, there's no proof that he was connected with what happened to me and The Prof. When I saw him with those guys – maybe they're just his suppliers.'

Which didn't explain why Larkin had seen Pierced Nipples strolling into Sir James Lascelles' lair. And Charlotte's lack of enthusiasm for his altruistic suggestion made it clear where her suspicions lay.

Charlotte was silent, musing. Then: 'Those men – the ones you saw with Charles – would you say they were definitely gay?'

Larkin shifted slightly, remembering. 'They're sadists, that's for sure. They might have attached themselves to the gay scene to get at men more easily.'

'Oh.' She went quiet again. And Lloyd Cole assured them that girls need guns these days, because of all the rattlesnakes.

'Charlotte?'

159

'Yes?'

'What about – Sir James?'

She stiffened at the mention of his name, involuntarily clutching the duvet to her chest. Larkin had only been going to ask her how well she knew him, but her manner made him ask something else entirely.

'He was your lover, wasn't he?'

She tried to look at him, brazening it out, but her eyes couldn't hold his gaze. 'Sir James has been a good friend when I needed one.'

'But he was also your lover?'

'What business is it of yours who my ex-lovers have been?' she exploded.

'OK.' He was angry too now. 'There's no need to blow your fucking top. If you don't want to answer, fine.'

There was a pause; the static in the air between them was almost palpable. Charlotte's body was rigid next to Larkin. Eventually, however, he felt her yield.

'I'm sorry, Stephen. Some aspects of the past I don't like to talk about.' She propped herself up again, adopting a deliberately seductive pose. 'Anyway, now I've got you.' Her smile was teasing, her naked body warm against his bruised skin. He felt an erection stir.

He smiled. 'You've got me.'

'I don't know for how long – if you've got to go back to London and be your boss's executive toy—'

'Don't worry about that. She's probably been auditioning replacements while I've been away.'

'She sounds charming... you know, I do think we came back together again for a reason.'

'And what's that?'

'I don't know. Yet. Do you . . . do you think you'll stay up here?'

'I don't know. Depends.'

'On whether you've got something to stay up here for?'

She was hedging, he knew it, but he wasn't going to say it for her. After all, he was hedging too. 'Something like that.'

160

'Or – someone?'

He paused; he had a feeling that any answer he gave would be the wrong one. 'Something like that.'

She slid her hand beneath the covers and reached for him. 'Something like – this, perhaps?'

'You don't need to be told what that is?' he said, grateful for her understanding.

'No. And I don't need to be told what to do with it, either.'

She demonstrated, and Larkin responded. And the darkness gathered outside the drawn curtains, and Lloyd Cole sang about how precious times together had been wasted.

19: One Bad Dream And A Few Good Mornings

The house was warm and bright, sunlight illuminating the airy, cheerful rooms. Laughing children were playing in the garden. His beautiful wife was sitting in the living room, and he was on his way upstairs.

His footsteps were light and brisk as he moved, taking the stairs two at a time. He didn't know why he was going upstairs, or what he'd find there – only that he had to go.

He reached the landing. In front of him was a choice of doors. He stopped. They were all shut, offering no clues, but he knew that something good would be behind at least one. Yet he was also aware of the possibility of something bad lurking there too. He shuddered. Through a window, he saw the sky darken as storm clouds moved overhead; then came the familiar sound of rain hitting the roof in a torrential downpour, followed by the wailing of children – *his* children – as they had to come indoors, their play ended. Which room? All he wanted to do was get it over with and go back downstairs to his family – but he couldn't. Not until he'd made his choice. He grabbed the handle of the nearest door, on his right, and turned it.

Immediately the rain hit harder, more violently, and was joined by deep, rumbling thunder. He looked down at his hand, illuminated in strobe relief by vicious fork lightning. He opened the door.

A tidal wave of dread engulfed him. He heard the

children screaming downstairs as the house was rocked by thunder, but he was forced to walk into the chosen room.

What confronted him was so unbearable, yet so intriguing, he couldn't pull away. He couldn't begin to describe it; he wasn't even sure he was seeing it. Black and iridescent, it rippled like velvet in a breeze. It turned on him when it saw him, swooped down to swallow him, overwhelm him. And just as he started to scream, it spoke. 'I'm *you*,' it said.

Larkin's eyes snapped open, sweat running off his body in rivers, panting for breath, as if he'd just run a marathon. He tried to move, but pain restrained him; he lay still, getting his breath back.

Turning his head to the side, he saw Charlotte lying facing him, in a deep sleep. Her soft, rhythmical breathing was comforting, and he allowed his own breathing to subside. Her arm had fallen across his chest; he enjoyed the comforting weight of it.

He smiled. For the first time in years, the thought of going back to sleep after a bad dream didn't seem so awful. He lifted her hand to his mouth, kissed it, saw a slight smile play at the edges of her lips.

He shut his eyes.

Next thing he knew it was morning. Charlotte was still in the same position: out for the count. Relaxing, he settled back and ran through the past twenty-four hours. They'd stayed in bed all day, making love twice; on both occasions Charlotte had dictated events. After that, she had knocked up a huge bowl of spaghetti which they'd wolfed down in bed, followed by a bottle of Chianti. Then they'd talked; nothing profound, just getting to know each other again. The awkwardness of the last week had disappeared, its tension dissipated by their lovemaking. Another bottle of Chianti followed, with some garlic bread, and eventually they had fallen asleep in front of the late film; Peter Cushing fighting a befanged Christopher Lee in order to make the world a safe-place for virgins with huge cleavages . . .

Charlotte stirred. 'What time is it?' she slurred.

Larkin had been on the point of nodding off again. He checked his watch. 'Half-nine.'

She groaned loudly and theatrically. 'Middle of the bloody night! What d'you wake me at this ungodly hour for?'

'I didn't wake you. You woke yourself.'

She sat up, hair mussed, eyes half-closed, lips in a sleepy pout. 'Don't look at me! I must look a complete wreck.'

Larkin thought she was the most beautiful woman he'd ever set eyes on. 'You look fine,' he said.

'Hmm. I suppose you want a cup of coffee?'

'If you're making one.'

'Urr.' And with that she got up, walking naked out of the room, tantalising Larkin all over again.

She came back with coffee and a mock-grumpiness that made her all the more attractive. They larked around for a while, teasing each other, seeing how far they could push their newly rekindled affection. Then Charlotte reminded Larkin that Moir wanted a word with him; she had tried putting him off, but he was proving very persistent.

'Just tell him I'm convalescing,' said Larkin, 'and I don't feel like talking.'

Charlotte smiled slyly, put her coffee cup down, pulled back the covers. She kneeled upright on the bed, breasts swaying, took Larkin's cup from his hand and put it on the bedside table. Her eyes trailed down to his rapidly engorging groin, her lips slightly apart.

'I know what you feel like . . .'

Sunday went well after that. They spent the day in bed; they chatted, ate more pasta, drank more Chianti. Listened to music; Larkin was devastated to discover that Charlotte owned the whole of the Simply Red back catalogue. He made her promise to try and mend her ways. They finished the evening watching television. Just like an old, married couple – but neither of them dared to say it.

Monday morning, and Larkin woke up feeling better than he had for a long time. He made an inventory of his body: his breathing was easier, the movement in his limbs was improving, his bruises were yellowing nicely. He still didn't want to confront the damage to his hand, but apart from that everything seemed to be healing well.

He turned to Charlotte. She had kicked off the duvet and was lying naked, the sheet twisted round her legs. She looked beautiful. He felt a twinge of guilt; he should be doing something instead of just lying there being waited on, especially after the promise he had made to himself at The Prof's bedside, but he knew he had to be in better shape than he was before he was capable of action. His conscience clear, he settled down to more sleep again.

When he next awoke, the curtains were open, the day was a nondescript misty-grey, and he was alone. He was about to call out when in came Charlotte, hair washed and blow-dried, dressed for work.

She told him there was cold pasta salad for lunch, CDs next to the player and books on the bookshelf. If he got really lonely he could phone Moir; failing that, he could watch 'Richard and Judy'. And she left.

Larkin lay, wallowing in the prospect of his new life. Things could be worse, he thought. Things could be a lot worse.

She'd been gone for a couple of hours, and Larkin had been drifting in and out of sleep, when the phone rang. He squirmed over to the side of the bed, grabbed the cordless from the bedside table, thumbed it on. A chill ran through him: what if it was Charles?

A man cleared his throat, then spoke. "Ello?"

'Andy!' Larkin's sigh of relief was audible.

'Where the bloody 'ell have you been, eh? What the fuck have you been up to, you dirty sod?'

Larkin found himself smiling. 'I don't know what you mean, Andy.'

'Come off it! I saw those curtains being closed pretty sharpish when you got in. They haven't been opened again till today, and then it was only cos she went to work.'

'You've been doing a good job.'

'Course I 'ave. I'm a professional, ain't I?'

'Aren't you just. How's it been over there?'

His voice dropped. 'Torture. Sheer, fuckin' torture. This place – I tell you, you wouldn't believe it. Makes Dachau look like Butlins. Woman in charge—'

His voice stopped abruptly; Larkin could hear a muffled conversation going on in the background. Eventually Andy came back.

'That her, then?' asked Larkin.

'Yeah,' said Andy, downcast. 'She heard me swearing, come to tell me off. Fuckin' radar.' Another muffle, then, 'Yeah! Sorry.'

Larkin was laughing.

'It's all right for you, innit? It's me who's suffering.'

'Well, I do appreciate it.'

'I hope so. Anyway, anything I should be doin'?'

'I don't think so. Just keep an eye out if you-know-who comes waltzing back.'

'Wilco. Well, I'd better be off.'

'Why, what are you doing?'

'I've got a nice little sideline going. I've got a commission for an art book on Newcastle – you know, black and white, moody shots of the bridges, that sort of thing.'

'Yeah?' Larkin was impressed. 'What's it going to be called?'

'*Arseholes With Daft Accents.* See you later.'

After a couple of hours lying in bed watching daytime TV, Larkin felt the need to empty his bladder. He painfully levered the top of his body up with his arms and slowly swung his legs to the floor. The expensively polished bare boards weren't as cold as he had expected. Gradually, he forced himself upright.

After the sudden, dizzying rush of blood to his head had cleared, he felt reasonably OK. He set off, gingerly placing one foot in front of the other, until he had reached the toilet.

Once there, Larkin was relieved to find he was no longer passing blood. His bruised kidneys seemed to be on the mend. He also realised he was hungry. He'd had his fill of pasta; he decided to throw caution to the winds and make himself a sandwich.

He slowly hauled his body downstairs, moving like an old man, clinging to the banister at every step. After a lifetime he shuffled into the kitchen. Although it was an interior designer's dream, it was lacking one essential ingredient: food. He rummaged around until he found an unopened can of tuna, a jar of mayonnaise and a couple of slices of bread that were arguably the right side of being stale.

He ate in the front room, which was also, like the kitchen, pristine but empty, as if no emotional investment had enabled it to become a home rather than a place to live. Larkin thought of his own flat. Although he made no claims to keep it tidy, he recognised the feeling.

Tuesday followed more or less the same pattern as Monday. Larkin could almost literally feel his body repairing itself: bones and muscles knitting together. Mentally too, he felt renewed. He figured that the time he'd spent with Charlotte had done that to him; he had forgotten how good it felt to share his life with someone. He found himself letting go, ready to allow someone else to fight his battles at his side. Or one step ahead of him, if Charlotte had her way. He made his way round the house with little difficulty now. He was beginning to feel at home.

Charles still hadn't returned. The police had finally been called, and discreet enquiries were being carried out. No leads yet. He could stay missing indefinitely, for all Larkin cared. He hoped Charlotte would receive a postcard from Charles in Acapulco, saying he'd found a new toy boy and had so much Columbian up his nose he'd created two extra nostrils.

The only thing that gnawed away at his conscience was The Prof. He called the General Hospital, got through to the ward sister. And was told that The Prof – or 'Graham', as she insisted on calling him – was out of his coma and resting comfortably. Larkin's whole body breathed a sigh of relief. He thanked her and said he would visit as soon as he could. He sent The Prof his love.

He put the phone down: one less ghost to carry round with him. Things did seem to be looking up.

Tuesday passed to Wednesday and Larkin was stronger still. And he was beginning to feel more and more at ease in Charlotte's company.

That night, having shared a couple of intense orgasms, they lay, postcoitally, Charlotte curled round Larkin. She spoke first.

'Are you happy?'

'Yeah.'

She looked up. 'I mean, *really* happy.'

'The happiest I've been for a long time.'

He could feel her smile into his chest, hug him a little tighter. She spoke again.

'I know you don't want to have this conversation – and you won't want to answer me when I ask this in case you get hurt – but I think that after the last few days, if you feel the same way that I do, then you've got no choice *but* to answer.'

Larkin steeled himself. 'Yeah?'

'Do you think there's – a chance? If there was no Charles, if you didn't have to go back to London, if all this was out of the way – if all the "ifs" disappeared and

169

there was just you and me. Do you think that we would have a chance?'

She was looking directly at him. He dropped his gaze.

'Charlotte . . .' he started, unsure how to go on. 'These last few days have been some of the best that I can remember. I feel like you've been healing me in . . . in all sorts of ways. It's difficult for me to say these things . . .'

'I know.'

The words felt like stones in his mouth, but he continued. 'What happened to Sophie and Joe – it was my fault.'

'What did happen? I've heard the facts, but I haven't heard them from you.'

Larkin lay back, staring at the ceiling. He had never told the story from his side. Perhaps now, if he truly wanted to go forward, bury the past, it was time he did. And it seemed like he was with the right person. He took a deep breath.

'I was working, being my usual cocky self, fuelled up on coke and ego. This was the late eighties, remember, when there was still an easy living to be made, providing you weren't too ethical.'

The room seemed to darken around him. 'I was working on a big exposé of some high-profile City guy, Ralph Sickert. The usual stuff: ridicule him, ruin his reputation. Always popular. People loved to read about the downfall of a yuppie, especially one who was mega-successful, like Sickert. So I obliged. Sickert's life collapsed, a lot of papers were sold, and I was handsomely rewarded.'

He sighed. Outside, a streetlight came on, but it didn't penetrate the gloom inside. 'Trouble was, Sickert took it personally. Now, you could say he shouldn't have put himself in a position where he could be exposed in the first place – or you could say I had no business doing what I did. But he blamed me for his collapse. And made me pay for it.'

He fell silent. 'So?' Charlotte prompted.

Larkin's breath caught. 'So he pulled up at my house

with a loaded double-barrelled shotgun. I wasn't there. But Sophie and Joe were. And he let them have it.'

The tears started to well behind his eyes.

'Where were you? At work?'

'No. I was . . . I don't even know. I'd been out the night before, stoned and drunk . . . I can't even remember the name of the tart I ended up with.' The tears, long-dammed, came silently. 'I killed them. It should have been me . . . I killed them.'

Charlotte pulled him to her, starting to speak. But he hadn't finished.

'And don't tell me it's not my fault and I shouldn't blame myself, because it *is* my fault. No one else's.' His body was racked with sobs now. 'I've never allowed myself to get involved since. Never wanted anyone close to me. In case it happens again . . .'

His voice trailed off; the sobs subsided. Charlotte held him.

'Until now,' he said, so quietly she could hardly hear him.

'Stephen – don't you think you've had enough suffering? It's time to let go. To share it.'

'Charlotte? I think we have a chance. I want a future with you in it, Charlotte.'

That was it. He'd said it now. She turned away; he took her face in his hand and held it. Her cheeks were wet with tears.

She half-laughed, half-snuffled, 'Oh, you beautiful, beautiful man. I love you!'

And in the gathering dark no one was more surprised than Larkin when he heard himself reply, 'I love you too, Charlotte.'

20: Nemesis

Larkin sighed, rolled over and woke up. He righted himself with a grunt and looked around: Charlotte's bedroom. As he was shutting his eyes to go back to sleep, he noticed something. Charlotte. Her absence. The room was crack-of-dawn dark and there was no sign of her.

The possibilities went rattling through his head. Perhaps she had gone to work early and hadn't wanted to wake him; perhaps it was later than he thought and it was an exceptionally dark day outside. Perhaps she'd gone to get a paper, or some milk. Perhaps she had gone to the toilet. Perhaps.

As his eyes accustomed themselves to the gloom, he looked around. The bedclothes had been thrown back on her side; the wardrobe door was slightly open. He checked the bedside table for a note: nothing but a half-drunk cup of coffee and *Tender Is The Night*.

He lay back. And as he did, a figure appeared in the dim light of the landing outside the open bedroom door.

'Charlotte,' he said, 'where have you been?'

The figure didn't stop. Larkin looked closer. It wasn't Charlotte. It wasn't a woman. It was a man. Because of the gloom Larkin couldn't make out his features but he could see that he was quite tall – nearly six foot – and smartly dressed.

'Charles?' said Larkin fearfully.

'No. It's not Charles.'

And suddenly Larkin knew who it was. With that realisation, the cold sweat of terror returned like an unwelcome friend from a dead and buried past. He felt helpless, trapped. There was no one he could call, nothing he could do. Right in front of him was the person he'd been looking for. And the last person he wanted to see. Terry.

He tried to get up.

'Stay where you are!'

Larkin did as he was told. But he felt he had to say something. He couldn't let Terry have it all his own way.

'Hello, Terry. Didn't hear you come in.'

Terry seemed taken aback, rendered speechless for a few seconds. 'You must be Larkin.'

'Yeah.' Larkin gulped. He tried not to show his vulnerability, knew he wasn't succeeding.

'I hear you've been looking for me.'

'That's right.'

'Why?'

'I wanted to ask you some questions.'

'What sort of questions?'

'You know what. About Mary.'

He looked thrown for a second. '*Mary*?'

'Yeah. Mary Torrington? Or Greene, when you knew her.'

Terry, even in the half-light, looked confused. 'What d'you want to know about her?'

'I want to know what you know about her death.'

'I don't know anything about her death. That was nothing to do with me.'

'That's not what it said in her diary.'

'What diary?'

'The diary she kept all about you.'

Terry was suddenly angry enough to explode. Or was it panic? 'She can't have kept a diary!'

'She did. I've read it.'

'Where did you find it?'

'In her house.'

174

'Liar!' He moved forward. Larkin could see his face, contorted by desperate rage, for the first time.

'It's true,' he said quickly. 'I found the diary in her house. And I've got a photo of you and her together. I must say it's a very flattering one.' He regretted the words almost as soon as he'd said them.

Terry stepped forward and pulled his fist back. There was nowhere for Larkin to move; he braced himself for the blow. When he finally found the courage to open his eyes, Terry was standing there, his arm at his side, his rage under control.

'Where's this diary now?'

Larkin opened his mouth to reply, then paused. 'I don't know,' he said.

'Come on!'

'Honestly, I don't. It must have got lost. With the photo, they were together.' He hoped he sounded sincere. 'But I have seen them.'

Terry seemed scared, almost desperate.

'Mary committed suicide. That's all there is to it. You think I killed her, is that it?'

'That's what it said in the diary.'

'Then you'd better find that diary, hadn't you? Because I didn't do it.'

'I'm not really in a position to go anywhere or do anything, am I?'

Terry came up close to Larkin's face; Larkin could smell cheap aftershave mingled with stale cigarette smoke and deodorised sweat. 'You listen to me, and you listen good. I had nothing to do with that. Nothing at all. And if you can't find me, it's because I don't want to be found. So stop trying. Or you'll be sorry.'

Larkin didn't respond. He couldn't think of anything to say that wouldn't get him hurt. Terry looked at him. 'Yeah?'

'OK.'

'Good. I'm glad you understand me.' He reached down for Larkin's bandaged right hand. 'Cos if you don't . . .' He grabbed Larkin's hand, pushed his thumb right into

175

the middle of the palm; Larkin felt the tenuously healed new skin rupture and break. His face contorted, neck muscles bulging, but he was determined not to scream. He wouldn't give Terry the satisfaction.

Blood started to ooze through the bandage. Still Larkin didn't scream. Terry pressed harder, blood pooling around his thumb. Larkin was just about ready to pass out, but he held on.

Suddenly Terry removed his thumb. Like a siren winding down, the pain in Larkin's injured hand slowly decreased and his breathing returned to something approaching normal. Terry stood up, wiping Larkin's blood onto a handkerchief. When he had finished, he tossed the bloody cloth onto the bed.

'Just remember what I said.'

Larkin stared at him.

'I don't want to be found. So don't come looking – right?'

The only thing that Larkin could use to threaten him effectively was his eyes. So he stared as hard as he could. Terry held his gaze for a while, but he wasn't a match for Larkin.

He tried to salvage his pride. 'Yeah, well. Let that be a warning to you.'

Larkin waited until he heard the front door slam and then let the pain and fear tumble from him. He started to sweat again. How had Terry got in? Why had he come here? He lay there not daring to move, not *able* to move, not even able to reach for the phone and ask where the fuck Andy had been. He lay there motionless, until the sky got lighter and the day started to break. Larkin had never been so grateful to put a night behind him.

21: An Inspector Calls

The knife-like ringing of the phone cut through the silence. Larkin's eyes opened to an atmosphere as charged with electricity as if a thunderstorm had recently passed overhead.

His left arm shot out, knocking his novel off the bedside table in his invalid scramble for the phone. It was the first time he had moved since the fear-induced paralysis of Terry's visit and his tense muscles had pins and needles, stabbing him all over. He grabbed the phone, pulling the aerial out with his teeth, pressing the talk button with his thumb. He didn't want to raise his right hand; he'd already glimpsed the fact that the blood and bandage had coagulated into a hard, dirty, red glove. He didn't dare look closer. He held the phone to his ear.

'Hello? *Hello*? Is that you, Stephen?' Charlotte's voice had an edge to it.

He finally spoke and the edge disappeared. She was phoning to apologise for leaving so early; she'd taken time off to nurse Larkin and had a huge backlog of work. The sound of her voice began to calm him. Then she said: 'Look, Stephen, there's a reason for this call. That policeman's on his way over. He's just called in to the office to pick up my spare keys – I didn't know if you'd be able to make it to the door. He says he's waited long enough for you to get better.'

'So I'm better now, am I?'

'You were fine last night.'

He chuckled in reply. He was building up to tell her about Terry, but something stopped him. Perhaps it was that he didn't want to worry her, to spoil their new relationship with too much reality.

'Are you all right, darling?'

'Yeah. Yeah.' The moment, if it had ever been there, had passed. 'Well, if I'm getting company, I'd better whizz round with the Hoover.'

She laughed. 'Don't forget the dusting. And I left you a pile of dishes in the sink.'

'Earning my keep now, am I?'

'I think you've done that already.' There was a pause; Larkin took a couple of deep breaths, willing the moment to return, but it was Charlotte who settled it. 'See you soon, darling. Look after yourself. Bye.'

Larkin sighed. Where the hell was Andy? He dialled the number of the guest house and spoke to a woman straight out of 'Dr Finlay's Case Book'. He asked for Andy Brennan. After a palaver which involved him being 'put on hold' (during which the woman covered the mouthpiece with her hand), Andy reached the phone. From the echoing of his footsteps it sounded as if he had journeyed from the far reaches of Gormenghast. 'Yeah?'

'Andy?'

'Yeah?' The voice was blurry; that explained a lot.

'It's Larkin. What the fuck happened to you?'

'When? Whassamatter?'

'I thought you were keeping guard.'

'I was. I am. What's up?'

Larkin sighed. 'Terry's been here.'

Andy's voice changed immediately. He was wide awake. 'What? When? Where?'

'Where d'you think? Here. When? I don't fuckin' know. You were the one supposed to tell me.'

'Must have dozed off. Had to sleep some time, you know. I tried me best, but even with the speed—'

'Yeah, well, you picked the right time to do it in.'

'Sorry. Won't happen again.'

'Fucking right, it won't.'

'So what happened?'

Larkin steeled himself and told him. When he had finished. 'Shit,' Andy said. Then, in the background, Larkin heard a stern Scottish voice. 'Please, Mr Brennan – not all our guests share your love of gutter invective.' Then Andy's shamefaced, mumbled, 'Sorry.' Larkin smiled despite himself.

He told Andy he wanted him to score him some heavy-duty analgesics and some amphetamines.

'What the fuck for?' There was a muffled noise. 'Sorry! I *know* there are. I won't say it again.' Then he was back. 'I was saying, what for? It's bloody madness. All *right. Sorry.*'

'I can't lie here any longer. There's things to do. If you score me some stuff I can do them.'

'Get stoned and take on the pushers? That your sense of irony, is it?'

'Fuck irony – this is personal. You said you'd help. So, you still in?'

Andy was silent for a moment. 'I don't like this.'

'I'm not asking you to like it. I'm asking you to do it. Please.'

There was a big sigh on the other end of the line. 'Oh, all right. But I'm not happy.'

'Look, Terry's been round once. He knows where I am. Who's going to come next?'

Andy thought for a moment. Finally he relented. 'It might take me a couple of hours. I'll see what I can do.'

'Cheers, Andy! You're a pal.'

'Yeah, right. You told Charlotte any of this?'

There was a pause from Larkin. 'I thought it best not to.'

'Probably right. For the time being. 'Ere, if you'd kept your curtains open, I could have had a nice little sideline going with some wank mags!' He chortled.

'Piss off, Andy.'

'Suit yourself. Fuckin' 'ell, most people would jump at

179

the chance!' There was more verbal sparring at his end; Andy made some placatory noises then, in a whisper that cut right into Larkin's ear, 'I'd do anythin' to get me out of this fuckin' madhouse! I'm goin' off me fuckin' rocker.' Loudly, 'Fuckin' *sorry*! All right?'

The birds were out in noisy, chirruping force; the sky was a crisp, autumnal blue. Just as Larkin was beginning to enjoy the morning, Moir arrived.

He entered wearing the twin brother of the suit Larkin had last seen him in – it may have been the same one – with a voluminous, dirty, Philip Marlowe trenchcoat thrown over the top.

Larkin smiled to himself. Policemen, he thought, fell into two categories: those who thought principles were a code to live and work by, and those who thought principles was a place to buy smart suits. Larkin reckoned Moir fell into the first category.

Larkin had pulled himself out of bed and dressed himself in a sweatshirt and Levis; bending down was still a problem, so his feet were bare. He sat on the sofa. 'If you'd given me a time I could have had the kettle on.'

Moir smiled and approached an armchair. His sweat stank like old kebab grease.

'So, Mr Larkin, I think it's time we had a wee chat.' There was a hardness and strength underlying his cosy words. For all his down-at-heel appearance, thought Larkin, he wouldn't want to go twelve rounds with him.

'Your friend came out of his coma,' said Moir.

'I know. I phoned the hospital.'

'Clever wee bugger, aren't you?'

'How is he?'

'Comfortable, as they say. He's been through a lot and he's resting. There may be some damage, both physical and mental, but they don't know if it's going to be permanent. He's going to be scarred, though. Nastily, too.'

'Has he said anything?'

180

'Well, we asked him how he got to the house – and he said that he was tipped off by someone he met in a pub. He followed it up, and then ...'

'Yeah?'

'He won't say anything more. He's blanked it out of his mind. Won't face it.'

'I don't blame him. I was there too.'

'That's right.' Moir sat forward. 'So what have you got to tell me?'

Larkin looked at him, instinctively wary. 'I'm taking a big chance, you know, if I tell you anything.'

Moir looked amused. 'Why's that?'

'Because I don't know you. Every man has his price.'

'That's true, Mr Larkin, and I doubt that I'm any exception. But ...' He trailed off, scrutinising Larkin. 'I think I can be honest with you. Yes, I'm sure I can.' He nodded to himself. 'Mr Larkin,' he began again.

'Look,' Larkin interjected, 'I hate to get overly familiar on a first date, but please, just call me Stephen or Larkin. None of this "Mister" business.'

Moir was clearly taken aback. He wasn't used to being interrupted. He reassembled his demeanour and continued. 'Stephen,' he forced out with some difficulty, 'let me tell you something. I'm from Edinburgh. Now, most people think of it as that quaint wee town with the Castle, the Tattoo and the Festival. And so it is. But, like most places, there's another side to it. And that, I'm afraid to say, is the side I know best. It's got one of the worst drug problems in Europe. Likewise AIDS-related diseases. Of course, the two are not unconnected.'

He looked at Larkin, gauging what to say next. Eventually he spoke. 'It's the children that get me,' he said. His eyes misted over; he was pulling out all the stops. 'You can see them on the housing estates, nine- and ten-year-olds, looking at you with these flat, snake eyes. I mean, you know what they're goin' to turn into. You know what kind of chances they've had, you know what they'll end up as. They're easy prey for the gangs and the pushers. For the kind of scum who did for you. Soon

181

they'll be so bored they'll be hooked on smack and crack and all sorts, dealing in school – if they're ever there – burgling, stealing, mugging . . .' He trailed off, lost in thought, shaking his head, as if he couldn't believe it himself. 'All to feed their habits. Oh, they hate themselves for it. And they hate everybody else too. You go onto housing estates where you've got fourteen-year-olds with AIDS, shooting up, sticking their used needles through the hand-rails, catching folk unawares, getting a twisted sort of revenge.'

He sighed and stood up. He walked over to the window, looked into the street, then turned round, his jaw set, his eyes hard. Larkin knew there and then that Moir would be a terrible man to cross.

'I can see it creeping in here, Stephen. And that creep will turn into a walk, and that walk to a run. And it'll be too late to do anything about it. You don't believe what I'm saying, look around you. You'll see I'm right.' He leaned in closer, his voice soft. 'Now, I think I know who they are. They like to think that they're untouchable – well, I'd like to prove them wrong. But I'm going to need your help.' Moir sat down again, wheezing; the trip to the window seemed to be the most exercise he'd had in ages. 'Does everything I've said make sense?'

Larkin bit his lip. 'If you've said all that just to make me open up to you and they find out, then you're a heartless bastard.'

Moir chuckled. 'True. You're quite right, I am a heartless bastard. But you have to believe me. I'm deadly serious.' And he looked it.

Larkin mulled it over. He was pretty sure that Moir was on the level. 'OK – I'll tell you.'

And he did. Starting with Wayne Edgell's funeral. He played down Charlotte's role as much as he could and played up Charles's, whether out of jealousy, or revenge for the bruises, he didn't know. He finished up his story on Woodcross Lane. Then breathed out hard, relieved to have got it over with.

Moir sat back, the cogs in his brain working almost

visibly. 'Right. Working backwards . . . this guy with the pierced nipples who did the number on you – his name, believe it or not, is Abel Cain Hutton.' He sat back, waiting for a response.

Larkin obliged. 'What?'

'Abel Cain Hutton. Like in the Bible. You know – Cain and Abel, the two brothers? The first murderer and the first victim?'

'Yeah, yeah, I know,' said Larkin impatiently.

'Well, our Abel was born in some weird religious sect, based on fear and flagellation. We've got a file on him as long as your arm. Started off torturing animals and birds – the usual stuff – but when he moved on to other children, that's when we became interested. He was taken into care, the child psychiatrist didn't know what to make of him.'

'Don't tell me – abused as a kid?'

'More than likely. Anyway, the sect's broken up now, and his parents are – dead.'

'Dead?'

'His father died in a fire, supposedly accidental; his mother fell down a flight of stairs. Both open verdicts, so work it out for yourself.'

'Oh.'

Moir nodded. 'Indeed. Well, to cut a long story shortish, Cain was eventually discharged into our wonderful care-in-the-community programme, where he got in with the scurviest lowlifes going. Like attracts like. He dropped the Hutton, attached himself to the gay boys and started to behave like a star.' He sighed. 'We've been after him for ages. This might be our big chance.'

'Why haven't you moved in on him before now?'

'Because it's not that simple. Up to a wee while ago Cain was just your average psychotic scum, but recently, he seems to have moved up in the world.'

'How?'

'Proper job, for a start. He claims to be in the import-export business,' said Moir with a sneer.

'Importing and exporting what?'

'What d'you think? Oh, it's all legit to look at – on paper anyway. Leather jackets, hold-alls. Taiwan's finest. We think someone is putting up the money, Cain's fronting it and the drugs are hitting the street through it. The money from the drugs is laundered through that many different sources, it would take years and more manpower and computers than we've got to track it down. He's got this thing sealed up tighter than a gnat's arse, and we want him out of circulation. But we need something watertight to pin him down.'

'Like my testimony.'

'Mr Larkin, I cannot impress upon you strongly enough that this man must be put away. This is strictly off the record – but if there's anything you can find out, anywhere you can go that I can't, then do it.'

Larkin looked at him. 'So you're asking me to risk my life against this bloke? After what happened last time?'

Moir's face was impassive. 'Yes.'

'And what do I get out of it?'

'Enough background information to write the feature of your career.'

Larkin thought for a moment, then sighed. 'Put like that, I've got no choice, have I?'

'I don't think so.'

'OK, then,' Larkin said, 'trade of information. It was on the gay scene that he met Charles Twigge?'

'Looks like it. By the way, we've got a warrant out for his arrest too. Conspiring with our friend to do you over.'

'Really?' Larkin couldn't disguise his joy.

'Thought that would please you. We talked to his wife today. Apparently, she knew he was gay—'

'I know.' Larkin was wary.

'Oh, well. Takes all sorts.' Moir looked round the room. 'What about this Terry guy? What d'you make of him, Stephen?'

'I dunno. I thought at first that he might be Gary Fenwick, but he looks nothing like him, and anyway Fenwick's still in Durham, isn't he?'

Moir stiffened.

184

'*Isn't* he?' said Larkin, a note of fear in his voice.

'Stephen, you've been honest with me, so I'll be honest with you. As a rule I don't like the representatives of the media, but I also pride myself on being a good judge of character. If I tell you this, you can't use it, OK? We've been trying to keep a lid on it, but I suppose it'll get out soon enough.'

'What? Tell me.'

Moir drew a deep breath. 'Well, technically speaking, Fenwick is still in custody. The only thing he isn't, is alive.' He fell silent, waiting for Larkin's reaction; Larkin didn't disappoint him.

'What? What happened?'

'Found only this morning in the showers. Apparently he slipped, hit his head on the wall.' Moir exhaled. 'From the look of it I'd say he was travelling at a couple of hundred miles an hour at the time. And he enjoyed it so much he did it again and again.'

'Didn't anybody see anything? Aren't there any witnesses?'

'Of course! But no one'll admit it. It'll be an accidental death, or misadventure – anything but the truth.'

'The truth being murder?'

'Spot on.'

'Why? Why him? Why now?'

'Because he was all set to turn Queen's Evidence, that's why.' Moir made an exasperated little noise in the back of his throat. 'It took us fucking ages to get him to do that. To talk. Even to acknowledge why he was there.' He sighed. 'Gone. The whole bloody deal.'

'Why was he going to inform? What did you offer him?'

'We worked out a bargain. Tried to get his sentence reduced to manslaughter, make it out to be a drunken brawl. In return he was going to tell us everything he knew about the drugs rings in Newcastle. It's a real bastard. Can't say I'm sorry about the wee bag o' shite, though.'

'So what happens next?' asked Larkin.

'That's up to you.'

'Will I have protection?'

'As much as I can give. Discreetly.'

'Meaning none at all.'

'Meaning as much as I can give. Discreetly.'

Larkin sighed. 'Fair enough.'

There was an uneasy silence, broken by Moir. 'You got a picture of this Terry?'

'Yeah, somewhere.' He attempted to look around. 'Try my leather jacket – wherever that is.'

Moir looked round the room until he found it, took the photo out and came back over. He looked at it. 'This him?'

'Yeah.'

'Who's this with him? His mother?'

'No, that's Mary. His girlfriend.'

'*Girlfriend*? He must like older women.'

Something tingled in Larkin's brain. He couldn't place it, couldn't name it, but it was there.

Moir handed him the photo. 'Anything else you have to tell me?'

Larkin thought for a moment. 'Yeah,' he eventually said. 'Not tell you – ask you.'

Moir braced himself.

'What's your opinion of Sir James Lascelles?'

Moir frowned. 'Some things are better left unsaid.'

Larkin was suddenly curious. 'Why?'

'He's a very wealthy, powerful man. And that's all I'm saying.'

'Tell me. Tell me what you know.' Nothing. Stonewall. 'Come on! I've told you everything, you give me this.'

Moir sighed. 'You're a persistent bastard, aren't you?'

'That's right.'

'Well – this is all conjecture, mind, but—' Moir sighed and continued. 'A property owned by Lascelles was turned into a nightclub. We got a tip-off about it one night, raided it, found an under-age girl ODing on heroin on the toilet floor. She was dead before she got in the ambulance. The manager was hauled in for questioning.

186

Eventually he cracked. He was an amateur. He said that Lascelles set him up in the club, told him to turn a blind eye to certain nefarious goings-on. We duly grabbed Lascelles, he claimed the manager's story was all bollocks. Of course, there was no evidence. The club's owner then changed his story, said it was was all his own doing, he'd been dealing on the side.'

'What happened at the trial?'

'There wasn't one. The manager was found dead a week before. Suicide – apparently. Left a note expressing remorse for the girl's death. End of story.'

'So you think Lascelles is dirty.'

'I *know* he is. But for all the damage I can do to him, I may as well try to demolish that godawful building of his with a toffee-hammer.' The admission was clearly a painful one.

Larkin sighed. 'Always the same, isn't it? The real villains always get off.'

Moir nodded sullenly. 'Aye. For now. That's why I do what I can. Try to make a difference.' Then he spat out, 'Bastards like him don't make it any easier.'

There was nothing to add to that. Moir looked at his watch and stood up.

'I'd best be off.' He passed Larkin his card – a well-thumbed specimen – thanked him for his help and clumped off into the street.

Surprisingly, Larkin had rather enjoyed Moir's visit. There was still something niggling, though. Something Moir had said . . .

And then, with an icy lurch in his stomach, he knew. It was the piece of the jigsaw with the complicated pattern on it, the one that looked like it fitted nowhere but, once in place, made the picture complete. He'd found it. And it was so obvious it had literally been staring him in the face all along.

He reached for the phone and called Andy's hotel. After the same rigmarole as before, Andy was on the line. He had managed to score; Larkin told him to get over to the house right away.

'What's the big rush?'

'The rush is, places to go, people to see!' Larkin could barely contain his excitement.

Andy was confused. 'What you on about?'

'What am I on about? I know who Terry is. Not only that, but I know how to find him. You coming?'

Andy was coming. And as Larkin rang off, he realised that, although he was unable to move without severe pain, although he had recently faced death, he had never felt more alive.

22: Jigsaw Pieces

'So tell me again, right, what we doin' now?' asked Andy, not for the first time.

He was behind the wheel of a hired Citroen, doing eighty down the southbound carriageway of the A1.

'Something we should have done in the first place. I haven't been thinking straight, Andy. I could have prevented a lot of trouble.'

'Oh, right.' Andy lapsed into silence again, pissed off with the fact that Larkin seemed to be speaking in code.

Larkin sat back and stretched, feeling his artifical life-support system kicking in. He was buzzing, highs and lows fighting each other for dominance. He felt as if he could slam his hand in a door and send himself into raptures about it. No doubt about it – Andy had scored some good stuff.

After leaving Charlotte's place, they had gone to see The Prof. He was propped up in bed, smiling; at first Larkin had thought it was because The Prof was pleased to see him, but he soon realised the beatific look hid a mind that was more offkilter than it had ever been.

He said hello. The Prof's smile stayed in place, unwavering. Larkin looked at Andy, who shrugged. He tried again.

'Prof, it's Stephen.'

The Prof's eyes immediately flashed with recognition and he nodded his head slightly, his mouth open.

189

Larkin stood silent, uncomfortable. 'Look, Prof, I'm sorry about—'

The Prof shook his head violently, his mouth trembling as he groped for the words. 'No! It was the cave . . .'

'*What*? What cave?'

'The cave . . .' He drifted off again; after a few breaths he came back. 'Entered the . . . cave. Faced fear . . . New man.'

Larkin could sense Andy's impatience. 'Listen, Prof, I wouldn't ask you if it wasn't important – but did you find out anything?'

Prof stared into space.

'Prof?'

Prof grabbed Larkin's arm. 'He's *bad*. But I was in the cave – he didn't know what I heard.'

'What did you hear?'

Prof's eyes were wide open, staring. 'Oh . . .' He shook his head.

'Prof, *what did you hear*?' said Larkin authoritatively.

Prof's eyes came back into focus. 'Sunday. Every . . . everyday is like . . . Sunday. Ships. Ship . . .'

'A ship coming in on Sunday?'

The Prof shook his head furiously. '*Ship*! Ship . . .' He paused. 'A shipment!' He sounded triumphant.

'Where? What time?'

The Prof shrugged.

'What is this shipment – d'you know?'

Prof creased his forehead, deep in concentration. 'It's London . . .'

Larkin and Andy looked at each other.

The Prof's eyes were clear as he imparted his last piece of information. 'London. Taking over.'

They left almost immediately, Larkin giving Andy directions and little else. They passed Durham, the Cathedral tower glimpsed distantly from the motorway; still Larkin wouldn't say where they were going.

'You know,' said Andy, making conversation, 'I always reckoned they should legalise drugs.'

190

'What kind?'

'All kinds, I reckon.'

'They should decriminalise cannabis. Even the police agree on that one. LSD too, I reckon. Can't ever imagine myself in favour of heroin and crack, though. All that real dodgy fuck-up stuff.'

'True . . .' Andy's voice trailed off. 'Hey, if they legalised it *all*, right, what would happen to the pushers and dealers?'

Larkin smiled. 'Dunno. Go into politics, maybe?'

They travelled further in silence until Larkin said, 'Turn off left.'

Andy looked at the sign.

'Darlington? Who do we know in Darlington?'

Larkin gave him a wide-eyed amphetamine smile.

'Terry.'

Larkin thought he had considered every angle, but when they pulled up outside the house, he was taken aback to find a white Lancia parked there. Seeing it again made his stomach turn over with fear and anger. Beside it, on the two-car drive, sat a Nissan Micra.

'Stop here,' he said to Andy, and the Citroën pulled up behind the Lancia. Larkin started to struggle out, still handicapped by the bandage he had refused to change. Shrugging off Andy's offer of help, he lurched down the driveway to the house, a detached mock-Tudor pile with exposed black beams over white stucco and period UPVC leaded windows.

Larkin rang the bell; its twee chimes could be heard reverberating all over the house. Eventually the door was opened by a middle-aged but well-preserved woman. The smile she gave them curled the corners of her mouth but didn't reach her eyes, as if it had been regularly used to wallpaper over a particularly persistent crack. She was wearing slacks and a pastel-coloured polo shirt; her hair had been bobbed short to disguise the flecks of grey.

On seeing the drug-addled Larkin and the hardly more

respectable Andy her smile threatened to leave her face. 'Hello? Can I help you?'

'Yes,' began Larkin. 'You don't know me – but I've met your husband. Is he in?'

The nervous glance behind her confirmed that he was. 'I . . . who is it that's calling?'

'You must be . . . Carol, right?' said Larkin, in what he hoped was his most charming manner. 'If you could just tell him that I'm here, and would like to see him?'

Carol looked even more wary when he mentioned her name. 'Just a minute,' she said and disappeared into the house, closing the front door behind her. Larkin and Andy had just sufficient time to exchange nervous glances when it opened again. And there stood Torrington.

He wasn't prepared for Larkin. His eyes widened and he stumbled back slightly. Larkin, inwardly shaking at confronting his attempted murderer, used this to his advantage. He smiled, took control.

'Hello, Phillip! Bet you didn't expect to see me again.'

Torrington tried to speak but the sound withered and died in his throat.

'Can we come in?' asked Larkin. Torrington mutely stood back and allowed them into the hall. Obviously he didn't want to make a scene where the neighbours might see it.

Torrington's wife hurried to his side. 'What is it, Phillip?' The fear in her voice was obvious.

Larkin turned round. 'How about some tea?'

'Yes,' agreed Torrington weakly. 'Could we have some tea please, Carol?'

She disappeared, leaving Larkin and Andy to make their way into the living room. It was a vast expanse – chintz curtains at the front window, gold-framed David Shepherd prints at the other. In between was a huge stone fireplace, complete with living-flame fire, a chintz three-piece and a cream-coloured fitted Wilton carpet. The only touch of individuality came from the shelved video collection behind the huge TV and video combination: David Attenborough, and golf, all neatly stacked and indexed. The whole room seemed somehow airless, untouched, as if it were being preserved for an occasion that would never arise.

Andy sat down on the settee. It was a wonder it hadn't been encased in plastic, thought Larkin. He stood, feeling the superhuman rush of chemicals pumping round his system once more. Torrington had followed them in.

'Didn't think I'd find you, did you?'

No reply.

'Suit yourself.' Larkin looked round, trying to stay calm. 'OK – where is he?'

'I . . . I don't know . . .' Torrington stammered.

'Oh, come on, Phillip, you can do better than that! You tried to kill me, didn't you? Don't try to deny it – the weapon's parked out front. Now, to do that, you must think I know something that would make life awkward for you. And, to be honest, I didn't, not before you tried to run me over.' He moved nearer. 'But I do now. I know plenty. So where is he?'

He stared at Torrington; Torrington couldn't hold his gaze.

'Please leave me alone. I can't help you. I don't know anything—'

'Oh, you do. You of all people. I want the address of your son. Danny, isn't it?' He was up close now, eyeball to eyeball, catching Torrington's flickering, cowardly gaze. 'Come on. You know where he is, you know what he's doing. Tell me.'

Torrington started to blabber his excuses again, but Larkin had had enough. He brought his fist down on a china vase sitting on top of the TV, sending it shattering. The blow made even Andy jump. It also brought Carol rushing from the kitchen, just in time to see a wild-eyed Larkin grab her husband by his shirt-front. And, in a voice that was all the more terrifying because of its quiet urgency, he spoke.

'Your son ran past me the night I saw Charles and

193

Hutton doing a deal outside a gay club. I saw him at Edgell's funeral, again with Charles. He's pushing drugs, Torrington – drugs. Not soft drugs, but the hard stuff. Crack. Heroin. D'you know what that does to you? Do you? The first time you take it, it feels like you've hit heaven, so you do it again. And again. And before you know it, it's stopped being heaven and it's turned into hell. And you can't fucking get out. Your arms look like a spastic spider's woven a web all over them, you can't shoot up there anymore, so you do your thighs. And when they've turned into bastard pincushions, you try your arse. And when that's used up you do the soles of your feet, or between your knuckles. Or your eyeballs. Anywhere, just so long as you get back that little piece of heaven. That's what your son deals in, Torrington. And if he's pushing it, chances are he's doing it. That loving, fucking scumbag you're trying to protect. That's what he does for a living. So I'll ask you again, and this time you'd better give me the right answer. Where is he?'

Torrington started to cry, big, blubbery sobs that twisted his face into an ugly mask.

'And you can stop that as well. It's too fucking late for that now.'

Torrington looked at Larkin, his eyes pleading for mercy. He found none.

'I'm sorry . . . I'm sorry . . .'

'Talk!'

Andy twitched uncomfortably on the settee, disturbed by a side of Larkin he'd never dreamed he'd see. There was silence in the room until, from the kitchen, the kettle started singing in a long, protracted whine.

'I'm waiting.'

Torrington heaved a sigh that seemed to take his soul with it. He opened his mouth and, as if finding his voice for the first time, began to talk.

'I've known all along . . . what he was doing,' he started weakly. 'The drugs. Everything. But it wasn't our fault! We brought him up as best as we could. We gave him

194

everything. It wasn't our fault that he turned out the way he did. That he was . . . queer.'

He broke off into self-pitying tears; Larkin's death-ray stare never left his face. Torrington composed himself and kept going.

'Well . . . I mean, it wasn't what we wanted . . . how he turned out. I can't help it. I . . .'

'You disowned your son because he was gay? You made his life hell so he had to move out, is that it?'

'I couldn't help it!' Torrington said between fragmented sobs. 'It was *his* fault – not mine.'

'Whose fault?'

'That solicitor. *Charles Twigge*,' he spat out. 'I wanted Danny to be a *man*, to stand up for himself. All my life I tried to instil that into him. I wanted him to be a good, honest, hard working boy.' Torrington gave a snort. 'I had it tough! Much worse than *he* ever did. Didn't make me turn out like . . . like *that*. Made me stronger! Made me the man I am today,' he said, a look of complacence creeping into his face. 'Gave me all this,' he said, with a sweep of his arm.

Larkin looked round the sterile room. He said nothing. Torrington's voice dropped.

'I wanted him to be the kind of son a father could be proud of,' he said. 'Go to the pub, have a couple of pints, go round the golf course. Man to man!' His voice trailed off again. 'Man to man.'

'So Charles,' said Larkin, 'what did he do?'

Carol Torrington took over. 'When we . . . when he left home, he went to stay with his Auntie Mary.' She looked pointedly at Torrington. 'He said she was more understanding. She took him to parties, tried to introduce him to people that were . . . better equipped to help him.'

'Which was where the photo was taken. The one you gave me. He went to a party hosted by Sir James Lascelles.'

'Yes.' Torrington again.

'And it was there that he met Charles?'

'Yes. And that bitch of a wife of his, the one who pretends he's not queer. Ruthless scheming bitch! She knew that, and still married him – she disgusts me.'

'And your son started to see Charles.'

Torrington turned on him, mania in his eyes. '*Seeing*? *Seeing*? Is that what you call it? What he did to my son, what that *bastard* turned him into, you call that "seeing"? That sick pervert got his hands on him and ... and ... I can't even say it!' Torrington turned away, shaking with rage. 'And he thinks he can get away with it! Well, let me tell you, he won't. He's going to pay!'

Larkin grabbed Torrington by the shoulders and stared into his zealot's eyes. 'I don't give a fuck what you think – or what you think you've lost. You forfeited the right to my compassion when you tried to run me over. I just want answers. Now, when your sister died you knew Danny was involved, didn't you?'

'Yes,' said Torrington, hesitantly.

'So you tried to hide any part of his involvement from me. Especially, when I'd mistakenly put two and two together and come up with six. Is that it?'

'Yes.'

'So where is he now?'

Silence.

'I'm not playing games, Torrington. Where is he?'

Again, nothing.

Larkin shook him, hard. 'Where *is* he?' he screamed, as loud as he could, using it as an outlet for all the rage that had been welling up inside him. Torrington looked terrified and slowly told him. The tension subsided a little; Larkin relaxed his grip.

'Why do you still protect him? You can't bear what he is, you hate what he's become – so why?'

The sobs started again.

'He's my son, isn't he?'

There was nothing more to say. Larkin motioned to Andy, who made a mumbled, inappropriate apology to Carol for not getting a chance to drink her tea, and they left the Torringtons standing amidst the wreckage of their life. Not wanting to face each other, not wanting to take responsibility for their complicity. Just dumbly listening to the wail of the kettle in the kitchen.

It was raining by the time Larkin and Andy reached their destination. Larkin had thought he would never see Grimley again – yet here he was.

They found what they were looking for: an upstairs flat in a stone terraced street. The curtain of the downstairs bay window twitched; Larkin didn't even acknowledge it.

There was the dull sound of feet descending carpeted stairs; Larkin braced himself. The door opened.

'Hello, Danny.'

Danny saw them both and froze. He assessed his chances and decided to make a run for it; but Andy was too quick for him, seizing him round his legs in a flying rugby tackle, bringing him down on the wet tarmac, leaving Larkin to finish the job by walloping him in the stomach with his size elevens.

'Come on,' said Larkin. 'Inside.'

Andy hauled Danny's defeated body to its feet and bundled him through the door. As they entered, Larkin allowed himself a look at the twitching net curtain; telling the occupant, in no uncertain terms, not to interfere.

They marched Danny up the stairs, threw him into the living room. It was better furnished than the outside of the building would have led them to suspect, but it still lagged some way behind the oppulence of a Columbian drug baron's mansion. *EastEnders* was on the TV, Kath and Phil gorblimeying at each other; Larkin switched it off. Andy guarded the door. Larkin remained silent until Danny's terror had grown to sufficient proportions, then spoke.

'Danny. Or do you prefer to be called Terry?'

A mumbled, inaudible response.

'Pardon?'

'Danny!'

'That's better! Now, we've met before, of course –
remember?'

Larkin held up his right hand where the corroded,
blood-soaked bandage had started to unravel.

No reply.

'You were looking for Charles, weren't you?'

'Yes.'

'And you had your very own key. Must have got the
shock of your life when you saw me!'

He didn't answer.

'All right, Danny – talk. Tell me everything.'

'Make me.'

Larkin gave a very unpleasant grin.

'If you want me to.'

He went up to the bedroom. He'd had enough. The
silence had eventually given way to shouting and he'd
been too weak to reply. Too weak. It was time he faced
facts. It was time he stood up for himself, did something.
Like a man should.

He closed the bedroom door behind him, leaving
Carol sobbing inarticulately downstairs. She hated him
now, he knew that. But he had a plan that would make
everything right again. She'd stop hating him. They could
be a happy family, as he'd always planned.

He opened the wardrobe door, looked in. It was so
long since he'd used it; he hoped it would still work.
He pulled out shoes and clothes, uncovered the locked,
stainless steel cupboard built into the back. He opened
the door with a small key. There it was – still looking
good. He had wanted to use it to go hunting and fishing
with Danny, like a father does with a son. No chance of
that now. He checked himself. He mustn't say things
like that! There *was* a chance, of course there was. That's
why he was doing this.

Yes, he thought, this would make them look at him
with respect once more. This time tomorrow he would
have his family back. And he tucked the gun under his
arm and left the room, making for the car outside.

Now, last time we met,' said Larkin to Danny Torrington,
'you had me at a disadvantage. Least I could do was
return the favour.'

Danny was sitting in the very centre of his living room,
tied to a straight-backed dining chair with whatever
Larkin and Andy had managed to lay their hands on:
string, parcel tape, sellotape, electrical wire – even a
length of clothes line. Danny couldn't move.

He had submitted willingly, as if to the inevitable; he
hadn't struggled at all while Larkin and Andy positioned
him on the chair. But his passivity extended to his mouth.
Larkin knew that drastic action was called for.

'Are you just going to sit there, Danny, and say
nothing?'

Danny was silent.

'OK, then, what we'll do is call the police. I've got a
friend on the force with a vested interest in all of this.
He'll make you talk.' Larkin stuck his face close to
Danny's. 'They *love* to get a gay boy down in the cells.'

Danny flinched, but remained silent. Larkin stood up.
'Still keeping mum? That's a shame. A real shame.
Because – as the saying goes – we have ways of making
you talk.'

He turned and left the room. Andy sat on the sofa, mind-
ing the immobile Danny. He picked up a newspaper that
had been left on the arm of the sofa and started to read.

From the kitchen there was a clatter of cupboards
being ransacked, drawers being rummaged through.
Eventually Larkin returned to the living room clutching
a can of lighter fluid, a box of matches and a couple of
firelighters. Andy looked up, and did a double take.

'What the *fuck* are you doing?' he said.

'This little bastard's going to talk. One way or the
other.' Larkin plucked the newspaper from Andy's hand.
'Very thoughtful,' he said, and began to wad the sheets
up into balls and place them at Danny's feet.

'Stevie, stop it,' said Andy, a note of panic creeping
into his voice.

Larkin didn't answer. He placed the firelighters on the newspaper and opened the can of lighter fluid; Danny began to look seriously scared.

'This ain't funny anymore,' said Andy.

'It never was funny,' said Larkin, and poured the lighter fluid over Danny's feet. Using the remainder, he made a trail across the carpet to the door.

'Right,' said Larkin, taking a match from the box, 'let's find out if we understand each other.' Danny began to pull, feebly, at his restraints.

'Tell me what I want to know, Danny – and you walk. No police. It's as simple as that. But fuck me about—' – he waved the match – 'and up you go. What d'you say?'

Danny stared at the match. 'You wouldn't,' he said in a cracked voice.

'Don't be silly, Danny. If I were you, I'd assume that I would.' Larkin held the match to the box. 'Well?'

Silence. No one dared to move. Eventually Danny spoke. 'All right – what d'you want to know?'

'That's better,' said Larkin; Andy looked distinctly relieved. 'Let's start with why you came to Charlotte's house before sunrise?'

'I was looking for Charles,' Danny mumbled. 'He'd been staying here, with me. He got a phone call in the middle of the night, said he had to go out for a while. When he didn't come back, I got worried.'

'And you were sleeping with him?'

Fire came into Danny's eyes. 'I *love* him! And now he's gone, and I don't know where.'

'OK,' said Larkin, 'We'll leave that aside for the moment. So how d'you know Edgell?'

'He was Auntie Mary's boyfriend. Charles knew what Wayne did for a living and he wanted a piece of it. He told Wayne he could introduce him to a lot of people.'

Larkin moved closer to Danny. 'So what's Mary's part in all this?'

Danny looked at the floor again. 'She was unlucky. The lot up here got wind that we were moving in. They

200

sent Fenwick to spy on Wayne. He went to Mary's house. I don't know what happened in there—'

'But Fenwick killed Mary with a shotgun.'

Danny nodded, sadly.

'And then he went after Edgell, found him in Grimley, in that tacky nightclub, and killed him.'

Danny nodded again.

Larkin breathed out. 'OK, Danny – one more thing and you can go. This shipment today – when and where?'

And Danny told him.

Andy went to get a kitchen knife; Larkin looked round, half-appalled, at the mess he had made of the flat. The relief he felt at getting the truth was almost post-orgasmic.

'So where are you going to go?' asked Larkin.

Danny raised his head. No longer the flash young man he had first appeared to be, he looked disappointed, defeated. Like the pathetic failure he was. 'As far away from cunts like you as possible,' he spat defiantly. Larkin almost felt sorry for him.

Andy came back, loosened one of Danny's arms and passed him the knife. They left him there, sawing at his bonds, trying desperately to make himself free.

Larkin held the crumpled card in the fingertips of his right hand and the receiver in his left. The phone box could only take one person, so Andy was in the car. Larkin stared, transfixed, at his own reflection; the rain bleaching down the side of the glass had distorted it beyond all recognition. He didn't know himself any more.

The phone was answered: a bleary, Scottish voice.

'Hello, Inspector Moir.'

'Who's this?' He sounded like a bear interrupted during hibernation.

'It's Larkin.'

'Where are you?'

'In a phone box in Gateshead.'

'What the fuck are you doing there? I thought you couldn't bloody move!'

'The miracle of modern pharmaceuticals. I've been out, earning my background information for the feature of my career. You want to know what I've discovered?'

Moir grunted.

'I'll take that for a yes. Actually, you gave me the clue yourself. You said Terry looked like Mary's son. Once that fell into place, the rest was easy.' Larkin told Moir everything that Danny had told him, barring the time and place of the drug pick-up; he was keeping that for later. Moir listened in silence as Larkin finished his story. When Larkin stopped speaking he grunted again.

'Where's this Danny now?'

'Dunno.' Larkin didn't want to admit to Moir that he had let him go. But Moir said, 'Fuck him, anyway. He's not important.'

Larkin tried to change the subject, just in case. 'What about Fenwick?'

'Bit of a mad bastard, all right,' said Moir. 'Eager to make a name for himself in the hard-man stakes. And what a cock-up he made. All he was supposed to do was ask a few questions. I doubt he meant to kill her.'

Larkin stopped. 'You *knew*?'

Moir made a noise, a cross between a gloating chuckle and a smoker's death rattle. 'Of course we fucking knew! How many women commit suicide with a shotgun? Statistically, none.'

'So why didn't you tell me?'

'Need-to-know. It's an ongoing police investgation. We were happy to let the suicide story go round – we're after bigger fish here. You'd have been told eventually.'

Larkin tried to regain some ground. 'Fenwick *was* killed in prison because he was going to turn Queen's Evidence?'

'Sort of,' said Moir. 'He thought he'd be rewarded for what he'd done. For killing Edgell. Trouble was, he made such a balls-up of what should have been a simple job that they cut him adrift. He was a bit of a loose cannon as far as they were concerned. Best get him out of the way.'

'OK,' said Larkin. 'You think you hold all the cards, and it must be great fun to ask me to risk my neck and not let me have the full story – but two can play at that game.'

Moir snorted. 'Oh really?'

'You see, I know where and when the next shipment arrives. And I'm not going to tell you unless Andy comes along and we get an exclusive on it. What d'you say, Henry?'

23: The Pay-Off

The rain was hitting hard now, roaring as the wind carried it, bouncing up into little crowns as it hit the ground. Moir was at the wheel of the car, Larkin beside him. In the back seat sat Andy, weighted down by cameras and attendant paraphernalia, which he nervously checked every few minutes. They had been in the car for the best part of an hour and beyond the merest civilities, it had been spent in silence. The air was thick with testosterone, tension and sweat.

Larkin had been told that the lorry would pull into Grimley motorway services at ten-thirty, in order to unload into the feeder van. It was now quarter to eleven and there was no sign of either vehicle. Larkin groaned quietly. He had topped up his artificial life-support until he was at screaming point; but from now on, he would have to use it carefully. There was only a little left, and coming down off each new jag was more painful than the last. The pay-off would come soon, though – he could feel it. Then all he'd have to cope with was coming down for good.

Through the rain he could just make out the lights of the cafe over the bridge, hear the mechanical drawl of the passing cars. They waited. At five to eleven an articulated lorry pulled into the parking area and stopped dead. Moir, Larkin and Andy hardly dared breathe as the radio crackled into static life. Moir acknowledged the distorted voice, told it to wait for the signal. They watched as the driver stepped down from the cab and walked over the bridge to the cafe. He didn't look back.

'That him?' asked Andy.

'Could be,' said Moir. 'We'll know for sure in a minute.' His face was granite-set.

They sat there like rabbits in the headlights. A minute or so later, a transit van pulled off the motorway and parked next to the lorry. They couldn't see the driver's side from where they were parked, but they heard the door slam. The radio crackled again; Moir responded. The second van driver had followed the first into the cafe.

There was silence in the car once more. A Ford Scorpio pulled up, a fair distance away from the two vans; the driver turned off his lights, but didn't get out. Probably a tired exec having a rest, Larkin surmised. He turned his attention back to the vans.

Then the static hissed out again. 'Right,' Moir said, excited. 'The second driver's swiped the keys from the first one's table. Classic switch. Here he comes now!'

The transit driver made his way to the back of the artic, started to open the doors. Larkin's heart did a double take.

'I know him!'

'What?' said Moir.

'Batman. One of Cain's buddies.'

Moir picked up the radio. 'Trap leader to all grey-hounds. The deal is on. I repeat, the deal is going down now. Wait for my word, then go.'

They watched as Batman opened the big double doors of the artic. Robin emerged from the back of the transit; another man, who could have been their clone, joined them. They began transferring boxes from the lorry to the transit.

Moir bellowed into the radio. 'Go! Go! Now! Get the fuckers!'

Suddenly the black, deserted car park sprang to life. Bushes, fences and walls spewed forth men. Moir was out of the car like an overweight whippet, followed by Larkin, and Andy, snapping away. Batman, Robin and their pal had time only to turn round and catch the merest glimpse of the police jumping them. Robin, nearest the van, tried to make a run for it; he was brought down by two cops who lost no time in educating him on the finer points of arrest procedure. It was the only time that Larkin had been glad to see evidence of police brutality. He hoped Robin wasn't enjoying it too much.

The three were quickly overpowered. Larkin, since he could do nothing but observe, did a bit of observation and went over to the lorry. It was piled high with boxes; ripping the nearest one open, he discovered hundreds of shrink-wrapped Game Boys, all stamped MADE IN TAIWAN. He tore off the polythene on one of them, prised the casing apart. Inside the game was hollow, but not empty. It contained a small bag of white powder. Made in Taiwan, with coke from Columbia, and heroin from Turkey: a truly international set-up.

The three pushers were being bundled into the back of a police van; Larkin felt a high that wasn't chemical at the sight. He walked back to the car. As he approached, he noticed that the quietly parked Scorpio was revving up, ready to leave. Larkin stared at the driver. Cain.

Without stopping to think, Larkin jumped behind the wheel of Moir's Rover, found the keys, started it up. He briefly caught sight of Moir, swearing and shouting, as he sped out of the service station. Heading north. After Cain.

Once on the road it was clear that Cain didn't have any idea where he was going, driving only to escape. Larkin clung to him with terrier-like tenacity, matching Cain's every move, windsceen wipers working furiously, keeping the Scorpio in his sights. He quickly realised that Cain was heading for the minor roads in the hope of losing him; he couldn't have bargained on Larkin's local knowledge.

They went round a roundabout, up a steep bank, to Wrekenton, another ex-pit village. Past rows of stone houses, past a preserved mine-working and coal railway. Larkin dogged the Scorpio's tracks until the road dead-ended into a cinderpath bridleway, and he found the car abandoned, the door swinging open, the motor chugging.

Larkin stopped the Rover and got out. He crossed to the Scorpio, hoping for a clue to the direction Cain had taken. The cindertrack bisected the overgrown remains of the railway line; it was a straight line down, exposed. No sign of Cain. Ahead were fields: again, no sign. Up the track to the right was a breaker's yard, the rusting skeletons of dead cars piled up high, forming a jagged skyline visible even in the dark. It seemed the likeliest possibility. Larkin snatched the keys from the Rover and followed.

The yard had a padlocked gate and a chainlink fence, but there were no signs warning of guard dogs so Larkin thought it would be safe to enter. After all, what could be worse than the psychotic hiding inside? He pulled himself over the high fence, and fell hard to the ground on the other side; fortunately chemicals blunted the pain of the fall.

He moved cautiously, eyes darting left and right, ears listening for the slightest noise. All he heard was the wind whistling through the bones of cars, like old ghosts: towering piles of rust, waiting for a strong breeze to topple them. The place had been abandoned to decay.

Larkin tried to move as silently as he could, knowing Cain would be doing the same. He knew he was a sitting target. A noise of creaking and rending startled him; he turned round and saw a precariously balanced pile of cars rocking violently backwards and forwards, about to shed its top load. About to bury him. He froze for a few seconds, paralysed by the image of the avalanche of twisted metal; then he came to his senses and looked for somewhere to shelter. There was a gap between two stacks directly in front of him; he squeezed himself between them as the cars hit the ground in a wet cloud of rust flakes, missing him by inches.

He crawled out, sweating. He followed the course of the gap until he came out on the other side of the stack. No Cain. With his heart still racing and his breathing in overdrive, he planned his next move. His inner voice screamed at him to get out of there, leave it to the police. But another voice was telling him to stay and fight. The scrapyard was an arena – and Cain was another fear to conquer.

He needed a vantage point; but climbing would leave him vulnerable, so he would have to be careful. Getting a toe-hold on the nearest car, he hauled himself up. Halfway he looked at his hands, studded with rust, wet with rain and blood. The climb was more arduous than he had expected. There was no shortage of protrusions for him to grab on to, but they were so old they had a tendency to flake away in his hands. He clung on though and eventually he reached the summit.

After he'd got his breath back he looked around rapidly. Nothing. He looked harder. There! On the perimeter, trying to scale the chainlink fence. Larkin knew he'd have to move quickly. There was only one way – over the roofs of the cars, jumping from stack to stack, hoping his foot wouldn't cave in on a pile of rust. Forsaking stealth for speed, he took a deep breath and jumped.

It was easier than he thought. He leapt from car to car, arriving on the final one, appropriately an Avenger, just in time to see Cain reach the top of the fence. Cain saw Larkin and started a desperate scramble; but Larkin was right behind him. There was a few feet between them, but Larkin had height on his side. He stood on the crumbling roof of the Avenger and savoured the moment.

'Hello, Cain,' said Larkin, his iceman cool giving way to lava behind his eyes. 'Fancy meeting you here.'

As Cain turned his head, Larkin swung a kick at his face. The blow sent Cain's head snapping back, but didn't loosen him from the fence. Blood seeped from his nose; he shook his head to clear it, and went on climbing. Larkin swung his foot again, connecting this time with the side of Cain's head. Cain's grip almost gave way, but he recovered sufficiently to get his arm over the fence. Larkin chose his moment carefully. Ripping free a bumper that was loosly attached to the rusting Avenger, he raised it up and brought it down onto Cain's arm. Cain screamed. He let go, flailing, wildly grabbing for the Avenger, losing the top layer of skin from his hand in the process. Somehow, he was still clinging on. Larkin felt the car shake, as if it were about to fall; he figured that his body-weight might be the only thing stopping it. He jumped onto the car behind, an old Zephyr; as he hit the roof, the impact of his jump caused the Avenger to dislodge. And, with rusted metal grinding in the rain, the car began to topple.

Larkin could only watch helplessly as the car, with the battered, rain-lashed body of Cain clinging to it, gave way and fell with an almighty, industrial groan.

For a few seconds all was silence, broken only by the ghostly wind and the insistent rain. Larkin slowly descended. He looked down at the tangle of metal.

Cain, in falling, had tried to throw his body away from the vehicle. As a result he had hit the hard-packed earth with a thud, twisting his arm under him. Larkin found him lying motionless, legs pinned down by the Avenger's empty bonnet.

Larkin crossed to the prone body of his victim, the corroded bumper still in his hand, consumed by rage, by a burning need for revenge. A momentary wave of panic passed through him; could he really allow himself to be responsible for another human being's death? Would he find out what he needed to know? As he stood there, Cain slowly regained consciousness, whimpering. His face and head were bloody from Larkin's kicks; his cheeks were cut and pockmarked from the gravel.

'Help me,' Cain cried. 'I'm hurting.'

Larkin was thrown. He'd been expecting some big

showdown, man against man, but he wasn't prepared for this. Cain spoke again, his face contorted with terror.

'Please! Please help me. I'm hurt. *Please.*' He sounded like a wounded animal.

'Can't take the pain, eh?' said Larkin. Now that he knew Cain was alive he felt his anger returning.

'Just help me. I promise not to hurt you ever again. I promise. Just help me.' He looked down at his body for the first time. 'My legs! My legs . . .'

Larkin was relentless. 'Bit late for that, isn't it? The damage is done. It's only right that you should get what you deserve.' He moved in closer.

The pathetic wreck on the ground started howling, bestially rolling his upper torso backwards and forwards.

'No! No, *please* . . .' Then he saw Larkin's eyes. He looked into them. And the howling started again.

Larkin stopped dead. He had wanted to hit him, cause him terrible pain, beat him to death if need be, pay him back – but the desperate pleading of the broken man touched him. Besides, he didn't want to think how Cain thought, do the things Cain might have done.

He bent down. With a pitiful shriek, Cain wriggled painfully away, sobbing, eyeing Larkin with mistrust.

'Come on, I'm going to help you. Come on,' he coaxed.

Cain stared at him suspiciously; he looked like a rat in a hole.

'Look, I won't hurt you. I'll *help* you. Yeah?'

Cain didn't react.

'OK?' Larkin put on what he hoped was, under the circumstances, his most winning smile.

Cain stared at him, his eyes wide, childlike. 'OK.'

'That's better! Now, you help me by telling me what I want to know, and I'll . . .' He paused. 'I'll help you out of there, yeah?'

Cain nodded his head.

Larkin looked down at the twisted wreck of the psychopath. Cain looked beyond saving. When he spoke, he kept his voice light. 'Good. All right, then – you tell me this . . .'

24: Rumours Of Death

He stood in the freezing cold and the pouring rain. The Tyne was slapping angrily at the soaked wooden jetty on which he stood, all weather-eaten and mossed, its banks perilously close to breaking. He was in the shadows, looking out. He could hear the occasional car passing overhead, see right along the waterfront. Directly in front of him was the Tyne Bridge, with the floating night-club moored beneath it; tonight it's half-hearted disco lights seemed to cast a depressing pall on the mud-grey water. On the other side of the river the bars and build-ings were in darkness; the last straggling Sunday drinkers had gone home hours ago.

He had figured that Cain would have set up a meet with his boss that night, after the drop; he'd wanted to find out the time and the place. It hadn't been easy. The hardest part had been promising to help Cain, coaxing him into supplying the information – then walking away, leaving him there, his trapped howls piercing Larkin's soul. He'd got the information, though. Half past mid-night, the jetty underneath the Swing Bridge. How ironic.

Informing Moir had been a different matter alto-gether. He had put a call out over the air via Moir's car radio, telling Moir where Cain was and that he needed urgent medical attention. He'd then appropriated Moir's car for the final time – in for a penny, in for a pound – and driven to the rendezvous.

Now he stared at the water, tried to keep warm by

stamping his feet. The pain was slowly seeping back into his body as the last of the chemicals dispersed. It was twenty-five to one. He didn't think he'd have to wait much longer.

As if on cue, he heard movement on the steps above him. Someone had swung over the rail and was coming down. Whoever it was walked straight out onto the exposed part of the jetty as Larkin emerged from the shadows.

'Hello, Charlotte.'

She turned. Surprise, terror and disbelief all crowded onto her face at once. She was dressed, bizarrely, for a rainy day in the country. 'What . . . what . . .' she began.

'What am I doing here? Is that what you're trying to ask?'

She stared dumbly.

'Were you expecting someone else?' Again, silence. 'Look, Charlotte, I've got it all sussed. You don't have to pretend anymore.'

She considered her options, then realised she had no choice. 'Where's Cain?'

'He's . . . incapacitated.'

'Have the police got him?'

'Probably, by now. Or the hospital.'

'Why? What happened to him?'

'A car fell on him.'

Her jaw dropped.

'Oh, I'm pretty certain he's not dead – but you'll find he's a changed person. Very much so.'

She sighed. 'I suppose this is it, then. It's all over.'

'Looks like it.'

There was so much that Larkin wanted to say to her, it hurt. Half of him – more than half – wanted to grab her, tell her that everything was going to be all right again, that they would be together and the future would be filled with love. But freezing on the jetty, in the pouring rain, all he could manage was, 'Remember the last time we were here?'

214

The slightest flicker of a smile crossed her features.
'Yes.'

'We were very drunk.'

'You tried to throw me over.'

'You started it!'

'I didn't! You did.'

Even at a moment like this, they could look back at the past with affection. But this was no time for nostalgia. Larkin looked into her eyes; they were red and sore, as if she'd been crying. He didn't want to ask the next question but he knew he had to.

'Where's Charles?'

She paused. 'He's – actually, he's dead.'

That came as no surprise to Larkin. 'What happened?'

She looked straight at him, her eyes wide. He still wanted to drown in them. 'I killed him.'

Even though he had been expecting it, it still cut him; he tried not to let it show. 'I figured that.'

'How much else did you work out?'

'A fair bit.'

'D'you want me to tell you all of it?' Her eyes flickered away, then back again.

'No, I'll tell you. You can fill in the blanks.'

She looked up at him, imploring. 'Before you say anything – don't judge me. You're a part of this too.'

Larkin's physical pain had returned, and with it something deeper that stabbed him to the heart. He tried to blot it out, but it wasn't possible.

'Where should I start?' he said. 'How about, Charles? One of Thatcher's children. Decided to move into property in the late eighties, lost everything in the recession. Not too bright, was he?'

Charlotte started to speak.

'Don't deny it. I went through his stuff at your place – it's all there. All his debts. Including the ones he owed Lascelles, and he's not backward in coming forward where money's involved. Charles needed cash, and quick. That's why he threw in his lot with Edgell and Danny Torrington.'

215

Charlotte flinched.

'Yes,' he continued, 'I know about Danny Torrington. Charles had been staying with him; when Charles went off after a phone call and didn't come back, Danny came looking for him at your place. He wasn't there, of course . . . And neither were you. Danny and Charles were in love.' He snorted. 'He may have been a bastard, but at least *somebody* loved him.'

She started to say something, but he cut her off.

'Don't. Don't make excuses. So how did you do it? Cain didn't help you – he'd have told me. So how?'

She seemed to have shrunk visibly. When she spoke it was with a quiet emotionless monotone. 'I did it. This morning, very early. I called him, said I had something very important to tell him, something I couldn't say over the phone. He had to come straight away, and he couldn't come to the house, because it wasn't safe. The sort of thing Charles has been up to – it was plausible enough. So I told him where to meet me, insisted that he didn't tell – Danny.' She put her hand to her mouth; Larkin thought for a moment she was going to be sick. 'So I – I lured him to his death. At the bottom of Forth Bank.'

The reality of her words hit Larkin like a blow. He swallowed. 'Why – why there?'

'I'd thought about it all very carefully. Forth Bank is steep and it goes straight into the Tyne. It's a good place. And there's never anyone around at that time in the morning. Charles drove there and parked his car at the bottom, where I'd told him. I rushed straight over to him. And as he opened his door, I hit him from behind with a wrench from the tool kit in the boot. He fell backwards, into the car. I don't think he was dead, then, but he was certainly unconscious. I hit him again, just to make sure. I took his handbrake off, took the keys from the ignition, locked all the doors. Then I pushed the car down the Bank, into the river. That was the hardest part, especially at first. But once it had gathered momentum it went quite quickly. I threw the keys in after it. It was still dark.' She looked over the water, in the direction of

216

Forth Bank. 'He's still there now, I imagine.' When she turned back again, tears had made silent tracks down her cheeks. Larkin chose to tell himself that it was only the rain.

'But why? Why now?'

After a long pause, she spoke. 'When I met Charles he was rich and successful. That made him very attractive. Like I said, I knew he was gay, but it was a strictly business arrangement. We were useful to each other. But then he lost everything. I was going to leave him – but he pointed out that the people who were after him for money might also decide to come after me.'

'Including Lascelles?'

'Including Lascelles. Charles said our best chance was to stay together. Watch each other's backs.'

'So how did the drugs come into it?'

She let her eyes trail along the quayside. Absently, she noticed a white car pull up and park; the lights were turned off and the driver got out. She turned her attention back to Larkin. 'He started using. Coke, mainly. At first it was just because he was depressed. Then, like a true entrepreneur, he spotted other possibilities. He saw his way out though dealing. Our way out.'

'So why did you kill him?'

'Because . . . I'd convinced myself that what was between Charles and me was purely professional. No more. I was happy to stay with him, while he was making money. He gave me a certain status. He was handsome. And if people want to mess up their lives with drugs, that's their decision. He wasn't corrupting anyone – we're all responsible for ourselves, and no one else.

'And then he told me he was in love. With Danny. Not just sleeping with him – I wouldn't have minded that – but in love!' She gave a bitter laugh. 'And I was *over-whelmed* with jealousy. I couldn't believe it. It wasn't the sex, we'd never had that – it was the power. The emotional power. I enjoyed knowing that I had that over him. And suddenly he no longer needed me.' Her voice became very small. 'I couldn't cope with that.'

She sighed, lost within herself. Larkin waited, she continued as if retelling a dream. 'Then I thought; if Charles was out of the way, I could run the Newcastle end of the London firm! I knew I'd be much better at it than he ever was. And he'd become so indiscreet – he was putting both of us in danger. So I . . .' Her voice faded into silence.

Larkin stood, not trusting himself to speak. Charlotte looked at him imploringly. 'Stephen, please – you've got to believe this. Once I'd been with you again, I tried to put things right. All that mattered then was you. I thought we could start again—'

Larkin rounded on her. 'Don't give me that. You set me up.' He stared at her, merciless. 'You were good, though. You had me fooled. I always said you should have been a politician. I'll tell you the rest, shall I? You told me you and Mary were great mates, and I would be doing you a favour – you even offered to pay me, just to make it legit. You had every angle covered. You invented Terry; you must have written the diary. All so your connection with the London firm wouldn't be discovered by Sir James – who you also happened to be sleeping with. A finger in every pie, eh? Sir James was the one trying to unite the Newcastle gangs, and Cain was his enforcer. But you persuaded Cain to double-cross Lascelles and come in with you, Charles, Edgell and Danny – controlled by the London mob. Lascelles suspected someone was trying to rip him off, so he sent Fenwick to investigate. After that balls-up, you had to protect yourselves, so you sent me looking for a non-existent person – just to take the heat off. Trouble was I met Torrington, who gave me a photo of Mary with Danny. I assumed he was Terry; you didn't argue in case I found out too much and it all got back to Lascelles. I was getting too close. I was thinking, and that surprised you. That party I was supposed to meet you at – you never intended to go, did you? It was just a way of getting me into the arms of Cain. And don't say you didn't think he'd hurt me – you knew fucking well what he'd do. I was just something else that had got in the way of you and your ambition.'

He looked at her. She was crying, her tears flowing freely.

'And don't insult me by crying. Don't make excuses. I'm right, aren't I?'

She nodded mutely.

'So why me? Was it just luck? I'll bet you were rubbing your hands with glee when Larkin the Ace Fuck-Up came back on the scene. Did you think I was so incompetent that I couldn't hack it? Is that it?'

She looked down, not wanting to face him. 'Something like that.'

'That's what you'd planned to do, wasn't it? You were going to find a private detective – either some bloke who couldn't find his arse with both hands, or someone who could file reports any way you wanted for the right price – and then, suddenly, who should appear? Me. The fuck-up. The burn-out. Your ex-lover, and drunk when you met him. What did you think it would take? You coming on to me? Money? Whatever, your curiosity got the better of you – and that was your big mistake. Because I wasn't quite the mess you thought I'd be, was I?'

She was crying again now. 'No . . . But that's not the way it turned out. I fell in love with you, all over again.'

Larkin turned away in disgust. 'Oh, fuck off, just fuck off, I don't want to hear that crap.'

'You've got to believe me, Stephen. I love you. When I saw you in the hospital, I realised what I'd done to you, what I'd become. And then I knew. I'm telling the truth. I saw a chance for us, a way of us both being happy together, a future with no worries. With Charles out of the way . . . The drugs drop tonight was it. Just one score – that was it, no more. We could have gone away somewhere, anywhere, started again. I just had to . . . to get rid of my old life first.' She grabbed him by the shoulders; he could feel her nails through his leather jacket. 'Stephen, you have to believe me! *Please!*'

He pulled her into his coat, comforting her. 'Oh, Charlotte . . .'

He had softened, found himself talking against his better judgement. Then he realised what he was about to say. 'How can I believe you? How do I know you're not lying? Not using me again?'

'I'm not! I *swear* I'm not. I love you, Stephen.'

Larkin tried to be the iceman again. 'You never loved anybody but yourself. You were always ambitious, always wanted to come out on top. That's all you were ever interested in.'

She started to cry again. 'Yes – and look where it got me!'

'What's that supposed to mean?'

The tears stopped and were replaced by a still, small voice. 'You read the diary. You know.'

'What?'

'I *did* write that diary. But it wasn't about Mary – at least, only the beginning and the ending. It was about me.'

Larkin was stunned. '*You*? Then – who's Terry?'

'Sir James's middle name is Terence.'

Larkin felt sick, as if he'd been punched in the stomach. 'That gear – in the wardrobe—'

'All mine.'

'But why did—'

Charlotte wouldn't let him speak. 'You said I was ambitious. That's no secret. But like you – like everyone – I had ideals too. Once.'

'You told me ideals were a luxury! One you couldn't afford.'

'Just let me finish! I was trying to justify myself – what I'd become. I'm trying to explain to you – I wasn't like this at the beginning. Oh, I've always wanted to do well, better than my parents ever did for themselves, but I wanted a career where ambition and integrity could go hand in hand. That was why I chose to study Law. And then I became a solicitor. And it wasn't all about defending the vulnerable, getting justice, righting wrongs.

220

Far from it. Everyone I saw was on the take, feathering their own nests. And they were the ones getting on! Not people like me – I was a bloody good solicitor, but who cared about that? I began to realise, if I was going to make a success of my life, something had to give. And I knew that I wasn't going to win power and respect by slogging away in a solicitor's office till the end of my days.

'Marrying Charles was just the first step. Then I met Sir James Lascelles – Terry. I did actually call him Terry when we were together – never in public, of course. He told me that his mother and his lovers were the only people allowed to call him that.

'Anyway, Sir James found me attractive and didn't hide the fact that he wanted to sleep with me. So I let him. He's very influential in this city – I thought it was bound to open a few doors. And it did.' Charlotte saw the look of contempt on Larkin's face. 'Stephen, it's not as bad as it seems! It wasn't just that. Remember, I had no love in my marriage. To all intents and purposes, I was alone. I wanted to believe that I could love someone, and that they could love me. I knew I was pretty worthless. And because I didn't have any self-respect, because I knew I'd let myself down, I let Sir James do whatever he wanted. I let him abuse me.'

She broke off; Larkin noticed that she was trembling. He waited for her to regain her composure.

'Believe it or not, I enjoyed the sex at first,' she said. 'It was so wild – it was like a drug. But when I thought about it afterwards, I hated myself. I hated the fact that I allowed this horrible, ugly, fat bastard to do those things to me.

'Writing that diary helped me to get it all out of my system. Free myself from it. Oh, it was also helpful as far as the thing with Mary was concerned – but that wasn't the only reason I wrote it. Perhaps I needed to let someone know what I had been through – someone who mattered.'

Larkin turned away from her. She grabbed hold of

him, swung him round to face her. 'You have to believe me! You have to trust me. I want to start again, with you. I need you to give me a chance.' Her eyes were begging him. He stared into them and found, perhaps because he wanted to, the truth. All he'd ever wanted to find in Charlotte's eyes. He relented.

'All right. I believe you.' He looked straight at her now, her mask ripped away. And for the first time in his life he saw her as she really was: pitiful, desperate, damaged. He couldn't turn his back on her. 'We'll do what we can. We'll get it sorted.'

She looked up at him, hope glimmering through the tears, the disco lights creating a halo around her head.

'Will we?' She looked like a child who'd been expecting punishment, spared at the last minute. Perhaps she was telling the truth, thought Larkin. Perhaps on this jetty, where they'd parted all those years ago, was where life could start again.

'We will. We'll do something. Come on.'

He put his arm round her. As they turned to walk away, their path was blocked. Larkin thought at first that the man was carrying a fishing rod, aiming to do a bit of late-night angling. Then, as he stepped into the glow cast by the disco lights, he saw who it was. Torrington. Carrying a shotgun.

'I thought I'd find you together. The two of you, you're as bad as each other. Oh, you think you're so clever. But you're not, are you? You, you bitch – I was tailing you, all the way from your house, and you never even noticed. You've destroyed my family. But you won't destroy me. I've got the better of you now.'

Larkin tried to be rational. 'Mr Torrington, what exactly is it that you're doing here?'

Torrington swung the gun at him. 'Don't. Just don't. Don't say anything. D'you know what you've done to Carol? Do you know the state she's in? Coming round, saying the things you said – you've no respect for ordinary people.' He gestured at Charlotte. 'And nor does she.'

222

'Just listen,' Larkin said frantically. 'Think of your wife, think of Carol. Think what you're doing to her.'

But Torrington would not be deterred. 'I heard her. I heard the two of you, scheming away. So she's killed him. She's denied me that opportunity. He deserved to suffer, for what he did to me and my family. To my son. But she got there before me. And you – you were going to help her get away with it, scot-free.'

He swayed to and fro unsteadily; Larkin wondered if he were drunk as well as unhinged. Whatever he was, he was dangerous.

'If I can't have that degenerate bastard,' Torrington continued, 'then I'll have the next best thing. Oh, yes. Either the murdering whore bitch –' he pointed the gun at Charlotte – 'or the big-mouthed piece of scum.' He aimed the gun at Larkin.

'Don't be fucking stupid.' Larkin had had enough. Pain was driving a bulldozer to his brain as he looked straight down the twin barrels of the shotgun. And up into the cold, killer eyes of Torrington, as his finger tightened on the trigger.

Larkin knew he only had one chance. He tried to move as quickly as he could, but his battered body telegraphed his intention and Torrington neatly sidestepped, his middle-aged reflexes sharpened by adrenalin. As if it were a slow-motion dream, Torrington pulled his gun out of Larkin's range and swung it at Charlotte. And emptied both barrels into her.

Larkin pivoted laboriously, the jetty now molten tar. He reached out to stop the shots. Too late. He saw the bullets fly into Charlotte—

Into Sophie—

Cutting her almost in half, launching her off the end of the jetty, into the air and down into the Tyne—

Cutting her almost in half, exploding in a blossoming fractal flower of red—

He heard a loud roar, huge, full of anger and loss, and realised it was his own. He turned and faced Torrington—

Faced Sickert—

Walked over to him, his legs working painfully, and grabbed the gun from Torrington—

From Sickert—

Grabbed the shotgun from his hands, hefted it up, and brought it down on Torrington's—

On Sickert's—

– face. Then again. Then again. Tears streaming down Larkin's face, anger and pain flooding his body, screaming at the top of his lungs—

'You've taken my *life*! You've taken my fucking *life*!'

Living every single second as if it were an hour. Oblivious to everything except revenge.

Twenty minutes later, the police arrived and found Larkin slumped over Torrington's prone body. He had nothing left to give.

25: The Beginning

He lay there in bed and stared at the ceiling. He'd been doing it for so long he knew it by heart, every contour, every slight bump. But if he shut his eyes, he couldn't even remember what colour it was.

He didn't know how long he'd been there. It could have been days, or hours. When he shut his eyes, all he saw was emptiness. Dark, swirling emptiness. He had stopped dreaming. When he slept, all he saw was black. He closed his eyes. If he had no more dreams left, he might as well look back. To a few days ago, just after he'd been let out of hospital . . .

'You didn't have to come and fetch me, you know. I can manage perfectly well on my own,' said Larkin, hobbling along outside the General.

'Believe me,' said Moir, 'I didn't do it out of compassion.'

'I suppose not.'

'You've got some very serious charges stacked up against you. Stealing police property, interfering in an arrest, assault probably with intent to kill, deliberately withholding evidence – and, above all, seriously pissing me off. That's the worst one. Believe me, you don't want me for an enemy.'

'I can imagine. So what are you going to do with me now?'

'Well,' he said, opening the door of the Rover so

225

Larkin could get in, 'by rights I should take you to the station and book you.'

'But?'

'*But*, I think we should talk about this somewhere quiet. Get in.'

'Nice car, by the way.'

'Don't push it, sunshine.'

They drove to a pub Moir knew, up by St James's Park. It was the kind of place committed drinkers went to when they had nowhere else to go – which was often, to judge by the clientele.

They got their drinks and sat down.

'So,' Larkin ventured, 'what's all this about?'

'Shut up and listen. And don't interrupt. I told you I don't like journalists – and I fucking hate vigilantes. But before I moved to Newcastle, I had a family. A wife, two lovely wee daughters. And personally I was on the up – a fast-rising star in the police department. I spent all my time working, I never got to see my family. But I didn't care – I was on the up. I courted the right people, went to the right parties, was a member of the right Lodge. I didn't see what was happening. I was so blind.' His eyes dimmed for a few seconds, lost in the past. 'My wife found it difficult to cope when I wasn't there. You see, my oldest daughter had started running with – how shall I put it? – the wrong crowd. Sheila, that's my wife – *was* my wife – asked me to have a word with her. I did, half-heartedly, but she got worse. And I couldn't see it. One night I was down at the station, just about to go for a few drinks with the boys, when they brought in some kids from a heavy drugs bust. And there was Karen.' He was breathing hard, the memories weighing heavily on him. 'What could I do? Nothing. Fucking nothing. I talked to her, got angry with her, but it was no good. She wasn't my daughter any more. She stayed away from home all the time and eventually she didn't come back at all. We caught up with her through an old friend of hers, last year.' His voice started to crack. 'She's HIV positive. Living in a squat somewhere. I don't know

226

exactly where – Karen didn't want me to have her address.'

'What about your wife?'

'She took our youngest and went. They blame me for what happened. But that's all right – because so do I.'

They drank in silence. Eventually Moir managed to go on. 'Moral of this story; look after your kids. If you don't, there's always some shitbag waiting to pounce.'

He didn't need to tell Larkin that.

'I'll be taking no further action over what you did. I'm not condoning it – I just wanted to let you know why.'

Larkin nodded. He knew how painful it must have been for a man like Moir to confide in him. His respect for the man was growing.

'But if you ever do something like that again, I'll come down on you so hard you'll wish you'd never been fuckin' born.'

Moir had asked if there was anywhere he could drop him; Larkin gave him Charlotte's address.

'Must be weird for you to go back there,' Moir said, when they were in the car.

'You could say that.'

'How're you feeling?'

'Physically better than I thought I would be – but the rest . . .'

'Give it time. You mourn, you grieve, you get on with life. That's the way it goes.'

'Yeah. That's the way it goes.'

Larkin found the lies strangely comforting, he suspected Moir did too.

'How's Torrington?' asked Larkin.

'He'll live. He'll stand trial for Charlotte's murder, but he'll live.'

'Is he going to press charges?'

'After he tried to kill you? What d'you think? No – he's on remand, pending a psychiatrist's report.'

'What about Cain?'

'It's doubtful he'll ever walk again – at least, not without crutches. He's got his charges to answer to.'

'What about his mental condition?'

'Oh, come on. You really prefer him the way he was?'

Larkin didn't answer; they drove on. 'And Danny Torrington?'

'Again, on remand. He didn't get far without loverboy to hold his hand. He broke down, told us everything. Apparently, he really loved Charles,' he said with a derisive snort, 'if they can call that love.'

They pulled up outside the house. It looked suddenly desolate, abandoned, a ghost house.

Larkin got out of the car.

'Nothing's changed, has it?'

'How do you mean?' asked Moir.

'We caught a few scumbags. That's all. Plenty more where they came from. The pyramid's still in place.'

'And always will be,' said Moir bluntly. 'The only way to change that, is to changed human nature. And until that happens . . .'

'Just keep on keeping on,' said Larkin.

'That's right,' replied Moir. 'Fight the good fight.'

'Thanks for the lift. And – for everything.'

'You're welcome.'

'See you again.'

'I fuckin' hope not,' Moir retorted, and sped off, breaking several traffic laws along the way.

Larkin turned to the house. He had Charlotte's old key poised at the lock when it was opened for him from the inside by a walking, suit-wearing slab of beef, all gristle and no fat. It loomed over Larkin. 'You Larkin?' it asked.

He decided that, in the circumstances, truth was the only option.

'I am,' he said. Then, trying to be cool, 'Who wants to know?'

From inside came a voice he recognised. 'Hurry up, Mr Larkin. We haven't got all day.'

228

He entered. In the living room sat another slab of gristle – and Sir James Lascelles.

'Come in, Mr Larkin. And don't worry – you've nothing to fear from Hector. He's here for my protection only.'

Larkin looked dubiously at the doorman's impassive face; he seemed to have had his last independent thought in 1986 or thereabouts.

'Sit down,' invited Sir James.

'I was going to,' Larkin said truculently and sat.

'Are you surprised to see me?'

'I'm wetting myself.'

'There's no need for vulgarity. We're all friends here.'

Larkin was about to argue, but Sir James cut in. 'Just listen, Mr Larkin. I owe you my gratitude. You saved me a lot of trouble. You also prevented a very nasty shipment of crack and heroin from reaching the streets. I'm grateful for that, too.'

'You're grateful for that?'

'Oh, don't misunderstand me – I'm not grateful from any philanthropic standpoint. That shipment will only be replaced by another – I realise that. But this time I'll be behind it. The Londoners have seen where we stand and they're ready to do business. On my terms. And I have you to thank for that.'

Larkin found disgust and rage welling up inside him. 'You're proud of your little empire, are you? Your shining city, built on wasted lives? That's what you're the Great Architect of, is it?'

Before Sir James could speak, Larkin went on. 'I'll fight you. The next shipment, or the one after that – it's personal now. And next time I'll have some help.'

'Oh, how very naive. I, to all intents and purposes, own this town – or at least a good percentage of it. Including its press and police force. You could never touch me. And this little chat? It never happened. I was never even here.'

'Is that all you wanted to say to me?' Larkin felt if

Lascelles didn't leave soon, he would probably hit him – Hector notwithstanding.

Lascelles gave him a thin smile and passed Larkin an envelope. It was addressed to him. He recognised the handwriting.

'Your mail. It was waiting for you when we arrived. Of course, I haven't opened it – a gentleman wouldn't pry.'

Larkin tore it open, his hands shaking. There were some documents – and a letter.

Dear Stephen,
If you're reading this, it means that something's hap-pened to me. Perhaps I'm dead – in which case I wanted you to know that I've changed my will. After tax, the rest of my estate will go to you. My savings, the house – everything. I want you to have something. You deserve it. And I've no one else to leave it to.

I'm not very good at saying how I feel – I think you know that. But I think I've always loved you. I tried to put you in a little box, file you away – but since you've come back I've realised just how much I've missed you. How much I care.

Read the diary again. It's the only way I can tell you what's happened to me, what I've become. Don't judge me too harshly. I was only trying to do what I thought was best.

I love you, always,

Charlotte.

Larkin put the letter down, tears in his eyes. He was determined not to let them show. He turned to Sir James, loathing his smug corpulence.

'Get out of my house. You cunt.'

Sir James smiled. 'Ah. I thought it might be something along those lines.'

'Get out – or I phone the police.'

Sir James stood up. 'We were leaving anyway. I'm a

230

very busy man, Mr Larkin. And I've done what I came here to do.'

'You'd better get used to looking over your shoulder, Sir James. Because one day I'm going to be right behind you. And you won't be able to shake me off.'

Even in the void the bell was ringing.

Larkin awoke from his doze. He pulled back the covers, and realised he was fully dressed – he couldn't even remember getting into bed. He went downstairs to answer the door and found Andy standing there, soaked to the skin in the pouring rain.

'Awright, mate? Mind if I come in?'

'What are you doing here?'

'Well – I just happened to be passing. Here.'

He handed him a brown paper bag; Larkin opened it. Jack Daniels.

'Oh,' said Andy in mock surprise, 'wanna hand with that?'

Larkin smiled for the first time in ages. 'Come in.'

The living room was a mess. Pizza boxes, beer cans and MacDonalds cartons littered the room. Charlotte would be spinning in her grave.

Andy sat down. 'You wasted no time in making yourself at home.'

'Fuck off,' Larkin shouted from the kitchen. He returned with two glasses: 'Here.'

'Ta,' said Andy, taking a glass and pouring a generous slug for himself; Larkin did likewise. He sat opposite Andy, the bottle between them.

'So,' said Andy, 'you heard from Lindsay lately?'

'Only to tell me I was fired. Took the huff because I wouldn't sell her my story.'

'You don't seem too upset.'

'I'm not. It was time for a change.'

'So what you gonna do now?'

'Don't know. Write a book, maybe? Might even become a proper journalist again. What about you?'

231

'Oh, you know me. Have camera, will travel. I just go where the work is.'

'Best way to be.'

'You miss her, then?' asked Andy quietly.

'I . . . yes, I do. Like hell. She came back into my life just to leave again. I can't hold on to anything for long.'

'Stop feeling sorry for yourself. You've got to keep going. You've got no choice.'

'I know that now,' he said. 'I'll go on. Don't know where, though.'

'No – but it's a start.'

They sat for a while longer, making considerable inroads into the bottle. The talk was as bitter as the whisky; they both knew any victory had been Pyrrhic. After a couple of hours Andy left, making copious, drunken promises to keep in touch.

Larkin was left alone. In his very own ghost house. He picked up a newspaper and started to read. Princess Di had, yet again, announced her retirement from public life: he reckoned she would end up making more comebacks than Status Quo. The Irish peace initiative had broken down – surprise surprise – a serial killer had been found guilty and condemned to life. He put the paper down. He couldn't read any more.

He thought about what Andy had said. He couldn't go back; he had to go on. That much was true. He aimlessly paced the floor, poured himself another drink. He thought of Charlotte, tried to ease her from his mind. But he knew she would always be with him. Just like Sophie, just like Joe. He thought of Cain, of Torrington and Danny, what they'd lost. Of Mary, the woman whose death he had thought he was avenging; he remembered Charlotte's prayer for her and silently added his own voice to it.

He found his jacket on the floor, picked it up and shook pizza crumbs from it. A crumpled piece of paper fell out of one of the pockets. He picked it up. It had two numbers on it and a message: *Jane. Call me, you bastard!*

232

He thought for a moment. Jane? It clicked: the girl from the party. Should he ring her? He found himself walking over to the phone, paper in hand, picking up the receiver. Then he paused. Probably not a good idea. He looked out of the window; behind the rain, and the clouds, he could see the sun, trying hard to shine. He looked again at the piece of paper. *No*, he thought. *Not now. Maybe later*. He left it by the phone. Yes, the sun was definitely struggling to break through. But it wouldn't manage it today. Not today.

He put a disc in the CD player, selected the track he wanted and sat down. *Tomorrow*, he thought, *if it's a good day, I'll phone her. I'll get myself sorted out. Tomorrow*. He leaned back, refilled his glass. He looked round the room, at all the ghosts. He knew they would always haunt him, no matter where he called home. He lifted his drink in silent acknowledgement as the song began. 'Are You Ready To Be Heartbroken'. Lloyd Cole And The Commotions. He listened. *Tomorrow*, he thought, as the silent tears ran down his cheeks.

The very best of Piatkus fiction is now available in paper-back as well as hardcover. Piatkus paperbacks, where *every* book is special.